James Elliott lives in Charlotteville, Virginia. He is the author of *Cold, Cold Heart* and *Nowhere To Hide*, also published by Piatkus.

Praise for *Cold, Cold Heart*:

'A hot, hot book. Wickedly entertaining . . . non-stop action . . . readers will stay up far into the night'
Publishers Weekly

'Elliott knows how to jump-start the action and keep it going at 90mph from start to finish'
Booklist

'An exciting thriller that moves with breakneck speed'
Library Journal

and *Nowhere To Hide*:

'Elliott's prose glides over the page . . . a deeply absorbing new thriller'
Publisher's Weekly

'Breathtaking thriller ... Highly recommended'
Publishing News

'Readers will be hard pressed to forget this first-rate thriller'
Booklist

Endgame

James Elliott

PIATKUS

For more information on other books
published by Piatkus, visit our website at
www.piatkus.co.uk

Copyright © 2000 by James Elliott

First published in Great Britain in 2000 by
Judy Piatkus (Publishers) Ltd of
5 Windmill Street, London W1T 2JA
email:info@piatkus.co.uk

This edition published 2000

A catalogue record for this book is available from the British Library

ISBN 0 7499 3185 X

Set in Times by
Action Publishing Technology Ltd, Gloucester

Printed and bound in Great Britain by
Cox and Wyman Ltd, Reading, Berkshire

Chapter One

Thirty-eight thousand feet above the northern Quebec wilderness, a lone aircraft streaked across a brilliant autumn sky leaving a thin, white contrail in its wake. Two hours and fifteen minutes out of St John's, Newfoundland, the sleek silver and black Lear jet was headed west on a flight path for Vancouver, British Columbia.

A trace of a smile creased the corners of the pilot's mouth as he reached over and turned off the transponder, eliminating the signal that revealed his position to those keeping track of his progress. He next changed course to a heading of 185 degrees, then cut back on the power as he began a rapid descent at six thousand feet per minute.

The co-pilot turned in his seat and called back to a man he knew only as Mr Ramsey, the sole occupant of the plush, tufted-leather passenger compartment.

'Estimated time of arrival is two hours and ten minutes.'

Ramsey removed a flip phone from his briefcase, tapped out the cellular number for the man awaiting his arrival, and activated the built-in scrambler. A nervous flyer at best, he stared uneasily out of the small oval window as the plane dove steeply toward the vast isolated area of dense forest and sparkling wilderness lakes.

Thirty seconds after the Lear jet's transponder signal disappeared from his radar screen, an air traffic controller in Toronto keyed his microphone.

1

'November four six seven Kilo, this is Toronto Center. We have lost radar contact.'

The controller waited fifteen seconds, but heard no reply from the Lear.

'November four six seven Kilo, if you read, please ident,' he requested, prompting the pilot to press the button on his transponder that would send out a steady identification signal and give the Center the plane's precise location and altitude.

Again, he received no response.

'November four six seven Kilo, this is Toronto Center. Do you read?'

The pilot of the Lear simply ignored the radio call. Once he descended below the secondary radar coverage, he knew he would disappear from the air traffic controller's screens entirely. He also knew that Toronto Center would attribute the problem to equipment failure and take no further action to locate the plane until if failed to arrive at the Vancouver airport that evening. By then it would not matter.

The pilot's plan was now to continue heading south, stay beneath radar coverage, and enter the United States undetected. He had only to drop off the passenger and cargo he knew nothing about to fulfill his lucrative contract; one hundred thousand dollars to deliver them from St John's, Newfoundland to a small county airport outside of Syracuse, New York.

The pilot and co-pilot were smugglers for hire; willing to fly anyone and anything to any location. No questions asked. For the right price. The Lear, for all intents and purposes, was a phantom aircraft. The tail number was changed frequently, and although the serial number on the metal plate riveted to the airframe could be used to trace the plane's origins, anyone trying to establish true ownership would find it next to impossible. Purchased used eighteen months ago by a shell corporation in the Cayman Islands, then leased to another shell corporation in the Netherlands Antilles, it was once again leased to a company in Fort Lauderdale, Florida, whose business address was an empty warehouse.

2

Chapter Two

Twenty-eight miles due south of where the Lear jet changed course and began its descent, Ben Stafford and Eddie Barnes sat at opposite ends of a canoe casting their lines onto the calm surface of a wilderness lake that mirrored the brilliant fall colors of the forest along the shore. It was late September, the final days of the fishing season, and the last day of the week-long camping trip for the two old friends who had not seen each other in six years.

Barnes, having caught and released four small-mouth bass in the past half hour, reeled in his line and put down his fly rod. He pulled in a small net suspended over the side of the canoe and removed two cans of beer from the six-pack kept chilled by the cold, dark waters of the lake. He raised his chin toward Stafford, who nodded, then caught the can as Barnes tossed it to him.

'It's been a good trip, pardner. Let's not wait another six years to do it again.'

Stafford popped the top on the can and took a drink. 'Same time next year.'

Barnes raised his beer in agreement. 'You got it.'

The sun began its slow descent behind the distant hills, bathing the lake in a soft crimson glow as Stafford cast a deer-hair bass bug into the rocky shallows off the bow of the canoe. Barnes pulled on a thick wool sweater and propped a seat cushion behind his shoulders, then stretched out to enjoy his beer and the cool, crisp evening air heavy with the scent of the autumn forest.

Leaves of red and gold dropped in graceful swoops and lazy spirals from the maple and birch trees at the water's edge. Off in the distance, a bull moose, only his head and massive antlers visible above the surface, swam across a narrow section of the lake. The only sounds were the whoosh of Stafford's fly line and the gentle lapping of the water against the sides of the canoe.

Chapter Three

The co-pilot of the Lear jet was the first to notice the severe icing problem on the leading edge of the wings as they descended through eighteen thousand feet. The plane's de-icing equipment was not working; the reduction of power for the rapid descent had prevented the engines from producing enough heat to melt the ice before it had a chance to accumulate. There was nothing they could do. At fourteen thousand feet, where the temperature was warmer, the ice began to peel off in sheets. The first few pieces clattered noisily off the tail section of the aircraft. Then, from both wings, large chunks broke free and were ingested by the engines, causing a flame-out and damaging the turbine blades.

In the rear passenger compartment, Ramsey, startled by the ice striking the tail section, dropped the cellular telephone into his lap. A few seconds later, the muted roar of the engines died.

Ramsey's voice was tight and strained as he picked up the phone to continue his conversation with Tony Kitlan, his contact at the airstrip in upstate New York, several hundred miles south of the Lear's present position.

'Ah, Jesus, Tony! I think we just lost both engines.'

'The engines quit?'

'I think so.'

Ramsey got up from his seat and knelt at the entrance to the cockpit to see the pilot turn on the auto-ignition in an attempt to restart the engines.

The pilot glanced over his shoulder, the look on his face alone telling Ramsey that the crisis was real.

'Get back to your seat and buckle in tight. We might have to land somewhere around here, and fast.'

Ramsey's eyes widened and his voice cracked. 'There's nowhere to land around here! There's nothing but woods and water!'

At the airstrip north of Syracuse, Kitlan overheard the conversation between the pilot and Ramsey. 'Stay on the phone with me. If you have to make a forced landing, I want the exact coordinates of where the pilot's going to put it down.'

Ramsey did not answer. His attention was riveted on the actions of the pilot, whose calm demeanor was visibly shaken as he continued to try to reignite the engines.

'Listen to me,' Kitlan shouted into the phone. 'If you go down in an isolated area, I've got to get to you before a Canadian search team does.'

'Right now that's the least of my worries, Tony. We're probably going to crash in the woods or sink in some damn lake.'

Kitlan heard the panic creeping into Ramsey's voice, but his real concern was not for him or the crew, rather for the cargo the plane carried.

'You've got to stay calm and keep me informed. If I know exactly where you go down, I can come in and get you out.'

Ramsey took several deep breaths and calmed himself as best he could. He kept the phone to his ear as he watched the frantic activity of the cockpit.

The pilot finally gave up trying to restart the engines and concentrated on leveling off the plane to establish the best angle of glide. He estimated they had six or seven minutes to find a place to land.

Maintaining an airspeed of 160 miles per hour would give him a maximum of another twenty miles in which to locate a suitable site. His eyes scanned the terrain below, knowing all too well that with the vast stretches of dense forest broken only by an occasional lake, he would have no alternative but to land on water.

Both the pilot and the co-pilot assessed two lakes that came into view. They were wide enough, but neither had an open area long enough. They needed at least three thousand feet, to allow the plane to get rid of most, if not all, of its speed before reaching the forest.

After one last futile attempt to restart the engines, the pilot was about to accept the lesser of two evils, a small lake off to his left, when the co-pilot pointed out a much larger lake that came into view directly ahead of them. The pilot quickly agreed. It was wide enough, and they could see what they estimated to be at least two miles of open water in a straight line. More than enough to stop the plane before it reached the trees at the shore.

The only drawback was the lack of time for preparation. They were closing fast on the lake, and had no time to go around and make a circular glide, or to get the airspeed down to at least 115 miles per hour for a full-stall landing. The pilot's only option was a straight-in approach at a higher than desirable speed for touchdown.

'We're going in!' Ramsey shouted into the phone.

'Get the coordinates off the GPS,' Kitlan ordered.

Ramsey leaned forward to read the information off the Global Positioning Satellite receiver on the instrument panel.

'Latitude fifty degrees, forty-two point three five one minutes north. Longitude seventy degrees, fifty point two four six minutes west.'

Kitlan wrote the coordinates down. 'Stay on the phone as long as you can.'

The pilot soon realized he had misjudged the length of the open water. In a frantic attempt to realign his approach, he overcompensated, gaining even more unwanted speed by putting the plane into a steeper descent in the hope of touching down as close as possible to where the woods ended and the lake began.,

Ramsey continued to look through the cockpit windshield as the plane made its straight-in approach. He had to look away and then back to be certain he wasn't imagining what he saw in the distance directly ahead of them.

'I can see two people in a canoe on the lake we're going to land on,' he told Kitlan his voice now filled with raw fear. 'And I think there's a red tent in a clearing on shore.'

7

With less than twenty seconds to touchdown, Ramsey hurried to buckle himself into the leather bench seat at the back of the plane to brace for the landing.

Chapter Four

Eddie Barnes was drinking his beer and enjoying the sunset when something just above the hills at the far end of the lake drew his attention. Little more than a distant speck at first, it continued to grow as he watched. He wasn't certain what he was looking at, then, for a brief moment before the object dipped below the hills on the horizon, he saw the setting sun glisten off its surface, and he knew what it was. He turned to Stafford, who was still working his bass bug across the rocky shallows.

'You don't happen to have any enemies who'd call an air strike in on us do you?'

Stafford laughed. 'Not that I know of. Why?'

'Take a look.' Barnes pointed to just above the trees at the far end of the lake.

Stafford stared at the fast approaching aircraft. 'Either he's playing some dumb-assed game, or he's going to try to land on this lake.'

'Since there isn't any noise coming from his engines, my guess would be the second one. And he's headed right for us.'

Stafford immediately put his fly rod down and both men grabbed paddles. They moved quickly into shore, pulled the canoe from the lake, then stared in disbelief as the Lear jet closed at a speed in excess of 170 miles per hour.

The powerless aircraft flared at the last moment and hit the water at the wrong angle of attack, sending a towering spray cascading out across the lake as the force of the impact bounced it one hundred feet back into the air where it passed directly over Stafford and Barnes as they stood beneath the trees along the shore.

The Lear was airborne for only a few seconds before it nosed down, rolled onto its side, and disappeared into the trees approximately one half mile from the lake. The terrible sounds of the crash filled the peaceful forest and traveled out across the water to echo off the distant hills. A powerful explosion followed, sending an orange and black ball of flame and smoke billowing into the sky.

Stafford and Barnes looked at each other for a moment, then headed off through the woods in the direction of the crash site.

Chapter Five

The last thing Tony Kitlan heard before the phone went dead was Ramsey screaming, 'Oh, my God! Oh, my God!'

He waited five minutes, on the off chance that the plane had not been completely destroyed and there were survivors, before dialing the number for Ramsey's cellular phone to no effect. He then immediately dialed a number on the thirty-fifth floor of a glass office tower one block off Battery Park in New York City to hear the voice of Paul Cameron, the man he least wanted to talk to at the moment.

'The plane went down.'

'What do you mean "went down"?'

'It crashed.'

'Where?'

'Somewhere up in the Canadian wilderness. In Quebec Province. I was on the phone with Ramsey until they went in.'

'No further contact after that?'

'Nothing.'

'Do you think you can find them?'

'Positive. I've got the coordinates. But we might have a problem.'

'What problem?'

'When the plane doesn't arrive in Vancouver according to the flight plan, the Canadians are going to assume it crashed. They'll send out search planes. If it had made it to New York that wouldn't have mattered, but it's down on their territory.'

'What are their chances of finding it?'

'If the emergency locator transmitter on board went off on impact, they'll just home in on the signal.'

'That's not what I need to hear.'

'I'll just have to get there before they do.'

'Then get on it. Now!'

'I'll drive up tonight and take Marcus with me. I'll find the closest airport to where they went down and get a bush pilot to take us in.'

'How soon do you think you can get to the plane?'

'No one will take us in at night. It'll have to be tomorrow morning. The upside is the Canadians won't get a search going until tomorrow either. By the time they're organized it'll be at least noon. If I'm lucky, I could be in and out before they get there.'

'Anything else I should know?'

'There were some campers on the lake they were trying to land on. They're a wild card. I'll just have to see how it plays out.'

Cameron fell silent for a long moment, then, 'You know what's at stake here, Tony. There's no margin for error.'

'Maybe it's not as bad as it looks.'

'Right now it looks pretty damn bad. Don't let it get any worse. You call me as soon as you know anything. And whatever else you do, sanitize the area and make sure there's nothing there that can lay this at our feet. You understand?'

'Understood.'

Cameron hung up and stared out the floor-to-ceiling glass wall overlooking Upper New York Bay, with the Statue of Liberty and Ellis Island off in the distance. He watched a ferry brimming with tourists pull into the pier at Battery Park after its last run of the day, then he started to dial the pager of the man he needed to speak with. He stopped halfway through the number, deciding to place the call after Kitlan had fully assessed the situation and reported in.

Chapter Six

Ben Stafford stood at the top of a ravine, peering over the edge at what remained of the Lear jet three hundred and fifty feet below. The towering evergreens at the bottom, and the scrub pines and underbush growing out of the crevasses on its sheer rock walls, all but concealed the smouldering wreckage from view.

The cockpit and most of the fuselage, along with the engines and the wings, had fallen into the depths of the ravine and landed in the middle of a swift-flowing stream. The churning water had all but extinguished the fire caused when the fuel tanks exploded, and the heavy rains from the previous evening that had soaked the forest floor gave the remaining flames nothing to feed on once the jet fuel was burned off. Had it not been for the spiral of black smoke rising through the trees, it would have been almost impossible to locate the crash site even when flying directly overhead.

The aft section of the aircraft, from the tufted leather bench seat at the rear of the passenger compartment to most of the tail section, had been sheared off when the plane was torn apart by the initial impact. It had remained intact and dropped part way into the ravine, coming to rest on a broad rock ledge sixty feet down from where Stafford stood looking over the edge.

Stafford had no doubt that whoever was in the forward section of the plane at the bottom of the ravine had been killed, if not on impact, then by the explosion and fire that followed. And, on the ledge below, he could clearly see

13

Ramsey's limp, seemingly lifeless body strapped in the bench seat by a shoulder harness and seat belt. He was slumped over, his neck twisted at an impossible angle. He looked to be dead, but Stafford was not about to leave him there without being absolutely certain.

The last of the evening light was fading fast when Eddie Barnes returned from the campsite with their climbing gear. Stafford, experienced at rappelling and descending from helicopters on fast ropes, did not bother with the harness and figure-eight descender he used for rock climbing. He instead secured one end of a rope to a large spruce tree at the top of the ravine and tossed the seventy-five-foot coiled length over the edge. After pulling on his gloves, he passed the rope through his left hand, under his arm and around his back, then under his right arm and through his right hand, using a simplified rappel to lower himself down the side of the ravine.

He leaned out from the near vertical rock face at a ninety degree angle and pushed off with his feet, expertly paying out the rope until he reached the ledge where the battered and twisted tail section had come to rest.

Ramsey's eyes stared directly ahead, the pupils fixed and dilated. Stafford moved closer, leaned into the wreckage, and placed his fingers on Ramsey's neck, feeling for a pulse. Finding none, he searched the dead man's jacket pockets and found a wallet with his identification. He slipped the wallet into his parka and, with nothing more he could do, was about to climb back up when he noticed a large black nylon equipment bag on the luggage shelf above and behind the bench seat. He reached over the seat and undid the leather cargo straps holding the bag in place, then pulled the zipper back a few inches to look inside.

His eyes widened in astonishment. He grabbed the handle of the bag and tugged, quickly releasing his grip and backing away when the entire tail section pitched forward, threatening to topple over and drop into the depths of the ravine, taking him with it.

As a safety precaution, he tied the end of the rappelling rope around his waist, then looked up to where Barnes was standing at the edge watching him.

'Throw the other rope down.'

'Get the hell out of there, Ben. That thing's going to go over any second.'

'I need another length of rope.'

'What for? He's dead, isn't he?'

'Yeah. But there's a bag in there I want to get out.'

'You're worried about the guy's luggage? Leave it for the search and rescue team and get your ass back up here.'

'Just throw the rope down.'

Barnes tied off another length of rope and tossed it over the edge. Stafford took the end and again leaned inside the Lear. He passed the rope through the handle on the bag, knotted it, then stepped back as he pulled it out of the compartment. The tail section creaked and rocked as he dragged the bag out onto the ledge.

He dropped to one knee and zipped it fully open to confirm what he had seen, slowly shaking his head in disbelief as he stared at the contents crammed into every available space. He got up and again looked inside the plane to see two more identical black nylon equipment bags farther back on the luggage shelf.

'Pull the bag up,' he called to Barnes. 'Then toss the rope back down. There's two more just like it still inside.'

'What, are you nuts?'

'Open it when you get it up there. Then ask me that again.'

Barnes hauled the bag up to the top of the ravine and looked inside. His reaction was a mirror image of Stafford's upon seeing the contents. He immediately untied the rope and tossed it back down to the ledge.

Stafford reached for the two bags crammed into the back of the luggage shelf; his body from the waist up inside the tail section as he ran the end of the rope through the handles of both bags and knotted it. He then backed out and stood a safe distance away as he tugged and pulled. The bags slid easily off the shelf, but hung up on the back of the bench seat. Stafford dug in his heels and pulled harder, finally wrenching them free.

As the bags were about to clear the wreckage, the forward redistribution of their weight caused the tail section to rock

15

and sway, then, with an ear-piercing screech of metal scraping against rock, toppled off the ledge. The bags came free as they went over the side, their combined weight enough to pull Stafford off his feet and drag him over with them.

Stafford fell free for fifteen feet, then the rope around his waist reached its end and brought him to a jolting halt, digging deep into his back and side before it slipped up underneath his arms. His weight and momentum pulled the rope over his shoulders and out of his grasp, and in the split second before he was about to fall to a certain death three hundred and fifty feet below, he reached out and grabbed the rope holding the bags.

Suspended in mid-air, he swung like a pendulum and was slammed hard against the rock wall of the ravine. He was momentarily stunned, but managed to hold on as Barnes pulled on the rope and got him into a position where he could throw a leg over the ledge and crawl back to safety.

Stafford rested briefly to shake off the effects of the blow, then climbed back to the top of the ravine where he and Barnes pulled the two remaining bags up to them.

The tail section of the Lear had dropped another forty feet before it lodged between the wall of the ravine and a jagged rock outcropping of scrub pines and thick underbush. Ramsey's body, still strapped in the seat, was now facing upward, his blank unseeing eyes staring directly at Stafford and Barnes as they stood on the ledge looking down.

Chapter Seven

In a windowless room in the basement of the new CIA head-quarters building in Langley, Virginia, eleven hundred miles south of where Stafford and Barnes stood at the top of the ravine in the Canadian wilderness, someone else was acutely aware that something had happened to Lear jet November four six seven Kilo.

The CIA's Counter Narcotic Center, with a staff of several hundred, including photo interpreters, political analysts, operations officers, and technicians, is tasked with collecting intelligence information on the smuggling and money-laundering operations of international narcotics traffickers. Through the use of satellites and an extensive network of agents and informants on the ground, they track drug shipments on the high seas, monitor known and suspected air and land smuggling routes, and locate drug-processing laboratories and growing fields, sharing that information with other federal intelligence and law enforcement agencies with whom they occasionally run joint operations.

Lou Burruss, the senior operations officer at the Counter Narcotics Center, stood watching Carole Fisher, a CNC technician and photo interpreter, recheck the coordinates of the steadily blinking pin-light on the large wall-mounted screen that displayed a map of eastern Canada and the north-eastern United States.

Fisher was monitoring the signal from a miniature transmitter hidden inside the lining of one of the black nylon equipment bags on board the Lear jet she had been tracking since it left St John's, Newfoundland. She was now certain that the signal was stationary, and that the aircraft was not where it was supposed to be.

Burruss, in charge of the joint CIA-Secret Service operation, had received an unexpected bonus when a Secret Service undercover agent had been able to place the transmitter in the bag when it was unloaded from a freighter in St John's harbor that morning. The agent had been unable to learn precisely where the Lear was to deliver its cargo, only that it was somewhere in upstate New York where it would then be transferred to ground transportation.

A Secret Service air and ground surveillance team that included a Cessna Citation equipped with state-of-the-art electronic eavesdropping and tracking equipment, and four surveillance vehicles to be guided by the Citation, was hastily organized and waited just across the border at the Watertown, New York airport ready to respond as soon as the Lear entered United States airspace. But all the indications now were that the pilot had changed plans, or the agent's information was wrong.

Burruss stared at the screen, watching the blinking light that indicated the position of the transmitter. 'You're sure it's not moving?'

Fisher checked the coordinates again. 'Positive. I had the tracking map set to only show movement every fifty miles until it entered the United States, so I didn't notice it at first. But with the map display set to a larger scale, I can track the plane's progress in increments of a quarter mile or less.'

Adam Welsh, the head of the Counter Narcotics Center, entered the operations room after just returning from a strategy session at the White House with the President's new drug czar, the FBI director, and head of the DEA. Burruss immediately briefed him on the developments. Welsh said nothing as he stared at the screen, then turned back to Burruss.

'Why wasn't I informed of the transmitter being put on board the plane?'

'We didn't learn about it from the Secret Service until a few hours ago. I didn't want to interrupt your meeting.'

Welsh simply nodded and watched intently as Fisher typed out instructions on her computer keyboard. The electronic wall map changed in scale, zooming in on the terrain features of an area three hundred and eighty miles north of Quebec City. The signal coming from inside the bag, bounced off a communications satellite and back down to the Counter Narcotics Center, clearly indicated the transmitter was in a stationary position in the heart of a vast wilderness area of lakes and forests.

Fisher looked at her watch. 'It's been emitting a steady signal from that location for the past forty minutes.'

Welsh studied the map. 'There's no airport anywhere around there.'

'No, sir. The plane either went down, or they kicked the cargo out.'

'Why would they make a drop in the middle of nowhere?'

'It's unlikely that they did. There aren't any roads into the area. It's as remote as it gets. And it's more than a little problematic opening the door of a Lear jet in flight, not to mention getting it closed again.'

Welsh stared thoughtfully at the map display for a long moment. 'Check the international distress frequencies. If they crashed, the search and rescue satellite will pick up the signal from their Emergency Locator Transmitter.'

'I already checked,' Fisher said. 'There's no distress signal coming from anywhere in Canada. Which doesn't necessarily mean they didn't crash. The ELT could have been destroyed on impact, or simply malfunctioned.'

'Then we have time before the Canadian search teams get in there.'

'If they get there at all.'

'What are you saying?'

'I was listening in on the Toronto Air Traffic Control Center. The last contact they had with the Lear was when it turned off its transponder. At that point it changed course and apparently dropped below radar coverage. That was here,' Fisher used a laser pointer to indicate a heavily forested area north of the blinking light, 'approximately thirty miles north of where the plane is now. Even if the Canadians had the right location they'd have a hard time finding it in that terrain.

Searching in the wrong direction, thirty miles from the crash site, it'll be next to impossible.'

'How precise can you be about the location of the transmitter in the bag?'

'When it's stationary like this? To within a few feet.'

Welsh's frustration was evident in his expression. 'I want a close-in look,' he told Burruss. 'Move a satellite into position as soon as possible.'

'It'll take about an hour.'

'Do it. And let me know when you have it set up.'

At the Satellite Control Facility in Sunnyvale, California, the technician who received the authorization codes from the Counter Narcotics Center swivelled his chair to a control panel on his left. He clicked on a series of switches, then turned back to his computer and typed out the commands that logged him on to the system.

On the wall above him, lights moved with varying speed and arc across a large projection screen, depicting the orbits and ground tracks of eight of the CIA's imaging reconnaissance satellites. The technician typed in more commands and began his electronic conversation with one of the satellites, sending a sequence of encoded digital instructions that were responded to instantly by the on-board computers operating the satellite's navigation and altitude control systems.

In the cold, dark silence of space, three hundred miles above the earth, the fifty-foot-long, ten-foot-wide black cylinder gliding over the South Atlantic fired its hydrazine thrusters and the change of orbit and ground track began.

Chapter Eight

The temperature had dropped twenty degrees since sundown, and Ben Stafford and Eddie Barnes sat before the campfire with their parkas zipped, watching the flames dance in the night breeze coming in off the lake. The large, black nylon equipment bags recovered from the plane were off to the side, open and empty. The money, all twenty million dollars of it, four hundred packets of fifty thousand dollars each in one hundred dollar bills, wrapped in clear plastic, were stacked beneath the rain fly strung from the trees at the edge of the campsite.

Barnes was the first to speak after a long silence. 'I say we keep it.'

'Forget it, Eddie. It's a nice dream, but it's not going to happen.'

'Give me one good reason why not.'

'There's only one reason that matters; it's not ours. Tomorrow the Canadians are going to find the crash site, they'll notify the families of the victims, and then whoever the money belongs to is going to claim it.'

'Yeah, well I've been thinking about that. And you know what? No one is going to claim that money.'

'And why not?'

'Who hauls that kind of cash around . . . in a private jet?'

Stafford said nothing.

'You know damn well enough who. Drug traffickers, or the people who launder their money for them. And they can't come forward and admit it's theirs because they can't legally account for it.'

'That's one possible explanation.'

'It's the only one that makes any sense. Twenty million all in hundreds. Wrapped in cellophane. Stuffed in nylon equipment bags. No bank transports money that way.'

'It doesn't matter. We don't need that kind of trouble. When the bush pilot comes to pick us up tomorrow morning, we take him to the crash site and have him radio the Canadian authorities. We turn the money over to them, and give them the dead guy's wallet. And that's the end of it.'

'Hey, Ben. We're talkin' the American dream here. The big score. Winning the lottery. We've got it right in front of us. And it's not even illegal ... At least we didn't do anything illegal to cause it to happen. It just fell into our laps, literally. And my gut says if we don't tell the authorities about it, they're never going to know it was on the plane. And the druggies are going to think it got burned up in the crash, or they'll figure the Canadians have it and are just waiting for them to show up so they can bust them. Either way, we take it back to the states and we're home free.'

Barnes paused and looked hard at Stafford. 'You're my friend. And I love ya, pardner. But you can't deny me this. That's not right.'

'We're not thieves, Eddie. The worst crimes we've committed are traffic violations. Neither one of us has ever stolen anything.'

'And we won't be stealing anything now. We found it. There's a distinction.'

'That's just semantics. If it's not ours and we take it, it's stealing. And as easy and clean as it looks sitting here tonight, it'll set things in motion we can't anticipate. We'd end up looking over our shoulders for the rest of our lives.'

'Maybe. Maybe not. But for ten million apiece, I'd say it's worth the risk. There's a very basic philosophy that applies to this kind of situation. If you're going to cross the line and do something illegal, do it once and do it right, and make enough doing it to change your life, so that you never have to do it again. Then get out and stay out. That's exactly the opportunity we've got here.' Barnes flashed a roguish grin. 'Hey. No chance. No victory dance.'

Stafford smiled, recalling the last time Barnes had said that to him, eight years ago, in the Iraqi desert during the Gulf War.

The relationship between the two men was far removed from the casual workplace or weekend sports-based friendships most men shared. Theirs was a bond forged in combat; the powerful emotional bond of those who had faced death together and depended on each other for their very lives. Primal in its strength and force, it was a bond that ran even deeper than the bond of family, between brothers, or father and son, or husband and wife.

They had spent eight years together in Delta Force, the US Army's elite counter-terrorist unit. They had gone through the selection process and training together, served in the same squadron, and taken part in top secret missions around the world that the public and press knew nothing about and never would.

During the war they and their Delta Force team had infiltrated behind Iraqi lines on highly classified covert operations, hiding during the day, prowling the desert at night in heavily armed dune buggies and camouflaged motorcycles silenced by powerful mufflers. They conducted daring, lightning-fast raids on enemy command and control centers and storage facilities, and tracked down and destroyed Scud missile launchers, depriving Iraq of its only effective weapon.

They both left the Army shortly after the end of the war, and since then circumstances and the directions their lives had taken had conspired to keep them apart. But nothing, neither time nor distance, would ever break their bond of friendship. The past week had, if anything, only served to strengthen it.

They had a deep and abiding trust and respect for each other, and during their years in Delta Force had learned well the other's weaknesses and strengths. Barnes was steady and dependable in high-pressure situations, but he had a mercurial and impulsive side that Stafford, on more than one occasion, had had to keep in check. His instincts, however, were good, and had never failed him in all the time Stafford had known him. Stafford's own strengths were in meticulous planning and precision execution of mission objectives; his primary weakness was in occasionally over-thinking a problem when immediate and decisive action would have served him better. It was at those times that Barnes' impulsiveness had provided the necessary balance.

Stafford considered all of this as he watched Barnes get up from the campfire and go down to the lake to return with two cold cans of beer. He gave one to Stafford, then sat back down beside him, his words now the voice of reason.

'Let's put this on a more personal and immediate level for the moment, and forget the morality of it. Okay? Just hear me out.'

Stafford nodded his consent.

'What were we talking about sitting around this campfire last night, huh? How shitty our lives are, right? How it seems our best days are behind us. Your wife's dead, your daughter's in a private hospital, maybe for the rest of her life. I mean, I hope not. But like you said, it could be. The insurance has run out, it's costing you eighty-five thousand a year to keep her there, and you're busting your ass to pay the bills with no end in sight.'

'I'm doing okay.'

'You're a bail enforcement agent. An independent bounty hunter tracking down bail jumpers. Not exactly a guaranteed income. What happens if you have a dry spell and can't find any bad guys for six months? You don't get paid, right?'

'I'll manage.'

'Managing isn't what life's supposed to be about, pardner. Look at me. I haven't been able to find a woman dumb enough to marry me. Postponing immediate gratification has never been one of my strong points, so I'm in debt up to my ear lobes. And I'm stuck in a nothing government job going nowhere, getting a little crazier every day from the mindless bureaucratic bullshit. There are times when I think I'm going to lose it and go postal; wipe out the whole damn office.'

'Everybody has problems, Eddie.'

'Well the answer to our problems is right over there,' he jerked his thumb toward the stacks of money at the edge of the forest.

24

Stafford stared into the campfire and said nothing. A vision of Annie, his eleven-year-old daughter, flashed before him and he felt a terrible sadness. This past week was the longest he had been away from her since the accident eighteen months ago, and he missed her and worried about her. But he had not had a vacation in four years, and for the sake of his own sanity, he needed the time to relax with an old friend and put his problems aside, no matter how temporary the relief was. He remained silent until he finished his beer, then turned to face Barnes and motioned with his head toward the stacks of money.

'That's about three hundred pounds of cash over there. How do you think we're going to get it out without the pilot being a little suspicious?'

Barnes grinned. 'Now you're talkin'.'

'I didn't say I want to keep it. Let's just talk about the mechanics of keeping it.'

'Okay. Three hundred pounds of cash. We can't use the bags, the pilot knows we didn't bring them in with us.'

Stafford thought for a moment. 'We can use two of them. They'll fit inside the canoe. We can use the rain fly as a tarp to cover them, tie it down tight. If we load it on the rack under his float plane ourselves, he'll never notice the weight difference.'

'Right. Then what about the money from the third bag?'

'We have our backpacks, the stuff bags for the tent and the sleeping bags and the other equipment we brought in. They should hold the rest of it.'

'What do we do with our clothes and camping gear?'

'We put some of it in the empty bag, weight it down with rocks, and sink it in the lake. Then we bury the rest in the woods.'

'What if the pilot spots the tail section of the Lear when he comes to pick us up? He'll radio it in right away. Then we get hung up here until the search and rescue team arrives and asks a lot of questions.'

'Odds are he won't spot it. The crash site is about a half mile northwest of here. When he brought us in he made a straight-in approach from the south. If he does the same thing again, he won't fly over the ravine.'

'And if the search team gets here before him?'

'I don't think we have to worry about that. It'll probably be midmorning before they get organized, and we told the pilot to be here at sun up so we could get an early start for the drive home.'

Barnes poked at the campfire with a stick, watching a shower of sparks rise into the night as he tried to think of anything they hadn't considered. 'You know, if we don't tell the pilot about the crash, when they find it, he's going to wonder why we didn't say something.'

Stafford nodded in agreement. 'I've got a more or less plausible explanation for that.'

'What? We were on a seven-day drunk and thought it was a thunderstorm?'

'I was thinking more along the lines that this is a pretty big lake. Over a hundred miles of shoreline, if you count all the bays, coves, and inlets. We could have been at the other end of it fishing in a hidden cove, or rock climbing or hiking miles from here. We heard an explosion, thought it was a sonic boom, didn't think any more about it.'

'Works for me.'

Stafford got up and walked down to the shoreline. Barnes followed.

'You know, Eddie, getting the money out of here is the least of our problems.'

'Yeah? What else do we have to worry about?'

'Spending it.'

'Trust me on that one, pardner. I won't have any trouble spending it.'

'That's what worries me. We can't draw any attention to ourselves until we see how this shakes out. And I remember your spending habits when we were in Delta. You never made it from one pay-day to the next without hitting the pawn shops, and you owed half the stores in Fayetteville.'

'I can be discreet if I have to.'

'Hey, give me a break. It's me you're talking to. You don't even know the meaning of the word discreet. And you've got to get it through your head, you can't all of a sudden start spending a lot of money.'

26

'Why not? Cash doesn't leave a paper trail.'

'It does a lot more than that. If you spend ten thousand or more in cash in one place at one time, like buy a car, the dealer has to report it to the IRS. It's the same if you deposit large amounts of cash in a bank. By law, they have to report it. So we both have to keep our share some place safe until I come up with a plan to launder it and have it come back to us as legitimate income.'

'You know how to do that?'

'I've got a pretty good idea. I tracked down a bail jumper in Mexico two years ago. A Wall Street investment banker specializing in acquisitions and mergers. He was under indictment for insider trading. Before the Securities and Exchange Commission got wise to him he managed to launder about fifty million by using offshore banks in the Caribbean and some shell corporations he set up.'

'But he got caught doing it, right?'

'He got caught for insider trading, not money laundering.'

'So he told you how he laundered it?'

'Yeah. It took me three days to bring him back from the place up in the mountains where he was hiding; he was the talkative sort. Actually he was a nice guy. I was halfway thinking about letting him get away, but he skipped on a two million dollar bond and I was looking at a six hundred thousand dollar pay-day for bringing him back. I don't get many of them.'

'So how long will it take to launder it?'

'I'm not sure. Maybe a month, maybe more before I get it worked out. But the first thing I'm going to do when we get back is check out the dead guy and find out who he's connected to. His ID says he's Jeffery Ramsey from New York City. I've got a friend there, a detective in the Intelligence Division, who'll run his name for me. If he's tied into organized crime or any heavyweight drug dealers they should have something on him.'

'So I couldn't spend any of the money right away?'

'If you're careful, sure. You can buy postal money orders or travelers checks for a few hundred dollars at a time, but no more than that, and not always at the same place. If you have to buy any big-ticket items, put a few hundred down in cash, then pay the rest off in installments with the money orders or travelers checks. But keep it down to a minimum until I get things set up to launder it.'

Barnes smiled broadly. 'So it's a go? We're going to keep it?'

'We've been friends a long time, Eddie. And you're right. Who am I to take this away from you? I still think it's wrong, and we're taking a chance on getting caught, but if it is drug money, the odds are pretty good we can pull it off.'

'You made the right decision, pardner. Count on it.'

Stafford walked back toward the edge of the forest and got a flashlight from the tent. He then took two folding shovels from their backpacks and gave one to Barnes.

'We've got some work to do before sunrise, so let's get to it.'

'No problem. It's not like I'd get any sleep tonight anyway.'

As they made their way through the moonlit forest behind the campsite, Barnes began laughing softly to himself.

'What's so funny?'

'My last date. The night before I left to come up here? I went over to pick her up at her apartment. She opens the door with a whip in one hand, handcuffs in the other, wearing nothing but a garter belt and a leather mask with a zipper for a mouth. Man, I don't know what it is about me that attracts those kind of weirdos.'

Stafford laughed. Barnes could always make him laugh. 'So you got out of there, right?'

'What, are you nuts? Wanna see my welts?'

Chapter Nine

The Satellite Control Facility in Sunnyvale, California had maneuvered the imaging reconnaissance satellite down from an altitude of 300 miles to 150 miles above the earth to get maximum detail of the targeted area. As it approached the northern Quebec wilderness, control of its cameras was now in the hands of the CIA's Counter Narcotics Center. Inside the control room, Carole Fisher's eyes were hard on the digital clock running in the top right hand corner of her console.

'Ten seconds to open-cover sequence,' she announced to Adam Welsh, the head of CNC. He stood behind her with Lou Burruss, the operations officer in charge of the mission, watching the forty-inch flat screen monitor where the images would appear.

'Four, three, two, one . . . say cheese Bullwinkle.'

Eight hundred thousand feet above the wilderness area the satellite's on-board microprocessors instantly deciphered the encoded sequence of commands from the CNC computer logged on to its operating system. An alloy shield on the undercarriage slid open, revealing a large, gleaming, electro-mechanical eye that quickly focused on the terrain below.

The latest generation of spy satellites, unlike its predecessors, it did not snap a series of still photographs in rapid sequence, but instead filmed its subject much the same as a video camera, transmitting the images down to earth to be viewed in real time and simultaneously recorded on tape for later in-depth scrutiny.

Its unblinking eye could detect objects as small as six inches in size and produce three-dimensional images of extraordinary resolution, sharp enough to read the name on a mailbox on a country road or the headline of a newspaper on a Manhattan street corner. Night was turned into day by infrared optics that penetrated the darkness and a thermal imager that captured the heat signature of the objects below.

Capable of detecting temperature variations as small as two degrees, the thermal imager delineated the invisible heat radiation of anything in relation to its surroundings, whether concealed inside a building or hidden under trees and underbrush, rendering them in shades of gray or white depending on the intensity of the heat they radiated.

Fisher, a photo intelligence specialist, smiled to herself as she studied the first video image to appear on the large-screen monitor. The brilliantly clear, cold, late September night provided the perfect conditions for the satellite to perform its magic, and she quickly spotted the first area of interest. She typed out commands to zoom the camera in for a closer look, then used the laser pointer to indicate a cylindrical white spot glowing eerily among the dark-to-medium-gray terrain features on the screen.

'That's probably the crash site at the bottom of that ravine,' she told Welsh. 'Looks like the main part of the fuselage, missing the tail section. It's still hot. There must have been an explosion and fire on impact.'

Welsh watched, transfixed. He was old enough at fifty-three to have witnessed the early rudimentary photo reconnaissance satellites evolve into what was available to them now, and the quantum leap in technology never ceased to amaze him.

Fisher continued to study the image before her. 'It's definitely the crash site. There's the tail section, on a ledge halfway down the ravine. Must have been torn off on impact.'

Her practiced eyes noticed something inside the gaping hole in the tail section and her fingers again danced quickly over the computer keyboard. The satellite camera immediately responded, zooming in further for an extreme closeup of what took on the appearance of a macabre amusement park ride.

'There's a body strapped into the rear bench seat. No significant heat signature, so whoever it is was probably killed on impact.'

She typed in another command and the camera zoomed back out to cover more of the terrain as the satellite moved away from the ravine toward the lake. Fisher's eyes quickly locked on two light-gray images as a small clearing at the water's edge came into view. The heat signatures were far less intense than the fuselage, but the thermal imager clearly defined their shape and size.

'And what have we here?'

Welsh leaned in closer to the monitor. 'What is it?'

'Two people. Putting something in a small boat. A canoe.'

Welsh stared at the ghostly images moving along the shoreline. 'Survivors?'

'It's a real stretch to believe anyone walked away from that crash.'

'Then who? A Canadian search team couldn't have gotten in there this soon.'

'No, sir. Not likely.'

Fisher used the pointer to direct Welsh's attention to the open grassy area along the shoreline. 'There's a tent and a campfire in the small clearing behind them. What we've got are a couple of campers. I'll give it a close look when I rerun it.'

On a hunch, Fisher looked up at the wall-mounted screen depicting the map of northern Quebec she had earlier used to track the transmitter on board the Lear jet. Her brow furrowed as she typed out a command on another keyboard at the control console, changing the topographic map to display only the immediate area around the crash site as she again looked at the blinking pin-light on the map.

'The bag with the transmitter has been moved about half a mile from where it was originally. It's now fifty yards offshore; probably at the bottom on the lake.'

Welsh glanced at the pin-light, then back to the monitor. 'What the hell is going on down there?'

'An educated guess? Those two people found the crash site and the money.'

Welsh continued to watch the two phantom-like images as

31

the camera moved across them. 'Then what's the bag with the transmitter doing in the lake?'

Fisher shrugged. 'I'll have to work on that one.'

'And how did those people get in there? By canoe?'

'Couldn't have. No navigable rivers run into that lake. Just feeder streams. And there aren't any roads, and the closest town is over two hundred miles away. So I think it's safe to assume they didn't hike in with a canoe on their backs. Someone must have brought them in by float plane.'

'Are they men or women?'

'They both appear to be about six feet tall, give or take an inch. Broad shoulders. So I'd say two men, unless they're really big women.'

One minute and eighteen seconds after the satellite arrived over the area it completed its first pass. Fisher transmitted the close-cover commands and the camera shut down as the alloy shield covering the ultra-sophisticated optics moved back to the closed position.

'Have Sunnyvale keep the satellite on its present ground track,' Welsh told Fisher. 'And I want the camera on for every pass . . . That's what?'

'Eighty-nine minutes. That's how long it takes for it to circle the earth. In its present orbit, I can give you two more passes at varying angles, then it'll be twenty-four hours before it's back over the target again.'

Welsh thought for a moment, then, 'Tell Sunnyvale to move another satellite into position to cover the campsite at first light tomorrow.' He turned to Burruss. 'Get someone from our Ottawa station to check out all the bush pilots in the area. Find out which one of them flew those people in to that lake, who they are, and when they're scheduled to be picked up. And tell our people to keep a low profile; I don't want the Canadians aware of our interest.'

'Wouldn't it be better to put a team in there at first light and get the money back from the campers? With the emergency locator transmitter on the Lear not working, we don't have to worry about a Canadian search team getting there anytime soon.'

'No,' was all Welsh said, ignoring Burruss's questioning look.

'And what about the Secret Service?'

'What about them?'

'This is supposed to be a joint operation. The agreement was to keep them informed.'

'I'll decide what information we give the Secret Service, and when we give it to them. For now, just tell them we have reason to think the plane may have crashed, nothing about what the satellite showed us.'

Burruss backed off, nodding his acceptance as Welsh left the control room. The previous week, when a CIA asset in The Netherlands reported that the money had left Rotterdam by freighter and was en route to St John's, Newfoundland, Burruss had informed the Secret Service. Welsh had gone into a rage, ordering him to clear all information with him before passing anything on to the Secret Service or anyone else.

Burruss did not approve of taking the Secret Service out of the loop. But as head of the Counter Narcotics Center, it was Welsh's call, and his responsibility, he reminded himself as he left the control room to telephone the CIA's Ottawa station.

Chapter Ten

With Welsh and Burruss gone for the night, Fisher, on duty until eight the next morning, closed the door and settled in to do the part of her job she most enjoyed, ferreting out whatever still-undiscovered secrets the satellite had captured. The control room glowed with the soft light of monitors and electronic consoles as she turned on the compact stereo system on her desk, cranked up the volume of her favorite Golden Oldies CD, and shoulder-danced to Wilson Picket's 'Midnight Hour' as she rewound the tape.

She played the 'take' over and over, watching for anything that had escaped her during the real-time transmission, finally pausing to concentrate on the two men at the shore of the lake. She reversed and advanced the tape four times until she found the frame that showed the clearest image of what they were loading into the canoe.

She next centered the computer's mouse arrow, depicted on the screen as a small telescopic sight with cross hairs, directly on the object being carried by one of the men. Each click of the left mouse button increased the magnification of the area within the cross hairs, and she quickly zoomed into level twenty, the highest level of magnification. She could now see that the object was approximately four feet long and three feet in diameter, and that the man was carrying it by a handle on its top.

Fisher noticed that another object of the same size and shape was already inside the canoe. She knew from the information the Secret Service undercover agent had given her that the money was being transported in three black, ballistic nylon equipment bags, and she was almost certain that she was looking at two of them. But why would the third bag, the one with the transmitter hidden inside, be at the bottom of the lake?

She puzzled over that as she backed off on the magnification and scrolled across the terrain. Something in the woods just behind the campsite caught her eye, and she again froze the frame. Beneath a thick canopy of autumn leaves and evergreen branches, the thermal imager had detected the fading heat signatures of two sets of footprints along a wooded path leading away from the lake. Fisher reasoned they were probably made within an hour of the satellite's arrival.

She followed the footprints to where they ended just off the path at what appeared to be a depression in the ground in a thinly wooded section fifty yards from the campsite. She again increased the magnification to the highest level and the depression revealed itself to be a freshly dug hole with small mounds of soil piled around it. The trees were far enough apart and the foliage sparse enough that she could just make out two unidentifiable objects lying near the hole. With the computerized lens at her disposal, she enhanced the image, adjusting the contrast and brightness and definition, until two small folding shovels were clearly defined, faint heat signatures still visible where hands had gripped them. It was then that Fisher realized what the two men were doing.

She remembered something else she had noticed when she was watching the transmission in real time, and she ran the tape back and paused on a frame with a tight shot of the campsite. She then zoomed in on the backpacks and stuff bags stacked on the ground near the tent. She had no doubts they contained the money that had been in the bag with the transmitter, and that some of the previous contents of the backpacks and stuff bags were now in that bag at the bottom of the lake, and the rest of it in the hole they had dug in the woods.

Her attention was abruptly drawn away from the screen, to a small red light flashing in the right-hand corner of her control console. It was the warning light for the countdown clock, alerting her that she had sixty seconds until the satellite was again over its target. She ejected the tape from the first pass and put in another, then set the equipment to the record mode and prepared to send the commands for the open-cover sequence.

Chapter Eleven

After stoking the campfire and adding enough logs to last well into the night, Ben Stafford crawled into his sleeping bag a safe distance from the flames but close enough to benefit from the radiated heat.

Eddie Barnes, visions of Porches, Armani suits, and a fashion model on each arm dancing in his head, was too wired to sleep. He sat at the water's edge drinking a beer and staring up at the brilliant display of stars. Free of distortion from smog and pollution and undiluted by the lights of civilization, the heavens sparkled as he recalled having seen them only once before, deep in the Iraqi desert eight years ago, when he had neither the time nor the inclination to appreciate them.

He had polished off a six-pack by himself and had a silly grin on his face as he looked back toward the campfire and called out to Stafford. 'Sweet dreams, pardner. We're rich. And nothin's ever gonna be the same again.'

'If you say so.' Stafford rolled over in his sleeping bag and pulled it snug around his neck against the cold night air that had dropped below fifty degrees.

The money was not real to him; he did not truly believe they would get away with what they had planned. That kind of luck had never been his. But in the event Barnes' reasoning and gut instincts were right, he saw no harm in waiting to see how it played out. They could always give it back.

Stafford closed his eyes and let his thoughts drift back to happier times. He had never considered money to be the measure or validation of a person's life, and he knew in his heart that he would gladly give any amount of money, his very soul, if he could only have things back the way they were before the accident; when his wife was alive and his daughter was whole and carefree and the joy of his life.

One hundred and fifty miles above the campsite, silent and unseen in the dark void of space, the photo reconnaissance satellite moved across the night sky, dispassionately recording all that it saw and transmitting it down to the CNC control center.

Carole Fisher watched the 'take' come in, paying particular attention to the wooded area behind the campsite when the camera moved across it. She zoomed in to see that the hole had been filled and covered with fallen leaves. She then backed off to a wider shot to view the campsite. The tent was gone, a tarp now concealed the bags in the canoe, and two fishing-rod cases and two tackle boxes had been placed near the shore. All telling her that the campers were planning to leave the following morning.

She could clearly see one of the men tossing inside his sleeping bag, and the other sitting at the water's edge star gazing, unknowingly looking directly into the camera as the satellite passed overhead. Operating conditions were so good that Fisher even saw the night breeze rustle the autumn leaves and flare the flames of the campfire.

She shook her head in amusement at their careful planning. Some small part of her felt sorry for them, their dreams of a life of luxury soon to disintegrate as quickly and unexpectedly as they had materialized. And they'll never know how close they came to pulling it off, Fisher thought as the satellite neared the completion of its second pass.

With the uncanny luck of amateurs, they had inadvertently discarded the one bag that would have allowed them to be tracked wherever they took the money. And with the aircraft's ELT malfunctioning, had the transmitter in the bag also been damaged in the crash and ceased to operate, no one would have known where the plane went down. But their luck had not held, and now all that remained was the relatively simple process of identifying them and retrieving the money.

'Sleep tight, guys,' she whispered as they disappeared from view off the right side of the screen. 'The best laid schemes of mice and men.'

Chapter Twelve

In the still, half-light of dawn, an autumn mist rose from the lake and drifted through the forest. It chilled Stafford and Barnes to the bone, their breath hanging heavy in the frost-tinged air as they rolled up their sleeping bags and tied them to the tops of their backpacks. They pulled on their parkas against the raw, damp cold and extinguished the last glowing embers in the campfire before making a sweep of the area to be certain they were leaving it as they had found it, free of litter.

Within the hour, the day broke bright and crisp as the first rays of sunlight rose above the distant hills. Stafford was checking the tie-down straps on the tarp covering the bags of money inside the canoe when he heard the low drone of an aircraft. He turned toward the sound and scanned the sky, half expecting to see a search plane. But, true to his word, the bush pilot had arrived on schedule, and moments later the old, twin-engine Beech 18 appeared low on the horizon. It made a straight-in approach from the south, its flight path well away from the ravine and the crash site.

Barnes turned to Stafford and winked. 'So far so good, pardner.'

They stood on the shoreline and watched as the pilot touched down, applied power, and taxied into shore. The moment he cut the engines, they picked up the canoe and waded into the shallows.

Marcel Drussard, a tall, slender man in a plaid wool shirt and faded jeans, stepped from the cockpit onto one of the floats, a cheerful smile adding to the creases on his leathery outdoor face.

'Let me help you with that,' his words heavy with a French Canadian accent.

'We've got it,' Stafford said, and raised the canoe in concert with Barnes to place it on the rack beneath the fuselage.

Drussard came over and attached the cargo straps to hold the canoe in place during the flight, then started toward the backpacks and stuff bags lined up on the shore. Stafford waved him off as he and Barnes shouldered their packs and split the bags between them, carrying them to the plane and putting them inside before Drussard had a chance to notice the peculiar bulges or heft the weight.

They were airborne within fifteen minutes of the plane's arrival, Stafford in the co-pilot's seat, wanting to see exactly what Drussard saw when they took off. He watched the ground as they climbed to altitude, relieved that with no wind to dictate the direction for the takeoff, Drussard had simply left on a reciprocal heading, taking him back out the way he had come in. The ravine was only one half mile off to their right, but the dense forest of towering evergreens completely hid it from view.

Stafford looked at his watch. It was six forty-five. In ninety minutes they would be in Chibougamau, the small town bordering the wilderness area where he had left his car. With a six-hour drive to the US border and another five hours to Chadds Ford, Pennsylvania, he estimated he would be home no later than eight o'clock that night. Too late to visit Annie at the hospital, he thought, but he would go to see her first thing in the morning. He glanced over his shoulder at Barnes, who wiggled his eyebrows and flashed a silly grin.

The second photo reconnaissance satellite Sunnyvale had moved into position was just beginning its first pass over the campsite when Drussard taxied the twin Beech away from shore. The camera was filming at a low oblique angle, and Carole Fisher was able to zoom in and get the tail number from the vintage aircraft as it made its takeoff run.

41

She wrote the number down on a pad and placed it with the photographs she had printed of selected frames from the videotape of the earlier satellite's two passes: closeups of the equipment bags in the canoe, the hole dug in the woods, and the backpacks and stuff bags which she felt certain contained the money from the bag at the bottom of the lake.

Adam Welsh and Lou Burruss entered the control room at seven thirty. Fisher gave them each copies of the photos, showed them the tape of the amphibious plane on its takeoff run, then briefed them on what she had learned and what she suspected.

'I'll get the plane's tail number to Ottawa,' Burruss said, and left the control room immediately to make the call to the CIA's Ottawa station.

'How much longer do you want coverage of the crash site?' Fisher asked Welsh.

'Tell Sunnyvale they can put the satellites back in their original orbits when they're ready. We've got what we need.'

Chapter Thirteen

At three o'clock the previous night, too tired to drive any longer, Tony Kitlan and Peter Marcus grabbed a few hours sleep at a motel in the small Gatineau River town of Maniwaki, Quebec. The following morning they wasted an hour waiting for a pilot at a local float plane dock who arrived a few minutes before eight o'clock only to tell them that his plane was down for repairs. He did, however, confirm that, with the exception of a grueling two hundred mile hike, the only way into the lake they had circled on their map was to fly in, and that the sportsmen going there usually chartered a float plane from either Chicoutimi or Chibougamau, both small towns on the edge of the wilderness area, the first being three hundred miles west of Maniwaki and the second about the same distance north.

Kitlan decided on Chibougamau, reasoning that since it was farther north, and therefore closest to the crash site, it was the most likely point of departure for the two campers who had been spotted as the Lear went down. To make up for lost time, he drove the silver Mercedes along the narrow two-lane ribbon of blacktop at speeds that had Marcus holding the armrest in a death grip on every curve.

Just north of the town of Val-d'Or, halfway to their destination, Kitlan sped into a blind curve taking his half of the road out of the middle. His quick reflexes were all that saved him from a head-on collision with a black Jeep Cherokee with Pennsylvania license plates and a canoe on its roof. The

Cherokee swerved onto the shoulder, rocked up on two wheels, and careened to the opposite side of the road before the driver regained control. In the split second that the Cherokee flashed by, Marcus saw the man in the front passenger seat give him the finger, a gesture he promptly returned.

Stafford, his adrenaline still pumping from the near collision, cursed under his breath as he slowed the Cherokee and pulled off the road. He was transporting the canoe upside down on the roof rack, with the bags of money underneath, still covered by the tarp. He got out to check the ropes holding the canoe in place, and saw that the erratic maneuver made to avoid the oncoming car had caused the bags to shift forward, unbalancing the load. He redistributed the weight, then let Barnes take the wheel when they got back underway.

They had gone no more than a mile when Barnes, losing his patience with a slow-moving flatbed truck loaded down with logs, floored the Cherokee and pulled out to pass. He swung back into his own lane in time to miss a pickup truck heading straight for him, cutting off the flatbed so sharply that he nearly ran it off the road.

'You see that moron! He should have slowed down and given me some room when he saw me coming.'

Stafford shook his head and laughed. 'Right. Where does he get off driving like that?'

Kitlan and Marcus arrived in Chibougamau shortly after noon. A sign on the outskirts of town listed a number of local businesses, among them Marcel Drussard's charter service. Kitlan pulled into a gas station and used the pay phone to ask information about other charter services in the immediate area. There were none, and they soon found Drussard's operations shack on a dock at the south end of the lake named after the town.

Drussard was refueling the twin Beech when Kitlan and Marcus walked out on to the dock. 'Are you available for charter?' Kitlan asked.

'That depends on where you want to go.'

Kitlan handed him the map and pointed to the lake circled with a felt-tip pen.

'Sure. I can take you there. One thousand five hundred dollars, US, round trip. When do you want to leave?'

'Now.'

'I need a few hours to take care of a personal matter. Come back around two o'clock; I can do it then and have you there well before dark.'

Kitlan removed a thick roll of one hundred dollar bills from an inside pocket of his leather jacket and began peeling off one at a time as Drussard watched. 'Three thousand if we leave now.'

Drussard shrugged and took the money. 'Okay. Get your equipment from your car and I'll load it on board.'

'It's just us. No equipment except this.' Kitlan held up a leather carry-on with a shoulder strap.

Drussard gave him a quizzical look. 'How long do you plan on staying?'

'Just a few hours. To look around. See if it's the kind of place we want to go for our fishing trip next spring.'

'That's a good thing. Because you're not dressed to stay much longer than that. It gets pretty cold up there when the sun goes down.'

'Like I said, just a few hours.'

Drussard considered telling them that since he would be bringing them back with him that day, he only needed to make one round trip, and the rate should have been half the price he had quoted them. But he decided against it; the Americans were in a hurry and willing to pay three thousand dollars, so who was he to argue with them. Five minutes later, with Kitlan in the co-pilot's seat and Marcus in the back, Drussard applied full power and the plane roared down the middle of the lake and took off.

As he reached cruising altitude at fifteen hundred feet, Drussard looked over his shoulder at Marcus and cast a sideways glance at Kitlan, appraising the two men. The stocky, powerfully built man with the scowling face sitting behind him looked like a humorless, no-neck, bar-room brawler. The one sitting beside him had a military bearing and hard unyielding eyes with a predatory glint; no more than six feet tall, and wiry, he emanated a sense of power and ability far in excess of his physical size.

Drussard did not entirely believe their story about scouting out the lake for a future fishing trip, but it was none of his concern. Business was slow this time of year, and the personal matter he had mentioned was to pick up his wife's anniversary present. The extra money meant it would not take him until their next anniversary to pay it off.

He was staring at the thin, jagged scar at the base of Kitlan's neck when Kitlan gave him a look that made him avert his eyes. He tried making small talk to break the tension.

'Popular place this week, that lake.'

'Why's that?'

'I just brought two Americans like yourselves out of there this morning.'

'Yeah? How about that. Where were they from?'

'One was from Pennsylvania. The other Virginia, I think.' Drussard did not miss the look the two men exchanged.

The Cherokee he had almost collided with flashed through Kitlan's mind. Two men in front. Pennsylvania plates. A canoe on the roof.

'What were their names?'

Drussard hesitated; the tone of the questions were laced with something more than curiosity. 'Bob and John maybe? I forget. They didn't talk much. Nice fellows though. Said they had a good week fishing and rock climbing.'

Kitlan knew Drussard was lying. He would have logged their names and addresses before flying them into the lake, in the event they were missing when he returned to pick them up. But at this point it was information Kitlan decided he might not need and could always get later, so he let it pass.

'What are your names?'

Kitlan fixed Drussard with a cold, hard look. 'We forget.'

Drussard fell silent and stared out of the window at the wilderness below. It crossed his mind that accepting their money might not have been the wisest thing he had ever done.

Chapter Fourteen

Marcel Drussard followed Kitlan's instructions, descending to one hundred feet above the trees and flying in ever-widening circles outward from the small clearing on the shore of the lake where Stafford and Barnes had camped. Drussard now knew with certainty that the purpose of the charter had nothing to do with scouting the area for a future fishing trip. What he did not know was exactly what the uncommunicative Kitlan and Marcus were up to, and it was making him increasingly edgy.

'If you tell me what you're looking for I might be able to help you.'

'You'll know when you see it.' Kitlan's eyes were intent on the ground, moving back and forth over the dense forest.

On the third time around something winked up at Drussard through the trees; a flash of metal reflecting the bright sunlight. He banked sharply to the left and descended to just above tree-top level.

'Is that it?' He pointed to the ground off the tip of the left wing. The battered tail section of the Lear jet could be seen on a rock outcropping partway down the ravine.

'Yeah. That's it.' Kitlan looked around and got his bearings. He estimated the ravine was no more than one half mile from the campsite over easy terrain.

Drussard gave Kitlan a puzzled look. He knew there was no search and rescue effort going on in the area, and he had heard nothing of a missing plane. 'How did you know about this? And how did you know where to look for it?'

'I called the Psychic Hot Line. Put us down on the lake at the campsite.'

'After I call this in to the Toronto Center.'

Drussard pressed the switch on the yoke that keyed the microphone on his headset. Kitlan reached over and turned off the radio. 'That can wait until later.'

'There might be survivors down there.'

'We can determine that once we're on the ground. Stay off the radio.'

Drussard's temper flared. 'Either I report this right now, or I head back to Chibougamau. It's your choice. I'll refund your money except for the cost of flying you in here.'

Kitlan smiled humorlessly. 'I can fly this plane if I have to, Drussard. So do what I tell you. You took my money, and you'll follow my instructions. Now put us down at the campsite.'

The veiled threat was not lost on Drussard. He looked over his shoulder to see Marcus leaning forward in his seat, ready to do whatever Kitlan told him. He again silently admonished himself for so eagerly accepting the charter, wondering just who and what he was dealing with as he leveled off and turned for a final approach to the lake.

Once on shore at the campsite, Kitlan pulled Marcus aside. 'Keep him away from the radio until I get back. And no rough stuff. I wasn't lying when I said I could fly the plane, but I've never taken off or landed on water, and this isn't the time or the place to learn.'

Deer and moose trails, worn and rutted and partially covered with leaves, cut into the forest in several directions, parting the underbrush and following the path of least resistance from the water's edge. Kitlan passed them by, walking the perimeter of the clearing until he found what he was looking for: an old, partially overgrown footpath leading away from the campsite in the general direction of the ravine.

Drussard started to follow him. Marcus put a hand on his chest, stopping him in his tracks. 'We'll wait here.'

Drussard shoved the offending hand away, but stayed where he was, not about to challenge the thick-necked man glaring at him.

An experienced woodsman and expert tracker, Kitlan set out through the forest like a wolf following a scent-marked trail. The fallen leaves had covered most of the boot prints, but he easily picked up other signs of someone's passing within the last few days. Trampled vines and underbush, an abrasion where a boot had scraped an exposed tree root, and pencil-thin branches of small saplings broken and bent where they extended out across the trail, all led him to the crash site and a heavy concentration of overlapping boot prints at the edge of the ravine.

One hundred feet below him, Kitlan saw Ramsey's body strapped into the rear bench seat of the Lear, his eyes open, staring vacantly into the sky.

Kitlan knew, from talking to the man in St John's who had transferred the money from the freighter to the plane, that all three of the bags were placed on the luggage shelf directly behind the bench seat. He took the binoculars from the carry-on bag slung over his shoulder and trained them on the shelf above and behind the body. He adjusted the focus on the powerful optics and saw that the shelf was empty, and that the leather cargo net used to keep the bags in place was unhooked and hanging off to the side.

Had the eyelets that held the cargo net in place been torn from their mountings in the fuselage, he would have accepted that the force of the crash had been responsible and that the bags had ended up in the bottom of the ravine with the main part of the wreckage. But unless the cargo net was never attached when the bags were loaded, which he had to admit was possible, someone had unfastened it after the crash.

The limited area of destruction at the bottom of the ravine indicated that the Lear had gone in nose first, and closer observation revealed the path it had taken as it plummeted to the ground. Silver paint from the fuselage had scraped off on the sheer rock walls in two places where it had slammed against the sides, and huge limbs were splintered and the tops torn from trees where it finally came to rest.

Kitlan saw evidence of an explosion and fire as he focused the binoculars on the depths of the ravine, three hundred and fifty feet below. The sections of the fuselage visible through the gaps in the thick stands of evergreens were charred along with the surrounding trees and underbush. The possibility of the pilot and co-pilot surviving the crash was non-existent, and if the money ended up there, he knew the odds were it had burned up in the fire.

He estimated it would take the better part of a day to get to the wreckage at the bottom, and that would require returning to civilization to get the necessary equipment to do it. Then there was the problem of Drussard, and the Canadian search teams which could arrive at any time.

Kitlan studied the ground in the immediate area, noticing that a number of boot prints, only partially covered by the falling leaves, led in the direction of a large pine tree set back from the edge of the ravine. He thought nothing of it and was about to return to the campsite when, out of the corner of his eye, he saw faint scrape marks a few feet off the ground on the bark of the tree. He knelt on one knee and examined the marks carefully, finding small strands of nylon filament imbedded in the bark. Strands, he realized, that could have been left by a climbing rope tied around the trunk if someone had gone over the side in an attempt to reach the tail section of the Lear.

Drussard had said the campers were rock climbers. They would have had the equipment they needed. One, or both of them, had probably climbed down to the tail section to see if the man strapped in the seat was still alive.

But had they found the money? Kitlan's instincts told him that they had. He got up and walked back to the edge of the ravine and thought about what he knew so far. The two men had to have seen the crash. Their campsite was only one half mile away. According to Drussard, they were the only people on the lake that week, and the passenger had reported seeing them in a canoe as the Lear tried to land on the water.

Drussard did not know about the crash. Why hadn't they reported it to him when he picked them up that morning? Two possible reasons. They had the money and wanted to get out without any questions being asked, or they had not found the money and simply did not want to get involved with the Canadian authorities for their own reasons. Kitlan strongly suspected the former, and if that was the case, Drussard had to have seen the bags if they were loaded on his plane when he flew the campers out.

Any lingering doubts Kitlan had were eliminated as he walked back along the path to the campsite. He saw something he had overlooked on his way to the ravine. The underbush and leaves on the forest floor were disturbed where someone had left the path and walked fifty feet into the woods to a small open area among a thin stand of trees. Leaves and pine needles had been gathered and purposely placed over a soft patch of earth approximately four feet in diameter, looking out of place with the natural pattern of the ground cover. Kitlan scraped the leaves and needles away with his foot and saw the freshly turned soil underneath.

Five minutes later, he was back with a small shovel Drussard kept with his survival equipment in the plane. He dug no more than eight inches when the tip of the shovel struck something metal. He cleared the soil away and saw a small propane camp stove and a fore-blackened coffee pot and frying pan. Continuing to dig, he found a two-man tent, rolled up and thrown in the hole with more camping equipment and some clothing beneath it.

Kitlan stopped digging, puzzled by what he had discovered. Why discard and hide perfectly good camping equipment and clothing? And then he knew. To put the money in stuff bags they had been in. But as he examined what had been buried, he realised that the bags that had contained the discarded gear would not be enough to hold all of the money. Some of it, yes, but they had to have devised another way of getting the rest out if they did not want Drussard to become suspicious.

Back at the campsite, after assuring Drussard that no one had survived the crash, he asked him what the two campers had brought in with them and what they had taken out.

'Do you mind telling me what's going on here?'

'Just answer the question.'

'They took out the same things they brought in.'

'And what was that?'

Drussard thought for a moment. 'A canoe. They each had backpacks and sleeping bags. A tent. Fishing equipment. Four

51

or five nylon stuff bags for their climbing equipment and I don't know what else was in them.'

'Did you notice anything different when you loaded it on the plane this morning.'

'They loaded their things themselves.'

'What about the canoe?'

'What about it?'

'Was there anything in it?'

Drussard paused to think. 'I couldn't tell. It was covered with a tarp.'

'And why was that?'

'I don't know. It wasn't covered for the flight in. So I guess there could have been something inside it.'

Kitlan believed Drussard was being truthful, and he knew that at least two of the equipment bags the money was packed in could fit inside a canoe. And the contents of the third distributed among the stuff bags and backpacks. They had found the money; it was the only reasonable explanation for what they had done.

'Let's go,' he told Drussard, and walked toward the plane.

'Can I report the crash site now?'

'Do it when we get back to your office and our business is finished.'

Thoroughly intimidated by the two men, Drussard said nothing and climbed back in the plane.

Chapter Fifteen

Shortly after two o'clock, Ben Stafford drove across the Thousand Islands Bridge and pulled the Jeep Cherokee into the Customs and Immigration station on Wellesley Island at Alexandria Bay, New York.

The traffic entering the United States was light, something that made him even more anxious than he already was; the customs inspectors would not be rushed. He had gone through this same station numerous times over the years, returning from fishing and camping trips to Ontario and Quebec. The routine had never been more than a few perfunctory questions and a quick glance inside the vehicle before being passed through. There was no reason to expect that this time would be any different. But then there was always Murphy's Law . . . and Eddie Barnes.

Barnes drummed his fingers on the dash as Stafford pulled into one of three open bays. 'All we have to do is act normal and we've got it made.'

'Then we may as well just give them the money and assume the position over the hood right now. You've never had a normal day in your life.'

Barnes laughed. 'Ten million apiece, pardner, and this is the last obstacle.'

Stafford had taken over the driving just before they crossed the bridge. The inspectors usually asked most of the questions of the driver, and Barnes had a problem with authority figures, especially those who abused their authority and tried to raise their self-esteem by stepping on his. He was taking no chances with Barnes' volatile temper and notoriously short fuse.

Stafford groaned inwardly at the sight of the customs inspector who came out of the station: a short, thin man with a fastidiously trimmed mustache on a narrow, pinched face that had officious bureaucrat written all over it. His uniform shirt was tailored and crisply starched, his slacks had sharp creases, his shoes were spit-shined to a mirror finish, and he spent way too much time on his hair. The name tag on his shirt read Dumpty, and Stafford would have bet all twenty million dollars that the man had been called Humpty since he was a kid; probably the Hump for short, leaving him with little in the way of a sense of humor.

Barnes rolled his eyes as Dumpty approached the Cherokee. 'Will you look at this guy? I can just see his closet; color coded and arranged by seasons. And I don't even want to think about his sock drawer.'

'Just shut up, Eddie. Whatever you do, don't bait him and don't let him think you're challenging his authority.'

'Wouldn't dream of it.'

Dumpty appeared at the driver's-side window, his chin even with the sill. His eyes narrowed into a practiced Clint Eastwood squint and moved from Stafford to Barnes.

'Good afternoon, gentlemen.'

Stafford offered a pleasant smile. 'Good afternoon, Inspector.'

Dumpty did not return the smile. He had not missed the derisive look in Barnes' eyes before directing his attention back to Stafford. 'And what was the purpose of your trip?'

'Fishing and camping.'

'Did you buy or receive anything of value while you were in Canada?'

'Just a few fishing lures.'

'Are you citizens of the United States?'

'Yes.'

'And where do you live?'

'Chadds Ford, Pennsylvania.'

Dumpty looked across to Barnes. 'And you, sir?'

'Reston, Virginia.'

Dumpty glanced at the rear passenger seat, and Barnes could have sworn he heard his heels click as he took a quick step back and looked up at the roof rack, taking in the canoe and the tarp covering the bags of money. He then side-stepped toward the back of the Cherokee, frowning at the heavily tinted windows that prevented him from seeing into the rear compartment.

'Pull the vehicle into the inspection bay on your right, sir.'

Stafford kept his tone casual and friendly. 'Is something wrong, Inspector?'

'Just pull the vehicle into the inspection bay, sir.'

'Hey, pal,' was all Barnes got out before Stafford shot him a warning look.

Dumpty had no reason to suspect Stafford and Barnes were other than what they claimed to be. They did not fit the profile he had been trained to use in evaluating drug smugglers, or the more recent addition to the list, cigarette smugglers. But he did not like the arrogance of the man in the passenger seat, and with a lull in the traffic, he had time to show him just how far his smart-assed attitude was going to get him.

Stafford pulled off to the right and cut the engine. He and Barnes got out and stood at the rear of the Cherokee waiting while Dumpty took his time sauntering over to them. Barnes glared at the pretentious little man, his disdain evident in his expression.

'Probably has a bag full of little boy's underwear hidden somewhere in his house.'

'Knock it off, Eddie. This guy can hurt us.'

'Then how 'bout I just deck the little pencil-neck geek wannabe and we make a run for it?'

'Yeah. That'd be one of your smarter moves. We've got another bridge to cross before we're on the mainland, and I guarantee you they'd have the other end blocked before we got there. And even if they didn't, they'd have our license plate number.'

Barnes flashed a mischievous grin. 'Your license plate number, Kemosabe, not mine.'

'Very funny.' Stafford felt his stomach tighten and sour as

he watched Dumpty approach. 'We've had it. You know that don't you?'

'Maybe. But hey, it was worth a shot.'

Dumpty reached the rear of the Cherokee and stopped with military precision. 'Open the tailgate and step back from the vehicle, please.'

Stafford did as instructed, casting a look of imminent doom in Barnes' direction.

Dumpty looked at the backpacks in the rear compartment, his eyes lingering on the odd bulges in the stuff bags crammed in among them.

'What do you have in the bags?'

'Some left over free-dried food, climbing gear, boots, clothes.' It was the best Stafford could come up with; not that it would matter if the bags were inspected.

Dumpty leaned into the rear compartment and shoved the tackle boxes and fishing-rod cases to one side as he reached for the stuff bag closest to him.

Stafford silently cursed his fate, and his being stupid enough to let Barnes talk him into keeping the money. And now the Hump was about to make the bust of his career. Twenty million in cash that screamed big-time drug trafficker. He caught Barnes' eye and slowly shook his head as Dumpty began to untie the draw cord securing the top of the stuff bag. Barnes looked as if he hadn't a care in the world.

As Dumpty was about to pull the top of the stuff bag open, sirens filled the air, wailing in concert and growing in volume as they sped toward the Customs and Immigration station. Dumpty looked up to see two state police cruisers screech to a halt. The two troopers jumped out, leaving their light bars flashing and engines running. One of them went into the station, the other spotted Dumpty and ran toward him.

Dumpty quickly lost interest in the stuff bag and turned his attention to the approaching trooper, young and intense and full of adrenaline. Dumpty puffed himself up to his full height, which was level with the trooper's shoulder. 'Can I help you, Officer?'

'Did you pass a dark-gray Ford Explorer with New York plates through here in the last half hour?'

'I don't recall the car, but who are you looking for?'

'Two men. White. Mid-thirties. One skinny, stringy blond hair and a goatee. One heavily built, biker-type wearing a leather vest over a black Harley-Davidson T-shirt.'

'What did they do?'

'Committed an armed robbery on the Canadian side. Killed a local cop, a clerk, and a customer; a pregnant woman for Christ's sake.'

Dumpty's eyes widened. 'I've been on duty since eight this morning and I haven't seen anyone matching those descriptions.'

'Good. The Canadians think they might be coming through here. We've got two more cruisers on the way, and we'd appreciate your cooperation in setting up a road block on the southbound lanes until the Mounties can get set up on the other side.'

'No problem.'

The trooper turned and jogged toward the station. Dumpty followed, taking two steps to the trooper's one to keep up.

Stafford seized the opportunity and called out. 'Inspector? You want us to wait here?'

Dumpty paused and looked over his shoulder at Stafford and Barnes, then back at the departing trooper. He summoned up his best command voice and barked out his decision.

'No. Go on through. And don't waste any time doing it. I've got an emergency situation here.'

Stafford and Barnes quickly complied, getting into the Cherokee and pulling out of the inspection bay.

As they drove off, Barnes turned in his seat and looked back to see the troopers angle-parking their cruisers to block entrance to the southbound traffic lanes.

'Damn, that was close! The gods must be looking out for us today.'

'Yeah. As opposed to the three people who got killed.'

Stafford saw that his hands were shaking as he reached to turn on the radio. 'When that pompous little shit started to open that bag I saw my life flash before me. Everything I worked for down the drain. My daughter in some snake pit of a state hospital while I sit in prison. I should have my damn head examined for listening to you.'

'Yeah, well, we made it, pardner. And it's all downhill from here.'

'Just remember that everything I told you still holds. We sit on the money until we see what happens and work out a plan to launder it.'

'Absolutely.' Barnes reclined his seat, stretched out, and closed his eyes. He went over the mental shopping list he had been working on since the previous night, making a few additions.

Chapter Sixteen

Marcel Drussard cut the engines on the twin Beech and drifted into the dock on the shore of Chibougamau lake. Tony Kitlan and Peter Marcus climbed out and waited while he tied the plane down, then followed him into the small chip-board shack at the water's edge that served as his office.

Kitlan went over to the cluttered desk in the corner and glanced at some of the papers scattered across the top.

Drussard stepped in front of him. 'Since our business is finished, I'd appreciate it if you'd leave.'

'We'll leave as soon as you give me the names and addresses of the two men you picked up this morning.'

'My agreement was to fly you in and out. Nothing else.'

'Make this easy on yourself, Frenchie. Just give me what I want. Then we'll be on our way. No harm. No foul.'

Drussard looked behind him to see Marcus positioned at the door to the office, his huge arms folded across his chest, barring anyone from entering or leaving. 'I told you, I don't know their full names. Just John and Bob, I think.'

Kitlan again smiled without humor. 'I know that every bush pilot is required to keep a record of his customers' names and home addresses so they can inform the authorities in the event they get lost or have an accident, or whatever. So do yourself a favor and don't insult my intelligence again.'

Drussard did not want trouble from the two men, but the stubborn, proud side of him, smarting over their stopping him from calling in the crash site, was not about to give in.

'I may have written their names down somewhere, I'm not sure. But even if I did I probably threw them out this morning after they left.'

'How did they pay you?'

'Cash. Like you,' he lied.

Drussard sat down at the desk and pretended to search through the clutter, purposely shoving a stack of unpaid bills over the black, vinyl-covered record book in which he logged all of his charters.

Kitlan saw what he had done and pulled him out of the chair by his hair, slamming a fist into his stomach and sending him to the floor doubled over. He picked up the record book and flipped to the last page of entries to find the two names and addresses he was looking for. The time and date Drussard had entered for their pick up at the lake that morning confirmed they were the right men.

Drussard struggled to his knees, putting a hand on the edge of the desk to pull himself up. He stood on wobbly legs, gasping for breath. Kitlan looked at Marcus and nodded, then walked over to the window to watch for anyone approaching the shack.

Marcus removed a semi-automatic pistol from the shoulder holster under his jacket and screwed a sound-suppressor onto the end of the barrel. The two shots he fired in rapid succession made no more noise than a car door closing.

Drussard was still leaning against the desk gulping in air, his back to Marcus, when the .380 caliber hollow point bullets tore into the base of his skull, killing him and blowing away part of his face when they exited.

Kitlan walked over to where Drussard had crumpled to the floor. He dropped to one knee, pulled the dead man's jacket open, and reached into an inside pocket to retrieve the three thousand dollars he had given for the flight. He then opened a small closet on the wall opposite the desk and dragged the body inside, folding it over and stuffing it in a corner so the door would close.

Marcus calmly unscrewed the sound-suppressor from the barrel and put the pistol back in his shoulder holster. He showed no more emotion that he would had he just swatted a fly. 'So what now?'

Kitlan tore the last page from the log book and put it in his jacket pocket. 'We go talk to the boss. See what he wants to do.'

Twenty-miles south of Chibougamau, Kitlan pulled off the narrow, two-lane road and removed the Quebec license plates he had stolen at a service plaza the previous night shortly after crossing the border into Canada. He replaced them with his New York plates, and once back in the car and underway, used his car phone to call Paul Cameron in New York City.

Chapter Seventeen

Gary McDermott arrived at Marcel Drussard's office at Chibougamau Lake at five o'clock in the afternoon, eight hours after leaving the CIA station in the American embassy in Ottawa.

That morning, a CIA asset with the Canadian Transportation Safety Board had put him in touch with a well-meaning but incompetent clerk to whom he had given the tail number of Drussard's aircraft. The Beech 18 had four previous owners, and the clerk mistakenly gave him the name and address of the man who had sold the plane to Drussard, another bush pilot, who ran a charter service out of Matagami, Quebec, one hundred and seventy miles in the opposite direction of Chibougamau.

The pilot was out on a flight when McDermott arrived, and he spent two hours waiting for him to return, only to learn that he had been waiting for the wrong man.

Four hours later, McDermott reached the small chip-board shack on the shore of Chibougamau Lake that served as Drussard's office. A car was parked in the gravel lot at the side of the shack, and the make, model and license number matched the information given him by another CIA asset with the Quebec provincial government whom he had called on his car phone when he left Matagami. The door to Drussard's office was slightly ajar, but McDermott still knocked. When he got no response, he stepped inside.

He looked around the sparsely furnished room and saw no

one. Thinking that Drussard might be somewhere outside since his car was there and his aircraft was tied down at the dock, he turned to go out the door. It was then that he noticed the stain on the floor in front of the desk. As his eyes moved upward, he saw that the surface of the desk, and the papers pinned to a cork board on the wall behind it, were splattered with the same dark red stain.

McDermott followed the smear-trail leading to the closet where a thick, coagulated pool of blood had seeped beneath the door. He had no physical description of Drussard, but he was certain that the body he found on the floor of the closet with half of its face missing was the man he was looking for.

Chapter Eighteen

One hour after McDermott found Drussard's body, Lou Burruss entered the anteroom to Adam Welsh's office in the CIA's Counter Narcotics Center. He nodded to Welsh's administrative assistant and entered the inner office without knocking.

'I just heard back from McDermott.'

'And?'

'And he found the owner of the aircraft that picked up the two subjects at the lake this morning. His name's Marcel Drussard, and he's dead. Two shots in the back of the head. Killed sometime this afternoon. Probably around three or four o'clock.'

Welsh raised an eyebrow and put down the intelligence report he had been reading. 'By the two men we saw at the lake?'

'McDermott doesn't think so. He spoke to Drussard's wife. She said they left Chibougamau around eight this morning. She saw her husband alive shortly after nine when he came home for breakfast. A local fisherman saw two other men show up around noon, then he heard Drussard's plane take off about fifteen or twenty minutes later.'

'Did he know the two men?'

'He only saw them from behind. He said their car had Quebec plates.'

'He didn't happen to get a number, did he?'

'No. He said the car was silver, either a Mercedes, BMW, or a Lexus.'

Burruss sat in one of the chairs facing Welsh's desk. 'We may not know who they were, but there's no doubt what they were after. McDermott says one of the pages from Drussard's log book, where he records the names and addresses of his charters, is missing. The last page. Which would have had the information on the two subjects we saw at the lake. So whoever killed Drussard knows who they are.'

'Did McDermott find out who the campers were?'

'That's where we got lucky. One of them paid the bill for the charter with a credit card. His name's Ben Stafford and he lives at 1200 Wylie Road in Chadds Ford, Pennsylvania. I'm having his name run through our files now to see if we get a hit.'

'And the other one?'

'There was no record of who he was.'

Welsh propped his elbows on the arms of his chair, steepled his fingers under his chin, and stared off in the middle distance. Then, after a long silence, he said, 'We're still in the game. The bad guys know who has the money, and now so do we. At least one of them. All we have to do is sit on him until they show up and we've—'

Burruss cut him off. 'We've got to bring the Secret Service back in on this now. Before it gets completely out of control with a momentum all of its own.'

'No. Not yet. You tell them only that we have reason to believe the plane crashed in Canada but we have no idea where it is. That's all they get for now.'

'They're going to be really pissed when they find out we cut them out of the loop. It's their case.'

'It's not their case until I say it's their case.'

'I don't have to remind you that we have no charter to operate domestically.'

'We're not running a domestic operation. We're following up on one that originated in Paris and in which the Secret Service asked us to intervene.'

'You're splitting hairs.'

'It's my call.' With that, Welsh got up from behind his desk and paced as he spoke. 'I want twenty-four hour surveillance on Stafford. And our people are not to interfere with anything that goes down. When the bad guys show up, I want the surveillance to follow them back to whoever they work for and we'll find out who's running the show.'

'That's a good way to get this Stafford killed. We've got to grab whoever it is that shows up at his place before they find the money. Once they have it, they won't hesitate to kill him any more than they did the pilot.'

'That's not our concern. I want to know who all the players are. If we grab the ones who show up at Stafford's, all we have is them and the money, with no guarantee they'll roll over on the man at the top. And that's the guy we want, not his soldiers. Whoever he is, he's been bearding us in our den for the past four years, and this is the best chance we've had at nailing him.'

Welsh paused and softened his tone to his subordinate. 'We'll do what we can to keep Stafford and his friend alive, but I'm not blowing this operation over two greedy bastards who tried to walk away with twenty million that doesn't belong to them.'

'I still say the Secret Service is better equipped to handle this.'

'They'll just treat it as a counterfeiting case.'

'It is a counterfeiting case.'

'And I say it's a national security case.'

'Adam, we're talking about twenty million dollars in super-notes that to the untrained eye are virtually undetectable from the real thing. If that money gets into circulation, and the Secret Service finds out we could have done something to prevent it, there's going to be one hell of a backlash.'

'I'll deal with that if and when it happens.'

Chapter Nineteen

Stafford lived in a two-story fieldstone house built in the late eighteenth century in the gently rolling countryside of Chester County, Pennsylvania. It was once a tenant house for a three-hundred-acre estate recently subdivided and developed into pricey townhouse clusters and tract mansions – million dollar homes on postage-stamp-sized lots – that served as a bedroom community for Philadelphia, only a half hour commute away.

Situated in the middle of six acres in a secluded corner on the back side of the development, the house was off a secondary blacktop road a few miles north of the village of Chadds Ford. The property had a peaceful, idyllic setting of fenced-in meadows dotted with mature trees, a bank barn, and a small pond overhung with weeping willows. The house was really too big for one person, but Stafford could not bring himself to sell it after his wife's death. Even with her work as an elementary-school teacher and the myriad school projects in which she and their daughter Annie were involved, she had somehow managed to find time to oversee the renovation and the decorating of the house. So much of her personality filled every room that Stafford could not imagine turning it over to strangers. And although there were times when he thought his daughter was lost to him forever, he still hoped against hope that someday she might return to once again fill the rooms with laughter, and to ride her horse through the meadows and wooded trails adjoining the property.

Upon arriving home that evening, Stafford had a beer and a

sandwich with Eddie Barnes, then helped him load his share of the money into his car and, before he left for the drive back to Reston, Virginia, gave him a final dire warning about spending any significant amount of cash until they worked out a plan. Stafford then took the two oversized nylon bags containing ten million dollars into the kitchen and placed them at the foot of the rear staircase leading up to the second-floor master bedroom.

The kitchen was a warm and inviting room, but filled with the memories of a life destroyed. The brick floor, the hand-crafted cherry cabinets, the granite countertops, and the gingham curtains were all painstakingly chosen by his wife. Photographs pinned to a cork bulletin board captured vivid, haunting images of Annie, and smiley-faced magnets held old school notices and test scores on the refrigerator door, the same as they had on the day of the accident eighteen months ago.

Stafford missed his wife and knew that he always would. He saw something of her almost every day: when the sky was the deep cobalt blue of her eyes, when a full moon rose on a cold autumn night like the night they first met, in the way a woman turned and waved, and in the smiles and looks and countless small gestures exchanged by people in love. He sometimes wondered why she had married someone like him, suspecting that it might have been a momentary lapse of good sense. Whatever the reason, he blessed the day he met her, and the day she gave him Annie, and he believed that his part of the deal was to keep them safe. He would never forgive himself for failing at that.

They had lived their lives doing all the things people do to fool themselves into believing there is a permanence to what they are building. And then one evening a man leaves a happy-hour drinking bout with his office buddies and runs a red light at a four-way intersection going ninety miles an hour. And your world is never the same again. And you are faced with the brutal truth that permanence and control over life are illusions, and that we are all just passing through at the mercy of chance or fate with no guarantee of tomorrow.

Stafford removed a photo from the bulletin board – a big, happy smile on Annie's face as she stood beside her horse and held up a blue ribbon. He remembered taking the picture and how proud he was of her. 'See you tomorrow, honey,' he whispered, then put the photo back in its place and went into his study.

The red light on the telephone answering unit was blinking as he entered the room. Stafford pressed the playback button, listening to the tape rewind as he booted up the personal computer on his desk. All four messages were from Tony Nardini, the Philadelphia bail bondsman who used him almost exclusively. Each message was more urgent than the last. He had to talk to him. Immediately. A drug dealer he had written a million dollar bond for had disappeared three weeks ago and was due in court next week.

Stafford smiled to himself, knowing Nardini well. The bondsman had not called him in as soon as he learned the man had jumped, hoping to use his police contacts or his network of street snitches to find him and avoid paying Stafford a commission that ranged from twenty percent of the full amount of the bond for in-state cases, to as high as forty percent for international cases. The urgent phone calls meant that the police and the informants had come up empty and, with the man's trial only a week away, Nardini was getting nervous, if not desperate. He was responsible for the entire one million dollars.

When the computer was ready, Stafford logged on and checked his e-mail. Again four urgent, pleading messages from Nardini over the past week. The absence of any messages of a more personal nature stood to emphasize how void Stafford's life was of anything but work.

He looked at his watch; it was nine fifteen. Nardini would still be in his office. He dialed a number in Philadelphia and heard the high-strung bondsman's agitated growl after the first ring. He pictured the man on the other end, the image always the same: feet up on his cluttered desk, a cigar in his mouth, and grease stains down the front of his shirt from the fast food dinner he had inhaled between gulps of black coffee.

'Yeah?'

'Stafford.'

'Oh, Ben. Thank God! I need you buddy. Boy do I need you, and fast.'

'Can't do it, Tony. I'm going to be tied up for the next week or two.'

'Not the words I want to hear. I'll give you twenty-five percent.'

Under normal circumstances, Stafford would not pass up the opportunity to earn a two hundred and fifty thousand dollar commission. But ten million dollars sitting on the floor in the next room were not normal circumstances.

'Can't do it. But I'll see if I can get Bob Burton for you.'

'He won't work for me anymore. We had a slight disagreement.'

'You stiffed him on a fifteen-thousand-dollar commission.'

'Like I said. He won't work for me and I'm in a world of hurt here if I don't find this mutt in the next seven days.'

'Burton will do it if I ask him. For the same twenty-five percent you offered me.'

'Ah, Ben, you're killin' me here. Desertin' me in my hour of need.'

'I'll have Burton call you in the morning.'

Stafford hung up and went back to the kitchen where he carried the bags full of money up the rear staircase to the master bedroom. He opened the door to the walk-in closet he had constructed himself, and pushed the clothes to one side. The other end of the closet had a virtually undetectable false wall with shelves. He took the boxes of his wife's shoes from the shelves and removed the floor-to-ceiling panel to reveal a large fireproof safe where he kept his pistols and shotguns. He then stacked the packets of money inside among the guns, using every inch of available space. When he was finished, he selected a mini-Glock nine millimeter semi-automatic pistol with an inside-the-belt holster to place on the night stand beside the bed, then replaced the false wall, put the shoe boxes back on the shelves, slid the clothes back in place, and closed the door.

A hot shower soothed his cramped and aching muscles after the day-long drive, and sleep came quickly. But it would not last through the night. The bitterness and anger over losing his wife, and over what had happened to Annie, would consume him again, as it had every night since the accident. It would come in the small hours of the morning, when the mind feeds on itself, rising like a bile from the depths of his soul to torture him. He would lie awake until the first trace of pale dawn light lined the horizon, then go for his morning run and force the anguish and sorrow from his conscious thoughts.

Chapter Twenty

Just before eight o'clock on Monday morning, Special Agent Tom Quinn pulled his car into the underground parking garage at the new nine-story Secret Service headquarters building on H Street and took the elevator directly to the fifth floor. He knocked once, then entered the office of Steve Jacoby, the Special-Agent-In-Charge of the Counterfeit Division. Jacoby was just finishing a telephone conversation and gestured to one of the chairs in front of his desk.

Quinn sat down, giving his boss an exasperated look as he hung up the phone. 'I just came from a meeting with Lou Burruss, our liaison at the Counter Narcotics Center. They lost the shipment of supernotes.'

'Lost how?'

'The plane crashed somewhere in the Quebec wilderness.'

'Somewhere? They don't know where it went down?'

'No. They lost contact with it shortly after the Canadian air controllers did.'

'What happened to the transmitter our undercover planted in one of the bags?'

'Apparently our transmitter, and the Emergency Locator Transmitter on board the plane, were both destroyed in the crash, so we have no way of locating the site.'

Jacoby raised an eyebrow. 'You believe them?'

'I don't know. They might be playing turf games; waiting to grab the money when it comes into the country to make a show of recovering it themselves. But there's also the possibility that the smugglers found the transmitter in the bag and disabled it; that would have dropped the plane off CIA's tracking screens.'

'Do they have any idea how much money was in the shipment?

'If they do, they aren't saying. But our undercover got a look inside one of the bags when he planted the bug; he estimated it could be as much as twenty-five million.'

'Christ! The shipments just keep getting bigger.'

'And they're coming in at a faster rate. Four in the past six months, that we know of.'

Both men knew why the pace had increased; the counterfeiters had changed the way they were laundering their money. The new one hundred dollar bill, designed specifically by the Treasury Department to prevent counterfeiters from copying it, had failed to achieve its intended purpose. Within six months a new 'supernote' – a one hundred dollar bill that was a near perfect replica of the newly designed bill, impossible to detect without knowing what you were looking for – began to appear in the international monetary system.

The casinos in Germany and Italy, and the banks in Switzerland, Austria, and Liechtenstein that were heavily involved in money laundering, charged large fees to handle the counterfeit currency, as much as seventy cents on the dollar, so the resourceful counterfeiters had looked for, and found, a new outlet for their product. International drug traffickers.

The target area for moving most of the supernotes now became the United States, where the drug traffickers would have no trouble filtering large amounts of it into the flourishing American economy. The counterfeiters were buying pure uncut heroin and cocaine with the supernotes, then, through their own contacts, reselling it at current full market value, essentially getting a dollar for dollar exchange rate for the counterfeit money. Fourteen million dollars in supernotes had recently been traced back to a bank in the Cayman Islands, and to another in Lugano, Switzerland, both banks known to launder money for the Mexican and Columbian drug cartels. But much of the money was being laundered inside the United States, through a long-established network of businesses set up for just that purpose.

73

The cartels, and the people who laundered their money for them, were completely unaware that the millions they were receiving for their high-grade, uncut cocaine and heroin were counterfeit; such was the quality of the new supernote. For the moment, the counterfeiters not only had a new market, but a far more lucrative one. By getting dollar for dollar value for their money, and discounts for buying the drugs in large quantities that allowed them to resell them for considerably more than they had paid, they had increased their profits by more than eighty percent.

Quinn and Jacoby believed that the counterfeiters were moving quickly to maximize those profits before the drug cartels caught on to what they were doing. The estimate of the amount of supernotes that had gotten into the American and international monetary system, in the last ten months alone, was in excess of one hundred and fifty million dollars. And as Jacoby and Quinn were painfully aware, they were no closer to catching the people behind it than they were nine years ago when the first supernote, based on the old one hundred dollar bill, began to appear. The current joint operation with CIA's Counter Narcotics Center was the first time the Secret Service had gotten close enough to even pick up the counterfeiters' scent. And now, despite a promising beginning, they had, it appeared, once again eluded them.

Current intelligence information was sketchy at best, indicating that the new supernote was being produced in either Syria or Lebanon, possibly by the Russian mafia. But there was nothing concrete or verifiable.

Jacoby shook his head in disgust at the thought of the latest shipment of supernotes making it into the country. 'If that plane hasn't crashed and they managed to elude our surveillance efforts, the money's going to start showing up within the next few weeks.'

Quinn nodded in agreement. 'I can alert every field office that the shipment might have made it through. And if the notes surface, we can flood the area with agents.'

Quinn got up to leave and paused before opening the door. 'I almost forgot. Another piece of encouraging news.

74

One of the intelligence analysts over at CNC told me they've received fairly reliable information that the people behind this are also buying weapons, mostly small arms, from international arms dealers; possibly reselling some of them to militant groups in this country.'

'Find the bastards, Tom. And fast. Before this turns into more of a disaster than it already is.'

Chapter Twenty-One

The offices of the security firm of Cameron & Associates occupied the entire thirty-fifth floor of the modern glass tower overlooking Battery Park and Upper New York Bay. Paul Cameron, the firm's president and founder, had a staff of forty-eight associates in his Manhattan office, with smaller, satellite offices in London, Paris and Rome. His employees were among the best in their respective fields, all formerly with federal law enforcement or intelligence agencies: field researchers and intelligence analysts from the CIA, data-base personnel and experts in computer fraud from the FBI, and communications intercept and electronic surveillance specialists from NSA.

Cameron & Associates dealt only with CEOs and their lead attorneys, and then only those who were vouched for and recommended by established clients. Most of the firm's sizeable income was derived from litigation involving large multi-national corporations, mergers and acquisitions, and the peculiar troubles of the very rich. They provided discreet, in-depth investigations and surveillance, with cases ranging from an investment banker's wife after half of her husband's assets in a divorce, to corporate espionage and hostile takeovers with the inherent threat of greenmail where the stakes were often in the hundreds of millions of dollars.

But Cameron's security business, though very successful, was not his main source of income, or his primary reason for being in business. His other activities, far more secret and nefarious than those of the corporate world, were carried out by an elite group of men, all former contract employees of the CIA's highly classified special operations section. These men were not to be found in Cameron's employee files or payroll records, and they were entirely unknown to the rest of his staff. Cameron's own orders and instructions originated with one of the most powerful men in the world; the man who had provided the funds to set up Cameron & Associates as a cover organization for his own ulterior motives.

A tall, broad-shouldered man with patrician good looks, Cameron's superb physical conditioning belied his sixty-two years. His penetrating pale-green eyes were his most dominant feature, and once fixed on someone in a firm, steady gaze, told even the least perceptive person in no uncertain terms that he was a man it was best not to anger. He was at the built-in bar in his large, luxurious, corner office, pouring a glass of mineral water for himself and two fingers of Bushmills for the most trusted and experienced member of his elite group of field operatives, Tony Kitlan.

Cameron crossed the plush, dove-gray carpet to where Kitlan stood watching the morning sunlight sparkle off the dark, choppy waters of the bay. He handed him his drink and raised his glass. Kitlan touched glasses, then tossed back his head and downed the amber-colored liquid in one swallow.

Cameron sipped his mineral water and stared thoughtfully out of the floor-to-ceiling windows, his gaze fixed on a ferry midway between the pier and Ellis island. 'You have no doubts that Stafford and Barnes have the money?'

'None at all.'

'And you don't think they're going to turn it in?'

'Why go to all the trouble they did to conceal it from the bush pilot if that's what they intended to do?'

'Point taken.'

'How do you want this handled?'

'I would like the money returned, of course. And it would be best if there was no one around to talk to the authorities about what happened.'

'I'll have three men at Stafford's home no later than four o'clock this afternoon.'

'And Barnes?'

'Peter Marcus and I will take the shuttle to Washington. I'll have one of my men there meet us at the airport. We'll be in Reston by early this afternoon.'

Cameron nodded his approval. 'Make certain your men understand that while the money is important, it's secondary; we can always print more. What I'm most concerned with is what else Stafford and Barnes might have learned at the crash site, and who they may end up talking to. So deal with them accordingly. Try to recover the money. But if you can't, don't let that prevent you from finalizing the matter.'

'Yes, sir. I'll give the men explicit instructions. I don't anticipate any problems.'

'We didn't anticipate the plane crash either.'

Chapter Twenty-Two

Ben Stafford pushed his daughter's wheelchair along a tree-shaded path through the campus-like grounds of the private psychiatric hospital in the Philadelphia suburb of Chestnut Hill. He stopped at the bottom of a ramp leading to the entrance to one of the stately brick buildings and a uniformed attendant approached to take Annie the rest of the way. Stafford knelt beside her and hugged her, kissing her on the cheek, and stroking her hair, hoping for some response, no matter how small, some recognition that she knew he was there and that she understood how much he loved her and that he would always be there for her.

But the beautiful eleven-year-old girl, so strikingly reminiscent of her mother, only stared blankly off in the distance, limp and seemingly lifeless in her father's arms, showing no indication that she was even aware of his presence.

She had been like that – a catatonic state, the doctors called it – since the accident. Miraculously thrown from the car with only minor injuries, the hand of fate that had saved her life had exacted a terrible price. Annie had watched helplessly as her mother, trapped inside the mangled wreckage, burned to death before her eyes. She had tried desperately to reach her, but an onlooker had intervened, pulling her away from the car just before the gas tank exploded and mercifully ended her mother's life.

The doctors held out hope that Annie would some day, with proper medications and therapy, return to a normal life, but there had been no indication of even the slightest improvement in the eighteen months since the accident. Occasionally, always late at night when the hospital was still and quiet, she would cry out for a few brief moments, screaming in terror, only to suddenly lapse back into the world of silence and immobility that held her captive.

'I'll be back on Wednesday, honey,' Stafford whispered as he held her tight, not wanting to let go. Wanting to take her home with him. To have things the way they used to be. But Annie only slumped unresponsively in his embrace. He watched after her as the attendant wheeled her back inside, deeply saddened and tormented by what had become of his little girl.

There were times when he wished she had died along with her mother, if only to spare her the prolonged agony of spending the rest of her life suffering the way she was now. But they were only fleeting thoughts. He loved her too much to even imagine what his life would be like if he lost her completely.

The visits to see Annie were always difficult, and Stafford struggled to regain control of his emotions, wiping away the tears with the back of his hand, as he drove off the hospital grounds and headed home.

The three men who had been searching Stafford's house for the past four hours were growing more frustrated and angry with each passing minute. Any thoughts of a professional search, of leaving things undisturbed without a trace of having been there, had long been forgotten.

The rooms looked as if a madman had gone through them in a rage. Furniture was overturned; the upholstered pieces cut open and the stuffing pulled out. Wall-to-wall carpeting and the padding beneath it was ripped up as the men looked for loose floorboards or trapdoors to secret hiding places. Paintings and pictures were torn from the walls in search of a safe, thrown to the floor, their frames splintered, their glass shattered.

The man searching the second floor, Jerry Hanks, had ransacked Annie's room, then turned his attention to the master bedroom walk-in closet. Finding nothing, he had

80

strewn Stafford's wife's clothes in all directions, ripping some of them as he tore them from hangers to check the shelves behind them.

Outside, the late afternoon sun slipped below the horizon, casting a deep reddish-orange glow over the fields and woods, darkening the house to the point where the men inside needed flashlights to continue their search. Hanks cursed under his breath at the problem he himself had created. He had let things get out of hand rather than following Kitlan's instructions to interrogate Stafford, using whatever force was necessary, until he gave up the money. But Stafford had not been there when they arrived, and patience had never been Hanks' strong suit.

Now they could not possibly leave and come back later. If Stafford returned and found the house in its present condition, he might panic and go into hiding, or run to the police and tell them about the money. Either way, there would be hell to pay with Kitlan if they let Stafford get away.

Hanks continued his search of the master bedroom, using a small Mag-lite as he opened a blanket chest at the foot of the bed and tossed its contents about the room.

Chapter Twenty-Three

Stafford slowed the Jeep Cherokee and turned off the secondary blacktop road that ran along the back of his property. He took a shortcut through the woods, down a gravel lane that came out behind his barn, where he usually parked his car, out of sight of the house and the main road at the head of his driveway. In a line of work where the friends and relatives of those he hunted down and locked up occasionally sought revenge, he had learned that it was best not to make it too easy for anyone to determine at a glance whether or not he was at home, or to observe any pattern to his activities.

The woods on both sides of the narrow lane were deep in shadow, blue-black in the evening light, and Stafford turned on his headlights as the car rocked in and out of ruts formed where recent heavy rains had washed away some of the gravel. The lane made a sharp bend to the left and, as he went into the turn, Stafford saw the silhouette of another four-wheel-drive vehicle, a Range Rover, pulled partway into an overgrown farm track that led to a large open meadow on the far side of the woods. The vehicle was almost completely hidden by thick underbush and the boughs of overhanging white pines, but, just for an instant, the cone of light from his high beams reflected off its tail lights and disclosed its presence.

Stafford first thought it might be a local hunter preparing for the upcoming season; working his dogs on the quail that populated the surrounding woods and fields. But the brief flash he caught of the color of the rear license plate raised his suspicions. He turned his headlights off and stopped just inside the tree line where the gravel lane ended and the woods opened up twenty yards or so behind his barn. He then turned off the engine and reached into the center console for the nine-millimeter Glock he had taken from the safe the previous night.

Stafford tucked the compact semi-automatic pistol inside his waistband at the small of his back and crouched low, staying in the deep shadows as he made his way over to where the Range Rover was parked. Up close, he saw that the license plate was from New York, and after a quick look in the rear window he was satisfied that no one was inside. Finding the passenger-side front door unlocked, he opened it and immediately switched off the interior lights.

Three of them, Stafford reasoned, as his eyes adjusted to the dim light inside the vehicle. He counted three empty Styrofoam cups and the discarded wrappers and containers of three fast-food burgers and fries. The registration card in the glove compartment showed the Range Rover was owned by Gold Star Leasing and leased to Global Imports Ltd, with an address in Brooklyn.

As Stafford went to close the door, he spotted a crumpled piece of paper on the floor mat. He unfolded it and felt a knot tighten in his stomach as he held it up to the faint light coming through the trees and read the neatly printed directions from the New Jersey Turnpike to Chadds Ford, and then, in darker ink and a different handwriting, specific directions to his house.

Stafford quietly closed the door and returned to the Cherokee where he got the night-vision/thermal-imaging binoculars he used for stakeouts from the center console, along with the extra magazine of ammunition for the Glock.

He considered calling nine-one-one and waiting for the police to arrive, but he did not want to take the chance of losing the money, or to have to explain how he got it if the police captured the three men and it came out what they were after. If they turned out to be drug dealers, he was more than familiar with their type and could contend with them, perhaps to his advantage. If not, he could simply return the money, convince Eddie Barnes to do the same, avoid any further confrontations, and the authorities would be none the wiser.

The last of the evening light faded as he started toward the house. He skirted the open grassy areas and stayed well inside the dark recesses of the tree line for cover, pausing every ten yards to observe and listen, and to check his back trail. He had no idea who these men were, but he felt certain he knew what they wanted, and what they might do to get it, and he was not about to take them lightly.

Jerry Hanks had been looking out the second-floor master bedroom window toward the barn when the woods off to the right were briefly lit with a flash of headlights and then went dark again. He hurried downstairs and alerted the two men with him, telling them to get into position: one at the front door and another at the kitchen entrance. Hanks then slipped out the front and hid behind a clump of shrubs at the corner of the terraced entryway where he had a view of anyone approaching from the direction of the barn.

Fifty yards away, concealed by thick underbrush, Stafford knelt at the edge of the woods, slowly scanning the immediate area around the side of his house facing the barn. The thermal-imaging binoculars quickly exposed Hanks; the heat signature from his body temperature in relation to the shrubs he was hiding behind giving him away.

Stafford next turned his attention to the kitchen entrance, focusing the binoculars on the wall just inside the door where the numeric keypad for his security system was located. It was visible through the small glass squares in the upper half of the Dutch door, and he could clearly see the green light was on, indicating that the system had been turned off. The disarming of the sophisticated system told Stafford that he was dealing with highly competent professionals.

He then trained the night-vision binoculars on the large picture window in the kitchen and waited. It wasn't long before he saw movement and the partial outline of someone's head peering around the edge of the window frame for a quick look out toward the barn. He guessed that a second man would be similarly positioned at the front entrance, and that the man he had already spotted outside probably intended to come up behind him when he approached the house. Which meant they had been alerted to his arrival.

Stafford again moved along the tree line, until he was on the opposite side of the house. He paused to use the binoculars and saw no one. The light from a rising full moon cast long shadows across the open areas as he left the woods and ran from cover to cover, using the trees and shrubs close to the house. He stopped at the front terrace where he positioned himself behind the man he had spotted hiding near the entryway. A night breeze through the trees masked his footfalls as he advanced, one slow step at a time, heel to toe, until he was directly behind Jerry Hanks.

Hanks was beginning to think the flash of light in the woods had been a false alarm, until he felt the barrel of the gun pressed against the base of his skull. He froze in position as Stafford, crouching behind him, spoke in a harsh whisper close to his ear.

'Put the gun down. Slide it back to me, then on your stomach and hands behind your back. Do it now!'

Hanks did as he was told, lowering himself to the ground. 'The people I represent only want their money. Give it back and we don't have a problem.'

Stafford slipped Hanks' pistol inside his waistband. 'You alone?'

'Yeah. Just me. I thought I'd try to reason with you before things got ugly.'

Stafford pressed the gun harder into the back of Hanks' head. 'You already underestimated me once, sport. Don't make that mistake again. Now tell your two friends inside to come out. Empty handed. I see a gun and you die first.'

Hanks raised his head and shouted. 'Mike! Johnnie! Come out. No guns.'

No sooner had Hanks finished calling out to his men, than the man waiting inside the front entrance, whose name was Lewis and who understood Hanks' coded warning, threw open the door and charged out. He immediately dropped into a shooting crouch, his sound-suppressed pistol in a two-handed grip, the red dot of the laser-sight searching for a target, following his eyes as he tried to locate Hanks.

Stafford's single well-aimed shot caught Lewis between the eyes, killing him instantly. Hanks took advantage of the distraction, rolling over onto his back and kicking Stafford in the chest, sending him sprawling on the ground.

Hanks immediately reached for his backup pistol, but before the gun cleared the ankle holster on his left leg, Stafford rolled onto his side and fired two shots into the center of Hanks' chest at near point-blank range and killed him.

Stafford immediately left the terrace when he heard someone come out the kitchen door. He ran back along the far side of the house and into the woods to circle around and emerge behind the third man, who, unaware of Stafford's position, was moving toward the front entrance and the bodies of his two friends. He was armed with a sound-suppressed sub-machine-gun and was holding it expertly in the shoot-back position. Thirty feet behind him, Stafford took cover behind a large maple tree off the kitchen entrance and called out.

'Put the gun down. Real slow.'

The man stopped and stood motionless, considering his chances, his back to Stafford, caught in the open in the light of the full moon.

Stafford held him in his sights, keeping pressure on the trigger. 'Don't be stupid. You'll die just like your friends.'

The man made his choice. In one quick, fluid motion, he dropped into a low crouch and spun around, firing as he did. He was remarkably accurate with his weapon. A barrage of rounds tore into the tree where Stafford had taken cover, and without the broad trunk of the maple for protection, he would almost certainly have killed him.

The man paused, wondering if he had misjudged Stafford's location. The momentary pause was all Stafford needed. Exposing little of his silhouette in the bright moonlight, he took aim from behind the tree and fired three shots in rapid succession, all of them striking his target in the chest. The man staggered backward and dropped to his knees, wavering for a moment before toppling over.

Stafford approached cautiously, keeping his gun trained on

the man as he kicked his sub-machine-gun out of reach and knelt down to feel his neck for a pulse. There was none. He stood up, removed the miniature cellular flip phone clipped to his belt, and dialed nine-one-one as he walked back to the kitchen entrance and went into the house.

The CIA surveillance team from the Counter Narcotics Center had watched the violent drama unfold using powerful night-vision scopes from a vantage point on a wooded hill a hundred yards away. The younger of the two men took his eyes from the viewfinder and stared at his partner when Stafford disappeared inside the house.

'You believe that guy? He took out three pros like it was nothing. I thought he was supposed to be some wanna-be bounty hunter who got in over his head.'

The second man smiled. 'Looks like he's a lot more than that.'

'It might be in our best interests not to piss him off.'

The second man took a cellular phone from his jacket pocket. 'I'll call it in to Burruss. I guess we follow the only guy left alive.'

'Sounds like a plan to me.'

The state trooper who was first to respond to the emergency call was the same man who arrived at Stafford's house eighteen months ago to inform him of the accident that had killed his wife. Stafford had not seen him since and, as they accompanied one of the detectives from the nearby state police barracks at Avondale through the house, he thanked the young trooper for the considerate way in which he had handled things that fateful evening.

The detective picked up one of the cushions from the living room sofa that had been cut open with a knife. 'Judging from this mess, I'd say they were looking for something specific.'

Stafford knelt and picked up a Christmas picture of Annie and his wife and put it back on the fireplace mantle. 'Or they just trashed the place to see what they could find.'

'So you think this might be payback from some bail jumper you tracked down?'

'That's the only thing that makes any sense.'

'Maybe.'

'Then you tell me.'

The detective stopped and fixed Stafford with a hard look. 'Okay. None of those three guys had any ID on them. NYPD ran the plates on the Range Rover. They're stolen. I just got off the phone with a friend of mine at the Brooklyn North precinct; the address for Global Imports Ltd, is an empty warehouse. And I'm willing to bet my next paycheck that none of the dead guys' fingerprints are going to be on file anywhere.'

'What's your point?'

'These guys were pros. Their weapons have no manufacturer's stamps or serial numbers; they weren't removed, mind you, they never had any to begin with. Plus they're all equipped with factory-installed silencers and laser sights. And the ammunition they were using is another matter altogether.'

The detective took a single bullet from his pocket and held it up to Stafford.

'Highly specialized stuff. Muzzle velocity just below the sound barrier for optimum silencing. Designed to mushroom inside the body. You get hit anywhere in the torso with one of these rounds you're going to die where you stand, even a grazing wound is going to immobilize you. Now, factor that in with their car being leased to a shell company, no personal ID, and they had no problems disarming your security system. Does that sound like some skell bail-jumper and his friends out to get even?'

Stafford shrugged. 'What do you want me to say?'

'How 'bout we start with what you've been leaving out?'

'I didn't leave anything out. I've hunted down and brought back a few heavy-duty drug dealers in the past year. Some of them could have this kind of talent working for them, or the money they have stashed away gives them access to it. Other than that, I have no idea who or why.'

The detective nodded, not convinced he was hearing the entire truth, but with no hard facts to disprove Stafford's theory or support anything else, he backed off.

The coroner's van was leaving with the bodies of the three

men, and the crime-scene unit was packing up as Stafford walked the detective to his car.

'You'll be around, right?'

Stafford smiled. 'You telling me not to leave town?'

'Something like that.'

'That's what I do for a living; leave town.'

The detective opened the door and slid behind the wheel. 'By the way, nice shooting. Especially on the guy with the sub-machine-gun. Good tight group.'

'I got lucky, I guess.'

'I've been in shoot-outs, Stafford. We both know luck had nothing to do with it.'

Stafford didn't respond.

The detective smiled and started the engine. 'I'll be in touch.'

Stafford walked back through the house, assessing the damage. The furnishings could easily be repaired or replaced. What upset him most was what he found upstairs as he stood looking at the mess in Annie's room. He had left her bedroom just as it was on the day of the accident, wanting everything to be the same when she came home. It bothered him more than it should that he didn't know if he could put it back together exactly the way it had been.

He went into the master bedroom and found his wife's clothes strewn about. Her favorite silk blouse, the one that still held a faint trace of her scent, was torn nearly in half. He carefully, almost lovingly, picked it up and laid it neatly across the bed.

Something even more disturbing troubled him. Eddie Barnes. He had tried calling him four times in the fifteen minutes before the state police arrived and got no answer. On the last call he left a message, but with Barnes being slow in returning anyone's calls, regardless of the urgency, he had no way of knowing if his friend had gotten it. He had to be warned. If they could find him, they could find Eddie. Unless they already had.

Stafford looked at his watch. It was eight fifteen. He tried the number again and got the same recorded message. He felt he couldn't risk waiting any longer. The drive to the Washington DC area was just over one hundred miles. He could be at Barnes' home in Reston in an hour and a half, less if he pushed it.

He reloaded the magazine in his pistol, hurriedly packed a carry-on with some clothes and toilet articles, and tossed in a full box of ammunition. He got an envelope with three thousand dollars in emergency cash that he kept taped beneath a desk drawer in his study, then on his way out rearmed the security system and locked up the house.

Something one of the men said that evening kept tugging at Stafford's thoughts as he pulled out of his driveway.

'*The people I represent only want their money.*'

But they hadn't found the money, and yet they were willing to kill him. Why? Who did they represent? And who in their right mind would write off twenty million dollars without making a serious effort to get it back? There had to be more to it than the money. But what? What had he gotten himself into? He was now at least certain of one thing, Barnes had been right about the source of the money being illegal. This was not how banks went about recovering their funds.

Stafford took Route 100 South out of Chadds Ford, pushing the Cherokee to its handling limitations on the narrow, winding blacktop road that followed the course of the Brandywine River to Wilmington, Delaware and Interstate 95.

The CIA surveillance team kept its distance, following two miles behind in a dark-blue sedan and feeling no need to keep the Cherokee in sight. The man in the front passenger seat simply watched the back-lit display of the direction-finding receiver mounted beneath the dash that was picking up a steady signal from the transmitter he had magnetically attached to the frame of Stafford's car.

Chapter Twenty-Four

Eddie Barnes used one of his never-miss pick-up lines on Misti, a tall, attractive, thirty-year-old brunette who smiled at him when he spotted her coming out of the Victoria's Secret store in the upscale mall at Tyson's Corner, Virginia.

'Do you believe in love at first sight, or do you want me to walk by again?'

She laughed and Barnes flashed his best roguish smile, and after a cup of coffee they left the mall together. 'That's Misti with an "I",' she told him as they crossed the parking lot on the unusually warm autumn night.

She paused and took off her leather jacket before climbing into Barnes' new, all-wheel-drive, metallic silver Porsche cabriolet. 'Nice ride.'

She was wearing a silk tank top under the jacket, and Barnes tried not to get too aroused by what the scoop-neck garment revealed. That was until he noticed her left arm. And then he knew he was in for yet another wild night. Covering Misti-With-An-I's upper arm, from her elbow to her shoulder, was a tattoo of a long, fat penis, complete with testicles and pubic hair.

'Nice tattoo.'

'I wanted to make a statement.'

Barnes thought of asking her what that statement might be, but decided against it. Instead, he asked a question that always tugged at the back of his mind whenever he ended up with edge-walkers like the girl sitting beside him. 'Do you mind telling me exactly what it was that attracted you to me back there in the mall?'

'I don't know. Something you gave off told me we were *simpatico*.'

'Yeah? Well, if you can think of what that was, you let me know, huh?'

It was nine fifteen when Barnes tossed the shopping bags he was carrying into the car, slipped behind the wheel, and roared out of the parking lot. With the top down and the radio blaring, he red-lined the powerful sports car through four of its gears and sped down the highway, weaving in and out of the heavy traffic. Misti, her shoulder-length hair blowing in the wind, winked at him and stuck out a long slender tongue pierced with a silver stud. Barnes winked back and made a strange, involuntary high-pitched sound at the back of his throat.

The rear seats and floor of the Porsche were stacked high with clothing bags full of an assortment of designer sport coats, slacks, and leather jackets, and under them, shopping bags stuffed with silk shirts and cashmere sweaters, and a host of other things Barnes had purchased on impulse.

He had done little more than shop all day. Starting with a car dealer he knew who had a serious cocaine habit, and who was more than happy to take the eighty-nine thousand dollars in cash for the Porsche and would have no trouble finding a way to hide the fact that he did it. Barnes estimated he had spent over one hundred and twenty thousand dollars since nine o'clock that morning. A hundred and twenty grand in twelve hours, he thought, now that's world-class shopping.

But he had been careful, he reasoned. The Porsche dealer wouldn't give him up. He probably never reported more than a third of his income to the IRS anyway; the rest went straight up his nose. And none of the stores had his name or address, and they hadn't been the least bit concerned when he counted off the one hundred dollar bills to pay them. He had approximately thirty thousand dollars remaining of what he took with him that morning, leaving him more than enough to buy a few things tomorrow, pay off some long-overdue bills, then lay low until good old dependable Ben worked out a plan to launder the rest of the money.

*

Tony Kitlan moved about the study in Barnes' townhouse, looking over the photographs and military decorations hung on the wall, while Peter Marcus and the man who met them at the airport systematically searched the rest of the rooms.

Kitlan picked up a photograph of Barnes and another man he assumed to be Stafford, taken at some remote desert staging area during the Gulf War. They stood side by side, their arms draped over each other's shoulders, victorious grins on their camouflage-painted faces. He could tell from their specialized equipment and weapons, and the heavily armed dune-buggy-type-vehicle they were leaning against, that they had once been members of the army's elite Delta Force. Another photograph showed both men, dressed in Class 'A' uniforms and standing at attention, receiving decorations at an awards ceremony.

The red light on the answering machine was blinking, and Kitlan crossed to the desk and pressed the playback button to hear three hang-ups and then Stafford's terse message.

'Eddie, we've got a serious problem. Call me on my cellular as soon as you get this message. But first get out of your house and stay out. Go someplace where no one would think of looking for you. And take some noise with you.'

Kitlan immediately realized that Stafford's message warning Barnes to go to ground and take a weapon with him meant that he had already had some kind of run-in with Hanks and his men. They should have reported in hours ago, and now, in light of what he just heard, he believed he knew why he hadn't gotten an answer when he called Hanks' cellular number twenty minutes earlier. He erased the answering-unit tape in the event Barnes called in for his messages, and in a flash of anger, he threw the framed photo of Stafford and Barnes across the room just as Pete Marcus entered the study.

'Something wrong, boss?'

'Unless I'm mistaken, Stafford took out Hanks and the two guys with him.'

'Yeah? I'm impressed.'

'Be careful with Barnes when he gets here, Pete. It looks

like he and Stafford are former Delta; most of those guys can shoot the eyes out of a snake at fifty yards.'

'I'll keep that in mind.' Marcus noticed the military decorations on the wall. 'Silver Star. Bronze Star for Valor. Purple Heart. A real hero, huh? Too bad.' He flopped into a leather recliner and raised the footrest. 'I don't think he's got the money here. But we can tear the place apart if you want to and make sure.'

'No. We'll talk to him first. See how it goes.'

Barnes lowered the volume on the radio in deference to his neighbors as he turned onto Brass Lantern Way. He drove to the last cluster of homes on the cul-de-sac and pulled up in front of the garage attached to the townhouse on which he was two mortgage payments in arrears – another bill he made a mental note to take care of first thing in the morning.

He helped Misti out of the Porsche and scooped up a load of clothing bags as they followed the path to the front door. By force of habit, he used the small remote control attached to his key ring to disarm his security system, then remembered that it had been out of commission for the past month. He hadn't had the money to get it fixed, and he reminded himself to take care of that in the morning, too, now that he had some stuff in the house worth stealing. He shifted the clothing bags to one arm as he opened the front door, then stood aside to let Misti enter first.

The door was slammed shut behind Barnes as he stepped inside and reached for the light switch. A hand was clasped over Misti's mouth, smothering her scream as she was dragged from the entryway into the kitchen.

In his peripheral vision, Barnes saw Marcus coming out of the study. He dropped the clothing bags and spun around to face him. In that same instant, he was punched in the kidney by Kitlan, who had been standing in the corner behind the front door. The blow stunned him, dropping him to his knees.

Marcus closed in, and Barnes threw a punch upward at his groin that was deflected and hit him in the thigh, making his leg go numb. As Barnes struggled to his feet, Kitlan helped Marcus wrestle him to the floor and pin him down. Marcus delivered another blow to the kidney that immobilized Barnes long enough for them to pull his arms behind his back and wrap his wrists together with duct tape.

Barnes managed to twist onto his side and kick Kitlan in the face, bloodying his mouth before the two men finally overpowered him and taped his ankles together. They then yanked him to his feet and shoved him into a straight-back wooden chair taken from the kitchen and placed in the center of the living room.

Most of the floor space in the room was taken up by Barnes' earlier purchases: two television sets, new stereo equipment and speakers for the study, bedroom and living room, and two computers, a laptop and a desktop model, and a printer, all still packed in their boxes and stacked around the room.

Barnes took a deep breath and winced at the pain in his side as he watched Kitlan approach and stand directly over him. Still smarting from being kicked in the face, he stared down at Barnes, working his jaw from side to side as he dabbed at the blood in the corner of his mouth with a handkerchief.

Barnes looked to his right and took in the no-neck Marcus with his twenty-inch biceps, still favoring his leg from the blow to his thigh. The third man had a knife in one hand and an arm wrapped around Misti's waist from behind, grinding his crotch into her and grinning as he held the knife blade close to her face.

Barnes met Kitlan's gaze. 'You want to rob the place? Go ahead. Just tell the psycho with the knife to leave the girl alone, huh?'

Kitlan dabbed again at the trickle of blood, then gestured around the room. 'It seems you've been on a shopping spree, Mr Barnes. A recent inheritance?'

'Something like that. So who are you? What do you want?' But he already knew the answer to that as he stared into Kitlan's hard, unyielding eyes.

'We want what's ours. Give it to us and we'll go away.'

Barnes offered his most innocent expression. 'You got it. Take anything you want. What's mine is yours.'

Marcus moved from where he was leaning against the wall

and stood beside Kitlan, who nodded to him and stepped back. Marcus caught Barnes with a vicious back-handed blow across the face, knocking him off the chair and onto the floor.

Misti screamed and the man with the knife shoved her down onto her stomach. With his knee in her back, he pinned her there and cut off a strip of duct tape, placing it across her mouth. She struggled briefly, whimpering, her eyes wide with fright, as he cut off more tape and bound her wrists behind her before dragging her into a corner.

As Barnes rose to his knees, Marcus grabbed him by the hair and drove a fist into his face, breaking his nose. Barnes groaned in pain as the squat, powerful man pulled him to his feet and sat him back down in the chair.

Kitlan waved Marcus off and stepped forward. 'Why don't we start over?'

Barnes shook off the effects of the blow to his head and sniffled at the blood running from his nose. 'You mean you want me to go back outside and come in again? Sure I could do that.'

'You've got a real smart mouth Mr Barnes. I'd try to control that if I were you. Now why don't you just tell me where the money is?'

'What money? I look like I have money? Huh? I maxed out my credit cards on this stuff. Get serious, will ya?'

Kitlan drew a semi-automatic pistol from the shoulder holster inside his jacket and threaded on a sound-suppressor. Without a word, he turned to Misti-With-An-I and calmly shot the terrified woman in the face, blowing away the back of her head.

'Is that serious enough for you?'

Barnes stared in disbelief. 'What's wrong with you? I just met her. She's not a player. She had nothin' to do with any of this.'

'That's unfortunate. But it's on you. Now, do I have your undivided attention?'

Barnes continued to stare at the lifeless body slumped in the corner, deeply sorry for what had happened to her. 'Yeah. No problem.'

'So where's our money?'

'You mean the twenty million?'

'That's exactly what I mean.'

'You're not very good at this sort of thing, are you?'

Kitlan's brow furrowed. 'What sort of thing?'

'Intelligent thought.'

Kitlan's face flushed with anger, but he restrained himself. 'And what makes you say that, Mr Barnes?'

'You killed that woman over there without giving it a second thought. Which tells me that's exactly what you intend to do to me as soon as you get your money back. Now how smart is that? I'd have to be a goddamn moron to tell you where the money is. And believe me, I'm no moron.'

'You're right. You're going to die either way. The question is, how are you going to die? My friend can make it quick and easy, or he can make it slow and painful.'

Barnes shrugged. 'Bring him on.'

Kitlan again stepped back as Marcus approached, a small, sick smile on his face. 'I like tough guys. I especially like to hear them cry and beg.'

Barnes flashed his trademark cocky grin at Marcus. 'Anybody ever tell you you look like a flounder. Hell, if your eyes were any closer together you'd have been born dead.'

Marcus started a left hook in motion, but the punch stopped in mid-swing when Barnes, mustering all of his strength, brought both feet up together, kicking Marcus in the groin with a solid thud. The loud, guttural sound that came out of Marcus' mouth as he dropped to his knees, his hands between his legs, was barely human.

Barnes smiled through his pain. It was one final, futile act of defiance he knew would gain him nothing and cost him dearly. But it felt good.

'Gotcha that time.'

Chapter Twenty-Five

Janet Barnes downshifted her primer-splotched, vintage Volkswagen Beetle, leaving a trail of blue smoke behind her as she turned onto Brass Lantern Way. She had been concerned about her brother from the moment she got home from the gym that evening and found an envelope containing ten thousand dollars in cash, along with a key and note that raised more questions than it answered:

> *Don't read more into this than it can support, Sis. I'm fine, I haven't robbed anybody, and the cops aren't looking for me. The key is for a self-storage space in Sterling. On the off chance that something should happen to me, the contents of the two bags there are all yours. In the meantime, buy yourself something nice. Real nice. There's a lot more where this came from. Talk to you later.*

Janet parked alongside the shiny new Porsche and, despite her concern, smiled when she saw the shopping bags crammed into the back of the car. Eddie's unofficial credo was 'tomorrow will take care of itself', and he always spent extravagantly, even when he was broke. But she knew that the luxurious sports car cost at least eighty thousand dollars, and where he managed to get even enough money for a down payment, let alone the ten thousand dollars in cash he had left for her, loomed large on the list of questions she had for him.

As she approached the front door, the sixth sense that had

saved her life on more than one occasion alerted her that something wasn't right. She could feel someone watching her. The blinds on the kitchen window overlooking the walkway were partially open, and at the same moment she glanced inside a shadow moved across the far wall.

It was then that she realized the lighting was all wrong. Ever since they were children, Eddie hated being alone in a darkened house. The idiosyncracy had nothing to do with fear of the dark. To Eddie, light meant warmth and comfort and companionship and made him feel less alone. He always kept lights on in the kitchen and the entryway when he was home, until he went to bed, and then the small lamp on the table just inside the door was left on through the night. The only light Janet could see through the kitchen window was a faint glow from the moonlight coming in through the sliding glass door that opened onto the deck off the living room.

She slipped her hand into her shoulder bag for the Sig Sauer .40 caliber semi-automatic pistol she had a permit to carry concealed and was never without – a necessary precaution against a past that could come back to haunt her at any time. She opened the door just enough to peer down the length of the entryway, through the living room, to the deck beyond. In the pale light of the moon, she saw a chair in the middle of the room and something lying on the floor close to it.

A sudden movement drew her attention out onto the deck. A figure seen only in silhouette vaulted the railing and dropped the eight feet to the small garden below. Then another followed. And another.

Kitlan and Marcus hit the ground running, crossing the garden to the wooded area that served as green space between two clusters of townhouses. The third man stayed behind to cover their withdrawal.

Janet ran through the house and out onto the deck, her pistol aimed where she looked as she came through the already open door and made certain the deeply shadowed corners of the deck area were clear. Below her, in the distance, she saw Kitlan and Marcus reach the stand of pines in the green space. The third man stood out in the open, looking up at the deck, the pistol in his hands aimed directly at her. He fired three rapid-fire, sound-suppressed shots that impacted in the side of the house only inches from her head.

Janet dropped into a shooting stance, quickly acquired her target, and fired two well-aimed shots in return.

The third man swayed unsteadily for a moment, a surprised look on his face. He stared at the two bullet holes in the center of his chest for the brief seconds before he fell forward and lay motionless on the grass at the edge of the trees. Janet's unsilenced shots had echoed loudly throughout the neighborhood. Concerned faces appeared at windows in a number of adjoining townhouses.

Kitlan and Marcus paused to look back, then disappeared into the deep shadows of the pines. Despite Marcus urging him to kill Janet and wait for Stafford, whom they believed was on his way to warn Barnes, Kitlan opted for leaving immediately. His inability to break Eddie Barnes had somewhat unnerved him, and he wanted time to regroup and to contend with Stafford when he was not dealing with unknown variables, like the woman who had showed up unexpectedly.

Janet was about to go off the deck in pursuit when she heard an engine start and tires squeal as a car pulled away on an adjacent street on the far side of the trees.

She went back inside, taking quick looks in the study and the kitchen before standing quietly in a dark corner for a count of thirty, listening, making certain she was alone. With her eyes fully acclimated to the dim light, she scanned the living room and saw the body of Misti-With-An-I slumped in a corner behind a stack of unopened boxes.

She checked to make certain the once-attractive young woman was dead, then moved cautiously toward the oddly shaped form partially obscured by another stack of boxes on the floor near the chair. It wasn't moving, and as she drew closer and the shape revealed itself, she felt a terrible fear grip her, followed by a wave of nausea and dizziness as she realized what she was looking at.

Eddie Barnes lay on his stomach, his head covered with a plastic bag. The length of rope tied round his throat in a slip knot also secured his arms and legs behind his back. Janet had seen the brutal torture done once before: a

Columbian drug baron had used it on a man he believed was stealing from him.

The plastic bag assured that the victim would struggle as he fought for air, and the more he struggled, the tighter the rope around his neck became. It was a particularly heinous and effective form of interrogation, used to slowly strangle someone over an extended period. When the victim was on the verge of blacking out, the interrogator would step in, remove the bag and loosen the ropes. Once the victim recovered, the bag was replaced and the process started over again. The numerous abrasions around Barnes' throat, wrists and ankles indicated that he had not been allowed to die quickly.

Janet immediately tore the plastic bag from her brother's head, then ran to the kitchen wall-phone. She dialed nine-one-one, her voice frantic, her words coming in a rush between gasps for breath as she explained the circumstances and pleaded with the woman on the phone to send an ambulance.

She ran back into the living room where she dropped to her knees beside her brother. His face was grotesquely distorted, blue and swollen, his eyes wide open in a look of desperation and panic. She cut the ropes with a folding knife she kept in her shoulder bag, then tried breathing life into him, again and again, finally accepting that she could do nothing to bring him back. Her body went limp as she sat back on her heels and sobbed, holding his head in her lap and feeling as though part of her had died with him.

They were the only children of an abusive, alcoholic father who moved out of their lives when they were too young to remember him, and a cold, dysfunctional mother who provided little more than the bare necessities and left them to fend for themselves. Two years apart in age, all they had had growing up was each other.

Eddie had been her source of strength, her compass through life when she was most vulnerable. He had protected her in grade school, taught her how to take care of herself in junior high, and let it be known that anyone who did anything to hurt his sister would have to deal with him. As a star linebacker on the football team, and known for punching first and asking questions later, his warning was enough to ensure that her worst date-related problem throughout high school had been a wilted corsage for her senior prom.

He had encouraged her to run track and to take up kick-boxing, and she had excelled at both. He had urged her to go on to college, and when he enlisted in the Army he helped support her through four years at the University of Maryland on his Army pay. He was a proud member of the audience when she completed her training and was sworn into the Drug Enforcement Administration, and he shared her pride when she was assigned to the DEA's New York Field Division and worked undercover on a joint narcotics task force with the NYPD. He was also there for her two months ago when she resigned from the DEA and tried to lose herself in a bottle over what they had done to her.

The thought of how her brother had died pained Janet terribly. The method of torture suggested they were after information, and if she knew Eddie they didn't get it. She had no doubts that what had happened was connected to the money he had suddenly acquired. But the fact that they had allowed him to die told her that the men who had done this, unless they were careless and stupid, were not just concerned with recovering their money. Eddie must have known something that was a threat to them.

Janet continued to sit holding her brother's head in her lap, rocking gently back and forth, her thoughts returning to the days of their youth. Eddie was pushing her on a swing. She couldn't remember how old she was; two or three. He was singing to her. She could hear him, but she couldn't make out the words, and that bothered her. She fought back the tears streaming down her face as, off in the distance, the wail of sirens drew closer.

Chapter Twenty-Six

Ben Stafford feared the worst as he turned onto Brass Lantern Way and saw the swirling light bars of the police cruisers angled into the curb in front of Eddie Barnes' townhouse. He parked across the street and got out of the car, hoping against hope that his friend was not in one of the three body bags he saw being carried down the walk and placed in the medical examiner's van.

A small crowd of onlookers was gathered at the crime-scene tape strung along the edge of the property, and Stafford crossed to where they stood and shouldered his way to the front. He was about to ask a uniformed Reston police officer what had happened when he saw Janet Barnes standing just outside the entrance to the townhouse staring at the ambulance as the bodies were loaded on board.

Stafford flashed his Bail Enforcement Agent identification card at the young cop, mumbled something that sounded like 'county attorney', and quickly ducked under the tape and started up the walkway before the ID could be scrutinized.

Stafford had only seen Janet once before, on the day he and Eddie returned from the Gulf War. She had driven down to Fort Bragg to welcome her brother home and to be at the awards ceremony for his Silver Star. And even though it had been eight years since he spent only a few hours in her presence, he recognized her immediately.

She was the most chameleon-like person he had ever seen. She could look like a tomboy, or the girl next door, or when the light played across her face in a different way her natural beauty could take your breath away. Her eyes were her most captivating feature. Dark brown and flecked with gold, they were like hands that reached out and grabbed your face and forced you to look at her and nowhere else.

Stafford had the answer he was afraid of hearing as he drew closer and saw that she had been crying; the grief evident in her expression as she continued to stare after the ambulance as it pulled away.

Janet saw Stafford approaching, her eyes questioning for a few seconds until the moment of recognition. 'Ben Stafford?'

Stafford nodded and motioned toward the departing ambulance. 'Eddie?'

'They killed him, Ben. Tortured him to death.'

And then she fell silent, looking uncharacteristically vulnerable and defenseless. Saying it out loud had made it all the worse, and she fought to hold back the tears, afraid that if she cried again she would be unable to stop. Stafford opened his arms and held her in a comforting embrace. She stayed there for only a moment before stepping back, her intense eyes searching his.

'What are you doing here?'

'I just came down to see him.'

She didn't respond immediately. Then a flash of anger darkened her expression and her voice took on a hard edge. 'Don't lie to me. You just spent a week together on a camping trip.'

Stafford looked at the cops standing nearby. 'Not here. Let's go inside.'

'Where did the money come from, Ben? Tell me. Eddie lived from paycheck to paycheck. He was always broke. Always in debt. How does he get a new Porsche and enough cash to give me ten thousand dollars like it was pocket change?'

Stafford took her by the arm and led her toward the front door, away from one of the cops who was looking in their direction. 'We'll talk inside. All right?'

Janet followed him into the study, away from the crime-scene detectives working in the living room. Stafford's eyes immediately went to the telephone answering unit. Making certain he wasn't being observed by any of the cops, he flipped open the top of the unit and removed the incoming-message tape and put it in his pocket.

Janet saw what he had done. 'What's on the tape?'

'I called to warn him.'

The mercurial temper she had shared with her brother flared. 'You knew this was going to happen?'

'They came at me earlier this evening. I got here as soon as I could.'

'What the hell did you two get involved in?'

Stafford took Janet by the hand and sat down with her on the sofa. He told her all that had happened from the moment the Lear jet crashed near their campsite to the attack on his life that night. When he finished, Janet told him what had been done to Eddie and the girl with him, and how she had killed one of the men running from the townhouse.

'How did they find you and Eddie so fast?'

'I haven't figured that out yet.'

'They weren't just after their money, Ben.'

'I know. We probably saw something we weren't supposed to see, but I'll be damned if I know what it was.' Stafford took her hand again and squeezed it. 'I'll do everything I can to find out who's behind this, Janet. And they'll pay for Eddie. I promise you that.'

'We'll do it together.'

'I don't think it's very smart to hang around with me right now. They're going to come after me again.'

'I can take care of myself.'

'I know that, but DEA isn't going to sanction you getting involved in this with me, considering the events that set it in motion in the first place.'

'Eddie didn't tell you? I resigned from DEA two months ago.'

'No. All he told me was how well you were doing and how much you loved the undercover work.'

'That part was true.'

'What happened?'

'I had a boss on the task force who thought he had the right to fondle me whenever he was in the mood. I told him to knock it off. He kept it up. I told him if he didn't stop I was going to bring him up on sexual harassment charges.'

'Let me guess. They set you up.'

Janet looked away for a moment, the old anger flaring in her eyes. 'Two weeks later a kilo of cocaine was missing from a bust I was in on; it turned up in the trunk of my car. I was given the choice of resigning or being turned in.'

'Why didn't you go over his head and tell your side of the story.'

'He was a highly decorated agent who made a lot of high-profile busts that in turn made the suits in Washington look good. When it came to who would go down, it would have been no contest.'

'I'm sorry.'

'Yeah. Me, too.'

'Eddie was really proud of you.'

'I know. He loved me. And I loved him. And with or without you, I'm going after the people who killed him.'

'All right. But I've got to take the initiative. I can't just sit around and wait for them to come at me again.'

'Have you got anything to point us in the right direction?'

'I've got the ID of the guy I found dead in the plane. He's from New York City. We can start there.'

'I'd like to make one stop first. A bar. An after-hours hangout for DEA, FBI, Secret Service, the whole alphabet soup of federal law enforcement and spooks.'

'What's there?'

'I still have a few friends in DEA. One in particular who might know if any large amounts of drug money are missing and if anybody's looking for it. Even the real heavyweights aren't going to write off twenty million if there's any possibility of recovering it.'

'Have you given the cops your statement about what happened here?'

'Yes. I'm finished with them for now.'

'You want to make arrangements for Eddie?'

'I already called a funeral parlor. Eddie wanted to be cremated. They'll hold his ashes for me. There's a special place I know he'd want them scattered.'

'I want to be there when you do it.'

Janet nodded in agreement as they left the townhouse and crossed the street to where the Jeep Cherokee was parked.

'Where's the bar?'

'In Alexandria.' Janet took the keys from him and slid behind the wheel. 'I'll drive. It'll save time.'

Janet took the entrance ramp off Reston Avenue onto the Dulles Toll Road. The speedometer read seventy-five and climbing as she wove in and out of the sparse traffic headed toward the airport. She watched the rear-view mirror as she suddenly backed off on the speed, slowing to forty miles per hour.

Stafford gave her a questioning look. 'What's up?'

'Maybe nothing. When we turned off Eddie's street, I spotted a dark sedan with two men in it parked just around the corner one block up.'

Stafford looked over his shoulder and out the rear window. 'A tail?'

'They looked like a surveillance team to me. Thought I'd speed up, then back off fast and see if I could catch them coming up behind me, but I don't see anything.' She accelerated to just above the speed limit, repeatedly glancing in the rear-view mirror. 'I've got one more idea. Buckle up.'

Stafford cinched his shoulder harness tight as Janet got off the Dulles Toll Road at the next exit. She followed a two-lane highway for a few miles, then turned onto a recently paved road leading into a sprawling industrial development site. It was almost eleven o'clock, and the area was completely deserted.

Janet floored the accelerator, taking the Cherokee into a ninety degree corner in a textbook example of how to four-wheel-drift a sport utility vehicle without rolling it over: a touch of trail-brake, rotate, then back hard on the throttle with the tires wisping smoke while the powerful V-8 did its best to keep them connected to the pavement.

Stafford had the hand-hold on the door in a vice-like grip. 'What are you doing?'

'Smoking them out,' was all Janet said as she concentrated on her driving.

The CIA surveillance team got off the Dulles Toll Road on the same exit Janet had used thirty seconds earlier. They pulled onto the shoulder and stopped, watching the display on the direction-finding receiver mounted beneath the dash. The signal from the transmitter attached to the under-side of Stafford's car was strong and steady.

'They've been making erratic changes of direction for the last ten minutes.'

The driver continued to watch the display. 'Maybe they made us and they're trying to get far enough ahead to switch cars without being seen.'

'Let's close in and get a visual. If they're on to us it won't matter if they see us. If they're not, we'll drop back and continue the surveillance.'

Janet Barnes was doing ninety-five miles an hour down a quarter-mile straight-away on a deserted dead-end road through a torn-up construction site. She snaked through a tight S-turn, across railroad tracks, into the air over a sharp rise in the pavement, then back down through a low section of the road flooded by recent rains.

Stafford stared at her in disbelief. 'You might want to slow down a little. I think you put enough distance between us and whoever's back there.'

'That's not what I have in mind.'

She continued to speed down another straight stretch of road, totally focused on what she was doing. Then, amid fading brakes and the heady stench of rubber, she slid to a panic stop a few yards from where a bulldozer sat directly in her path. She immediately put the Cherokee into reverse and planted the throttle to the carpet. Coming sharply off the gas, she spun the wheel hard to the right and pirouetted into a gut-wrenching one hundred and eighty degree turn that put her in the middle of the road, facing in the opposite direction. It was an impressive demonstration of high-performance emergency driving techniques.

Stafford's head had bounced off the passenger-side window during the maneuver. 'What the hell was that about?'

'Separating the men from the boys.'

'Or the living from the dead.'

She sat with the engine idling, staring straight ahead. Then, as though in response to the report of a starter's pistol only she could hear, she floored the accelerator and roared back through the water and over the jump, pushing the Cherokee for all it was worth. Off in the distance, a pair of headlights appeared, coming directly at her.

Stafford's apprehension grew as the two cars sped headlong toward each other. The oncoming car finally slowed and moved partway onto the shoulder, but could go no further without dropping into drainage ditches lining both sides of the road. Janet made a small correction that again aligned the Cherokee for a head-on collision.

By now Stafford was alarmed by the anger and intensity emanating from her as she fixated on the lights coming closer by the second. He reached over and grabbed her arm. 'Hey! That's enough of this. Back off!'

Janet shook off his hand without taking her eyes from the road. 'Not to worry, Stafford. I got it under control.'

At the last possible moment before the two cars collided head-on, the CIA car swerved hard to the right and down into the drainage ditch, the rear wheels spinning in the soft, muddy ground as the driver tried to pull back onto the road.

Janet slammed on the brakes and skidded to a stop. She was out of the Cherokee in an instant, her gun in her hand, aimed at the driver of the surveillance car as he climbed out.

'On the ground!' she screamed, grabbing him by his hair and shoving him down. She held the gun on the passenger until he got out and lay on the ground beside the driver.

Stafford, his gun drawn, was standing behind and to the left of Janet, covering her. He moved closer and spoke to her so as not to be overheard by the two men on the ground.

'We'd better find out who these guys are before you take this any further.'

'Good idea.' Her eyes burning with anger, Janet placed the gun at the base of the driver's skull. 'Who are you?'

'I strongly recommend you cut and run while you still can, lady. You're in way over your head here.'

Janet's response was to again grab the driver by his hair and turn his face to hers. 'As far as I'm concerned, you and your sidekick are responsible for torturing and killing my brother. And in case you haven't noticed, there aren't any witnesses around here. So either you convince me I'm wrong or so help me God, both your brains are going to be smeared all over your nice, new gov-car.'

The driver saw the rage in her eyes and yielded to it, reaching inside his jacket and slowly bringing out a leather ID case. Janet took it from him and flipped it open, holding it up to the glow from the headlights of the car in the ditch.

'You're CIA?'

'And we had nothing to do with your brother's death. We don't even known who he is.' The driver pointed his chin toward Stafford. 'We got to Reston at the same time he did.'

He rose to his knees holding his hands where Janet could see them. His partner followed suit. 'You mind if we get up now?'

Janet motioned for them to stand, backing out of their reach. Stafford had not missed the significance of the driver's explanation.

'Why does the CIA have me under surveillance?'

'I have no idea. I just drew the assignment.'

'You followed me from Pennsylvania. Which means you were at my home when those three guys tried to kill me. Now you're here when Eddie gets killed.'

'One has nothing to do with the other.'

'Yeah, huh?'

Stafford moved closer and frisked both men, tossing the pistols they carried on their hips into the drainage ditch partially filled with water. He reached in and grabbed the car keys, doing the same with them.

'I'll give you some good advice. Stay away from me. Even if you're not the bad guys, you could still get caught in the crossfire.'

'We don't respond to threats, Stafford.'

'Make an exception.'

110

Janet had gone back to the Cherokee and was looking underneath it. She soon found the transmitter and held it up for Stafford to see before tossing it in the ditch.

Stafford ordered the two men back on their knees. 'Stay put until we're out of here.'

He walked over to where Janet stood, looking at her with genuine admiration. 'How did you know about the transmitter?'

'They were parked two blocks away from Eddie's place. Which means they didn't have to maintain visual contact. A transmitter's the only way they could do that and not take the chance of losing you.'

'Eddie said you were good.' He reached out and took the keys to the Cherokee from her hand. 'But I'd feel a whole lot better if you weren't behind the wheel.'

As they drove off, Stafford remembered something else Eddie Barnes had said about his sister: she was excellent at assuming characters. Blink and she's a Wall Street yuppie. Blink again and she's a crack whore or a high-school teacher, a nurse or a nun. Stafford could easily understand how her physical beauty, practical intelligence, and mental toughness, had made her a natural for the dangerous undercover work she had done for the DEA.

He smiled to himself as he recalled another remark Eddie had made about Janet; that as tough and cyncial as she was, inside was a sweet and wonderful little girl who would make a great mother and wife. Stafford had no reason to doubt that, but he felt sorry for the man who tried to domesticate and tame her.

They drove in silence for a long time before Janet turned to him with something she had been mulling over. 'If it's drug money, those two spooks are probably from the Agency's Counter Narcotics Center. They could have been using you and Eddie as bait.'

Stafford nodded. 'Speaking of the money, what do you want to do about it?'

'We can burn that bridge when we come to it. First let's find out who and what we're dealing with.'

Chapter Twenty-Seven

Adam Welsh turned off the tree-lined cobblestone street in the heart of the exclusive Georgetown section of Washington and parked in an alley at the rear of one of the elegant homes. It was eleven fifteen when he entered the walled-in garden behind the narrow, four-story brownstone and crossed to the terrace where the French doors of the lower-level study were open to the cool autumn night.

Inside, the dying embers of a fire glowed in a corner fireplace, and John Galloway sat before it sipping twenty-year-old Scotch, neat, from a cut crystal glass and listening to classical guitar music playing softly in the background. Galloway, a fit and trim man who looked ten years youngers than his sixty-one years, was a clotheshorse who could not pass a reflective surface without admiring his appearance. He was dressed in his usual fashion, which meant he was overdressed for a casual evening at home. He had on light-grey cashmere-and-wool-blend slacks and an impeccably tailored, tan tweed sport coat with a trace of pale blue threads woven through it. The collar of his custom-made blue shirt – the exact shade of blue found in the weave of the sport coat – was buttoned at the neck, and his silk regimental stripe tie was knotted in a perfect half-Windsor and pulled snugly in place.

Clothes were Galloway's one and only passion outside of his work; a passion that was a curious paradox for a man who had spent most of his career in the jungles of Southeast Asia during the height of the Vietnam War, and in the alleys and back streets of Eastern Europe before the Cold War ended and he found himself on the career fast track at CIA headquarters where he soon rose to head the Agency's Directorate of Operations.

Galloway looked as though he had just stepped out of one of London's best Savile Row shops as he put down his drink and, without a word of greeting, rose to close the terrace doors and draw the draperies as Welsh entered the cozy, book-lined study. He put another log on the fire and stoked it until the flames flickered, then returned to his chair and motioned for Welsh to sit opposite him. He pointedly did not offer his subordinate a drink as he picked up his own glass and gave him a disapproving look.

'What's so important that it couldn't wait until morning?'

'We may have more of a problem than we first thought. A temporary one, but nonetheless a problem.'

'I take it that means Cameron's men haven't recovered the money or dealt with the people who found it?'

Welsh nodded and then spoke in the manner in which Galloway insisted on hearing reports: concise and to the point, with no self-serving spin or embellishment.

'Barnes has been dealt with. Stafford has not. I accessed Stafford's Army records. He's former Delta Force. Highly decorated. Boxed as a light heavyweight on the Army team before being selected for Delta. He's a professional Bail Enforcement Agent now.

'A bounty hunter?'

'Yes, sir. And Barnes has a sister. A former DEA agent who worked undercover operations. They seem to have teamed up.'

'To do what?'

Welsh paused for a moment and considered his answer. 'I don't think it's just about keeping the money now. I think the sister will want to avenge her brother's death, and Stafford probably feels the same way. He and Barnes were close. Everything about them says they're going to come after us.'

'And you don't think Cameron's people can handle them?'

'I think their special-operations skill levels are at least the equal of Cameron's people, with the possible exception of

Kitlan and Marcus. So we aren't dealing with novice civilians who are going to scare easily or panic under pressure.'

'Well if you're right about them coming after us, we'll soon find out just how good they are, won't we?'

As the CIA's top spymaster, Galloway was one of the least known, yet arguably one of the most powerful men in the world. His super-secret Directorate of Operations was where all of the Agency's black operations were conceived and carried out: espionage, counter-intelligence, paramilitary actions, and covert activities that included the overthrowing of governments, bribery, kidnapping, assassinations, and a multitude of other 'black ops' that would never see the light of day.

Galloway was a true believer, among the last of the old school, adventurous Ivy Leaguers. The wealthy trust-funded sons of old-money families who joined the CIA for all the right reasons: duty, honor, country. And after a thirty-four-year career spent entirely in the clandestine services, it was Galloway's unshakeable belief in what he was doing that had led him to do the things that could now destroy him if discovered.

Five years ago, the anti-covert action analytical side of the Agency decided that the Directorate of Intelligence should receive the lion's share of the CIA's funding. Galloway's budget for the operations directorate was slashed by more than forty percent, forcing him to cut back on programs and operations, resulting in good men being summarily dismissed or forced into early retirement. The cuts, he was told, would be even deeper for the foreseeable future.

Galloway immediately began to see the results of the turn away from covert operations. The adverse effect on the recruitment of foreign agents, and the steady decline in the quality and quantity of the intelligence information he was receiving were only the beginning. After a year of watching his beloved operations directorate being emasculated, his own power-base eroded, and what he perceived as a dangerous weakening of national security, he decided he could no longer stand by and do nothing.

Fourteen months after the initial cutbacks in funding began, an opportunity presented itself and Galloway seized it. One of his agents in Paris, while on the trail of a safehouse being used by a Middle-East terrorist group responsible for a series of recent bombings, inadvertently discovered a counterfeiting operation being run by Iranian nationals in a farmhouse in the countryside south of the French capital. The Iranians were producing near perfect copies of the one hundred dollar bill. The quality of the engraving, and of the paper on which the notes were printed, were so good that when the Secret Service first learned of the bill's existence, four years before Galloway's agent discovered the counterfeiting operation, they dubbed it the 'supernote'. At the time the counterfeit was being produced on a small scale and was not a major concern for the Secret Service, but that was soon to change.

Galloway immediately recognized the counterfeiting operation as the solution to his long-term problems, and a way to circumvent those who would destroy what had taken him years to build. He buried the intelligence report and kept the information from his superiors and from the Secret Service, then tasked Tony Kitlan, a loyal and long-time special operator, with putting together a team to assault the farmhouse.

Kitlan and his team seized the presses, engraving plates, and the high-quality paper, and, with the exception of the master engraver who had made the plates for the supernote, left no one alive to tell what had happened. Two days later the French agent working for the CIA's Counter Terrorism Center, who had initially discovered the counterfeiting operation, was killed by a hit and run driver on the streets of Paris.

Deciding that the Counter Narcotics Center was the perfect place from which to control his rogue operation, Galloway appointed Adam Welsh, another like-minded loyal and trusted employee, to head the CNC and took him into his confidence. The final step was to set up Cameron & Associates as a cover operation to launder the money, and to staff it with personnel vetted and approved by Kitlan and Cameron; all dedicated former CIA field officers who had lost their jobs due to the cutbacks. When the new one hundred dollar bill came into circulation, Cameron had the master engraver, now working for him, make plates that were equal to the quality of the old ones.

115

Unknown to the CIA director, or to anyone else inside the Agency other than Welsh, for the past four years Galloway had orchestrated the printing and laundering of in excess of one hundred and twenty-five million dollars a year in supernotes, depositing the laundered money in secret numbered accounts in offshore banks and using it to fund highly successful black operations around the world. Operations for which he did not have to answer to anyone, and whose origins were completely unknown to his superiors at CIA or to the rest of the intelligence community. And now his brilliantly conceived and executed plan was threatened by the unforeseeable synchronicity of two events: the crash of the Lear jet in the vast wilderness of northern Quebec, and the presence of two old friends who happened to be on a fishing trip at the exact time and location of the crash.

Galloway got up to pour himself another drink, then slowly paced the room. 'How the hell did that transmitter get in one of the bags without us knowing about it?'

'A Secret Service agent from their Paris office found out about the shipment of supernotes from one of his undercovers working another counterfeiting case.'

'Can they walk the cat backwards to our operation?'

'No. We're too compartmented and have too many cut-outs for that to happen. They have no idea where the shipment originated. The undercover only knew it had been put on board a freighter in Rotterdam and was en route to Newfoundland. That's where the Secret Service put the transmitter in the bag.'

'And you couldn't contact Cameron and warn him about the transmitter?'

'I didn't find out about it until after the fact.'

'How much does the Secret Service know?'

'Only that the plane went down in an unknown location in the Quebec wilderness.'

'Did the satellite film Cameron's people going into the crash site?'

'No. I pulled both satellites as soon as Stafford and Barnes left the area.'

'Where are Stafford and the Barnes woman now?'

'I don't know. They made the surveillance Burruss put on them, and we've lost them.'

Galloway held Welsh's gaze. Welsh answered the unspoken question. 'I couldn't keep Burruss from putting Stafford and Barnes under surveillance without him getting suspicious. And I'll have to let him run with it for a while for appearance's sake. I'll shut him down if it even looks like he's getting anywhere near the truth.'

'I want Stafford and the Barnes woman dead, Adam. Without any consideration given to recovering the money. Is that understood?'

'Yes, sir. We do have one thing in the plus column,' Welsh offered. 'Their actions indicate they've decided to keep the money, which means they aren't going to be talking to anyone about what happened or what they know.'

'And how long can we count on that?'

Galloway opened the drapes, and Welsh took the not-too-subtle hint that the meeting was over. He got up from his chair as Galloway opened the French doors to the terrace and followed him outside.

Galloway fixed him with a cold hard stare. 'No more mistakes, Adam. The longer Stafford and the Barnes woman are out there as loose cannons, the greater the chance of them drawing the attention of people we don't need looking too closely at our operations. Particularly the Secret Service.'

Chapter Twenty-Eight

Located only a short distance from the Pentagon City office complex in Alexandria, Virginia, Whitey's is the closest thing federal law enforcement officers have to a cop bar. A sign over the door that says 'Eats' sets the tone for the hole-in-the-wall restaurant and bar complete with pool tables, a dart room, an occasionally hilarious karaoke night, and a rock and roll band on most other evenings. With the exception of a few truck-driver types and a steady stream of young, attractive groupies, it is primarily a watering hole and haven for off-duty FBI, DEA and Secret Service agents; a place where they come to dull their senses, vent their spleens, and relax among like-minded patrons who understand the unique pressures of their jobs.

The crowd was thinning out, the bar stools and booths mostly empty, when Janet Barnes and Ben Stafford entered Whitey's front room. Janet paused to scan the remaining customers, then led Stafford into the rear area where she spotted the man she was looking for. His name was Josh Grady, and he was sitting alone in a booth finishing off a pitcher of beer and watching two groupies wearing low-cut tops and mid-thigh skirts play a game of eight-ball – his interest heightening whenever they bent over the table to make a shot.

Grady was a big, rough-hewn man, who looked more like a knock-around biker than the DEA agent that he was; an image that had served him well in the days when he worked the street. His tie was loosened and his shirt collar unbuttoned, and he seemed uncomfortable in the suit that he was now required to wear to work each day. Neatly coiffed and clean shaven, it had taken Janet a few moments to recognize him without the ponytail and goatee he had when she last saw him.

Janet and Grady had graduated from the same DEA training class, were sworn in together, and subsequently assigned to the New York Field Division. For more than two years they worked dangerous undercover assignments on the same joint DEA/NYPD task force, until Grady was transferred to head-quarters shortly after Janet was forced to resign. They had been in numerous tight situations where their lives had depended on each other, and they had once been close friends. That was before push came to shove and Janet learned that their definitions of friendship differed widely.

Grady sat up straight when he saw Janet coming his way. The sheepish smile on his face told Stafford that the two had at best a complicated history.

As they approached the booth at the back of the room, Janet nudged Stafford. 'Let me do the talking. The less he knows the better.'

Grady took a long drink directly from the pitcher, draining the last drop as Janet and Stafford slid into the booth to sit across from him. Janet slowly shook her head as Grady thumped the empty pitcher down on the table.

'You always were a class act.'

'Yep. A prince among men.'

'I need some information.'

'Just like that? No how are you, Josh? How's it going, Josh?'

'It's almost twelve o'clock on a week night, you're slumped in a booth in this shitty dump drinking yourself into oblivion because you miss the street action and you hate the fact that you've been transferred back to headquarters and have to take crap from a bunch of suits who never had their asses on the line in their lives. That about cover how you are and how it's going?'

Grady shrugged. 'Pretty much.' He jerked a thumb toward Stafford. 'Him I don't know.'

'Ben Stafford. He's a friend. He's okay.' The two men

nodded to each other, forgoing a handshake. Grady got the attention of a waitress and pointed to his empty beer pitcher. She nodded and went out to the bar.

'So let me tell you what I've learned about the war on drugs since I've been transferred down here, Barnes. It's a goddamn joke, and we're losing it. Big time. Despite what the asshole suits and politicians say.'

'You just figured that out?'

'Yeah, well maybe I didn't want to believe it before.' Grady suppressed a belch and continued, his words beginning to slur. 'Did you know that worldwide more money is spent on illegal drugs than on food, and that virtually every bill in circulation in this country bears microscopic traces of cocaine? Boggles the mind, huh? But it's the truth. Along with the fact that the economies of a couple of dozen Third World countries would collapse if it weren't for drug money. And it's getting worse, not better. Makes you want to puke. Or on a real bad day, eat your gun. If you give a shit. Which I don't, anymore.' He leaned across the table and locked slightly bleary eyes with Janet. 'How many damn times did we almost get shot full of holes? And for what?'

Janet looked away, scanning the room as the waitress returned with a full pitcher of beer. Grady immediately poured himself a glass. 'I'd offer you guys some, but I'm working on getting seriously fucked up here.' He took another long drink, then studied Janet's face for a moment. 'So what is it you want?'

'You're assigned to the Operations Division, right?'

'Right. But don't ask me about anything I shouldn't be telling you.'

'So you'll tell me what you can.' She lowered her voice as she spoke. 'Have you heard of any big shipment of drug-related cash that's gone missing or stolen in the past few days?'

'How big are we talking?'

'Maybe twenty million.'

'Missing or stolen from where?'

'What difference does it make from where? Either you heard or you didn't.'

120

'Christ, lighten up, Barnes.'

Janet softened her tone. 'Sorry. It hasn't exactly been a good night.' She considered telling him about her brother, but decided against it. 'All I heard is CIA might be involved in some way. And their Counter Narcotics Center is supposed to keep DEA informed about any operations they're running, right?'

'Supposed to. Sometimes they aren't real big on sharing. But it doesn't make sense they'd be involved in any large shipments of cash. They don't run interdiction raids or buy-bust operations. They pretty much track drug shipments, monitor smuggling routes, and trace laundered money, then pass the intel on to us or whoever has the jurisdiction to deal with it. So I doubt it was CNC. But then who the hell knows? I wouldn't trust them any farther than I could spit them.'

'And as far as you know it didn't involve a DEA operation?'

'No. That much cash disappears, somebody's going to make a lot of noise, and I would have heard it.'

Janet slid out of the booth and Stafford followed. 'I'll check back with you in a couple of days. Maybe something will surface.'

'You care to tell me why you're asking?'

'You don't want to know.'

'If I can help you, I will. You know that.' Grady's expression changed to one of genuine affection. 'I'm really sorry about what that pig Burns did to you, Janet. You deserved better than that.'

Janet's voice took on a sharp, bitter tone. 'Is that right? You know, maybe my memory's failing, but I don't remember you going to bat for me when that rotten son of a bitch set me up.'

'What was I supposed to do? Go down with you? He had most of the agents there believing him. Only a couple of us figured you were set up. I couldn't prove what he did. And if I'd have taken him on he would have turned on me next. He knew I knew, that's why he had me transferred down here.'

'You're a real stand-up guy, Josh. My hero.'

Grady averted his eyes. 'He'll get his sooner or later.'

'Yeah, huh? How come that doesn't make me feel all warm and fuzzy?'

'You know, right after you left? That prick started hitting on one of the administrative assistants. She didn't have your guts and she wanted to keep her job. So she shacks up with him a couple of nights a week in a splash pad he's got on East Fifty-First.'

Janet's eyes hardened. 'He should die in a fire.'

She and Stafford turned to leave and Grady called after her, louder than he intended. 'Hey, Janet. I'm sorry. I really am sorry.'

'Me, too, Josh.'

Grady's eyes welled with tears. 'You forgive me? Huh? Do ya?'

Janet kept her back to him and left the room without responding. Outside, in the parking lot, it was Stafford who broke the strained silence.

'We'll get a few hours sleep, then drive up to New York, see what we can find out about the dead guy from the plane.'

Janet, still angry from the memories Josh Grady brought back of the humiliating experience of her resignation, said nothing as they got in the Cherokee and pulled away.

Chapter Twenty-Nine

Joyce Linkowski had two rare and peculiar gifts: the ability to memorize long strings of numbers at a glance, and an unerring eye for proper alignment and order. Something that would go unnoticed by most people would stand out like a sequoia tree in Death Valley to Joyce's organized and precise mind. If a painting was hung as little as one half inch off center, or out of plumb by a single degree, she noticed it. If a series of numbers were out of their intended sequence, or a list meant to be alphabetical had a name out of order by virtue of one letter, she noticed that, too. At times, given an imperfect world, she saw her unique gifts as nothing but an annoyance, but at other times, as on this second morning at her new job at the First Union Bank in Reston, they proved quite useful.

Joyce had spent the past six years working at the Federal Bank in Richmond, Virginia, helping to process the tens of millions of dollars that flowed through the federal reserve system on a weekly basis. She left that job, and a city she never really liked, to escape an unfaithful, abusive husband, and to make a better life for herself and her four-year-old daughter. Just prior to leaving, she had read a Secret Service advisory on counterfeit money, in particular the new super-note and the difficulty in recognizing it. The micro-printing, the color-shifting ink, and the security thread embedded in the paper that glowed red when the note was held under an ultra-violet light, were all perfectly replicated, according to the advisory, making it extremely difficult to tell the counterfeit version of the new one hundred dollar bill from the real thing.

For the most part, the counterfeiters had produced a near perfect copy that would fool all but the experts, with the occasional exception of someone who noticed things that made the bills stand out for reasons other than the quality of the printing. Someone like Joyce Linkowski.

Joyce had just opened her teller's window when a handsome, Armani-clad young man wearing a diamond-studded solid-gold Rolex handed her a cash deposit of eight thousand dollars in one hundred dollar bills. He flirted with her as he gave her instructions to deposit the entire sum in his money market account, and Joyce, who had only recently begun thinking of herself as a single woman again, self-consciously touched her hair and offered a shy smile in return. She began counting out the bills, efficiently flicking through them with a steady rhythm until she noticed something unusual.

The bills all showed a uniformity of wear, or more precisely, a uniform lack of wear. As though they had all been issued at exactly the same time and seen the same amount of use. But there was something else. Something that at first glance registered only in Joyce's subsconscious, at the back of her orderly mind, and caused her to pause and then stop counting altogether.

'I'm so sorry. I lost count,' was the excuse she gave as she feigned a helpless shrug and began again. This time, a third of the way through a slower, more deliberate count, she realized what it was that had caught her unerring eye. The serial numbers on the bills were sequential, and at least six of them had the exact same serial number; both positive indications that the bills were counterfeit.

Joyce finished the count and smiled pleasantly, maintaining her composure as she gave the man his deposit slip. She watched him cross the lobby, feeling a touch of remorse at the prospect of losing what had held the promise of being her first date since beginning her new life. But she dismissed the wistful thought, and the moment he was out the door she alerted the bank manager, who immediately called the Secret Service.

Two agents from the counterfeit squad arrived at the bank within twenty minutes. Upon identifying the bills as supernotes, they notified the Special-Agent-In-Charge of the Washington field office, who promptly called the SAIC of the Counterfeit Division at Secret Service headquarters, who in turn called Tom Quinn, advising him of the situation.

Quinn had no trouble locating Peter Duncan, the man who had the misfortune of encountering Joyce Linkowski when he deposited the eight thousand dollars in supernotes. Quinn ran an NCIC check on him and learned that within the past two years Duncan had a misdemeanor arrest for possession of marijuana, resulting in a fine, a felony arrest for possession of a small amount of cocaine that got him six months community service and a one year suspended sentence, and two arrests for aggravated assault, the charges later dropped when the victims refused to testify. All of which made Quinn believe that Duncan was a small-time, up-scale drug dealer careful enough never to get caught with significant weight, and had thus managed to avoid getting arrested for the far more serious 'with intent to distribute' charge.

Less than two hours after Duncan deposited the money, Quinn had him picked up and brought to the Washington field office for questioning, where he now sat in a suspect interview room nervously tapping his foot and staring at the additional fifteen hundred dollars in supernotes found on him and placed in the middle of the table. Quinn leaned against the far wall of the interview room, his arms folded across his chest and a bemused look on his face as he watched Duncan's mind work, trying to come up with an explanation that would put the right spin on whatever he was about to say.

'I'm telling you, man, I swear to God, I didn't know it was counterfeit. I mean what am I? A moron? Take counterfeit money to a bank?'

Quinn believed him. Duncan was nothing if not street smart, and he would have to have been a low-grade moron to knowingly deposit counterfeit money directly into his own bank account. Regardless of how good the quality of the bills were, a pro would have limited his personal exposure by using a network to pass them on the street. Even a half-smart, inexperienced amateur would, at the very least, have made small purchases in a variety of stores at peak business hours, knowing that it was highly unlikely that a harried clerk at a crowded sales counter would remember him, or notice the counterfeit money as he waited for his change.

Less than five minutes after entering the interview room, Peter Duncan did the two things Quinn knew he was going to do from the moment he laid eyes on him. He said that the money came from a friend. And he gave the friend up without a second thought.

'Anthony Baldini. He's a car dealer in Reston. Porsches. That coked-up fuck owed me ninety-five hundred ...' Realizing the implications of the statement he had just made, Duncan quickly backtracked and clarified it. 'He owed me ninety-five hundred for a personal loan and paid me back last night with the money you're saying is counterfeit.'

Quinn smiled knowingly, strongly suspecting that the payment was for cocaine. But he had no interest in Duncan's drug-related offenses, and convinced that the total of ninety-five supernotes were all that he had ever had, he released him.

Anthony Baldini stepped out from behind the desk in his office at the Porsche dealership on Reston Boulevard and greeted Tom Quinn with an outstretched hand and a broad I'm-your-new-best-friend smile. The hand fell to his side and the smile quickly faded when Quinn flashed his credentials.

Baldini, with a slightly bewildered look on his face, retreated back behind the stylish marble and glass desk and sank into his gray-leather Recaro swivel chair. He had no idea why the Secret Service was interested in him, but he did know they were part of the Treasury Department, as was the Internal Revenue Service. And the IRS could have any number of reasons for wanting to talk with him. But he was fairly certain that the Secret Service did not investigate for the IRS. But then there were phony titles and questionable lineage of some of his used cars.

Baldini tried not to panic as the tall, muscular Secret Service Agent with the steady, penetrating eyes calmly explained the reason for his visit as he sat in one of two beige leather armchairs set before the desk. Baldini listened with rapt attention, working on a convincing expression of wide-eyed innocence.

'I don't know any Peter Duncan. At least I don't think I do. I guess I could have sold him a car, but I'd have to check my records.'

Quinn smiled patiently. 'Are you sure this is the way you want to play it, Mr Baldini? Because if you are, I'm sure I can convince the federal prosecutor to make every counterfeit bill you passed to Duncan a separate count, in and of itself. That would be ninety-five counts. Each count carrying a sentence of five years. You do the math.'

Baldini quickly abandoned any pretense of innocence. 'Okay. Okay. I got the money yesterday from a guy named Eddie Barnes. Lives here in Reston. He bought a new 911 cabriolet all-wheel drive and paid cash. I hardly know the guy, and I promise you, I did not know that money was counterfeit, or why the hell would I have accepted it?'

'To launder it for him?'

'Hey, no way. Jesus. Where'd you come up with an idea like that?'

Quinn suppressed a laugh. 'Right. What was I thinking?' He leveled a hard gaze at Baldini. 'Where's the rest of the money?'

Baldini slumped in his chair, a thoroughly defeated man. 'Ah shit. I guess you took the ninety-five hundred back from Duncan, too, huh?'

'Good guess.'

'So now I'm out the whole eighty-nine grand that bastard Barnes gave me.' Baldini thought for a moment, then his mood brightened. 'But I can get the car back, right?'

'I don't see why not; if everything you've told me is true.'

'Absolutely. The whole truth and nothin' but.'

Hanging on the wall behind Baldini's desk was a large oil painting of him in a one-piece driving suit, one hand on his hip, the other holding a helmet, as he posed before a Porsche race car. Quinn was reminded of the paintings of Elvis on velvet he had seen for sale at truck stops. Baldini got up and removed the almost comical portrait from the wall, revealing a small safe. He dialed in the combination and took out the

127

$79,500 that remained of what Eddie Barnes had given him. He stuffed the money into a small back canvas tote bag bearing the Porsche logo and the name of his dealership, then handed the bag to Quinn.

'That's all of it?'

'Absolutely. And you can keep the bag. My compliments.'

Baldini tapped out a command on the computer keyboard on the desktop in front of him, squinted at the flat screen monitor on his right, then wrote down the address Eddie Barnes had given him. He handed it to Quinn with a hopeful smile. 'So I'm straight with the Secret Service now?'

'If nothing else turns up during our investigation.'

Quinn got up and walked out through the showroom, pausing to admire an outrageously expensive bright red turbo-charged Porsche. He felt certain that the moment he was out of sight Baldini would be laying down lines of cocaine on the glass top of his designer desk, using the snowy white powder to bolster his courage for the inevitable, and probably imminent, confrontation with Peter Duncan, a man whose record indicated he did not hesitate to get up close and physical with those who angered him.

Quinn knew that eighty-nine thousand dollars in supernotes appearing in the same place, at the same time, and originating with the same person, indicated one of two possibilities: Barnes was printing the notes himself, or he was part of the distribution and laundering network set up by the counterfeiter. Quinn doubted that it was the former; the printer and the passer were seldom the same person when it came to large quantities of high-quality notes. It was more likely that Barnes was a passer, albeit a careless and unsophisticated one. But still another question loomed even larger in Quinn's mind as he drove to the address Baldini had given him.

Was it possible the supernotes he had just confiscated were part of the shipment they had been tracking from Rotterdam? The coincidences and timing were impossible to ignore. But if the notes were from that shipment, a shipment the CIA's Counter Narcotics Center claimed was lost in a plane crash in the Canadian wilderness, the crash site still undiscovered, how had the money surfaced in Reston, Virginia, forty-eight hours later?

Less than an hour after finding the front door of Eddie Barnes' townhouse sealed with crime-scene tape, Quinn had the answer to that question and more. He had called the Reston police and learned of the torture and murder of Barnes the previous night, and of how his sister, a former DEA agent, had killed one of the intruders. No, the intruder was not carrying any form of identification, nor were his fingerprints on file anywhere.

A neighbor in an adjoining townhouse told Quinn of Barnes' recent return from a fishing trip in the Quebec wilderness with a friend. An Army buddy he hadn't seen since his Delta Force days, the neighbor recalled Barnes telling him.

Quinn had the Secret Service Intelligence Division access Barnes' telephone records for the previous month, along with his military service record. He soon had the intersect he was looking for. A telephone number Barnes had called the morning he left for his fishing trip linked him to a Ben Stafford in Chadds Ford, Pennsylvania, who, according to a Secret Service contact at Delta Force, had served in the same squadron with Barnes.

Within minutes of learning Stafford's identity, Quinn instructed the Special-Agent-In-Charge of the Philadelphia field office to have Stafford brought in for an interview, and to hold him until he got there. Within the hour, Quinn arrived at the Philadelphia airport in a Customs Department jet and was met by two agents who told him of the shoot-out at Stafford's home the previous night, and that Stafford had disappeared.

With the knowledge that the two men had been camping in the wilderness area where the Lear jet was believed to have crashed, and that Barnes had been tortured and murdered and an attempt made on Stafford's life within twenty-four hours of their return from the trip, Quinn now believed he knew what had happened to the shipment of twenty million dollars in supernotes.

But there were still unanswered questions. Who had tracked down the two men? And how had they managed to do it? Had they recovered the money? And if not, where was it? Quinn knew that in order to get the answers to those and other questions, he needed to find Ben Stafford. Quickly. Before whoever was trying to kill him succeeded. He began his search by calling the Secret Service Intelligence Division at Washington headquarters, requesting a complete background check on Stafford, including the numbers of all credit cards he had been issued, along with any vehicle registrations and cellular telephone numbers in his name.

Quinn then directed a thorough search of Stafford's Chadds Ford home by agents from the Philadelphia field office, while at the same time agents from the Washington field office conducted an equally thorough search of Barnes' townhouse. Both searches turned up nothing useful. A local sheriff's deputy, patrolling the area around Stafford's home, stopped when he saw all the cars and activity. He told Quinn about the tragic death of Stafford's wife. Quinn lingered in the house after the agents from the local field office had gone, studying photographs and other memorabilia as well as looking through Stafford's desk and computer files in an effort to learn as much as he could about the man he was now hunting. He saw the photographs of Stafford with his daughter, and the records of monthly payments to the private psychiatric hospital on the Philadelphia Main Line, along with the less than encouraging reports from the doctors, and he believed he knew what may have tempted this otherwise honest man to cross the line.

All the indications were that Stafford and Barnes had been best friends. And the sense of the man Quinn had gotten from what he had learned made him wonder how Stafford was going to react to the torture and murder of his friend. But then he thought he knew.

Eight hours after arriving in Philadelphia, Quinn boarded the Customs Department jet for the short flight back to Washington. Hoping to catch a quick nap, he settled back in his seat and closed his eyes as the aircraft roared down the runway and lifted off. He had considered calling Lou Burruss at the CIA's Counter Narcotics Center, to tell him the supernotes had surfaced, but he decided against it for the time being. His instincts told him that Burruss had been less than forthcoming about what CNC knew. And if they wanted to keep him out of the loop, it was fine with him, but that worked both ways.

Chapter Thirty

Tony Kitlan drove the dark-blue van north on Amsterdam Avenue, expertly maneuvering it through New York City's hectic morning rush hour traffic. He stopped at the light at the corner of 84th Street, waiting for the intersection to clear so he could make a right turn. His destination was an apartment building near the end of the block where Jeffery Ramsey, the man who died in the crash of the Lear jet, had lived. Cameron had ordered him to sanitize the apartment and to make certain nothing remained that could connect Ramsey to Cameron & Associates or to his former employer, the CIA.

Peter Marcus sat in the front passenger seat of the van chewing on a hangnail on his right index finger and casually watching the parade of mostly thirty-something pedestrians proceeding in a purposeful, take-no-prisoners march past the upscale shops and restaurants that lined the sidewalks of the trendy Upper West Side neighborhood.

Kitlan looked over and frowned at the sight of Marcus chewing his finger. 'That's a disgusting habit.'

Marcus shrugged and stopped what he was doing. He turned his attention to the attractive female passenger in a black Jeep Cherokee that was stopped broadside in the middle of Amsterdam Avenue, directly in front of the van. The driver was also waiting for the cross-street traffic to clear so he could continue on 84th Street.

Marcus' eyes widened with surprise when, for a moment,

the woman in the Cherokee looked directly at him. He quickly looked away, then realized that she could not possibly have recognized him. She had never seen him, or Kitlan. But they had seen her.

'Tony. Check out the broad in the car in front of us.' As he spoke, the Cherokee inched forward in an effort to clear the avenue before the light changed. 'Am I imagining things, or is that the bitch who killed Larry last night?'

Kitlan immediately recognized Janet Barnes as the woman they had watched approach the Reston townhouse the night before. The driver turned to talk to her, and the quick glimpse Kitlan got of Stafford's face was all he needed to identify him from the photos in Barnes' study. The Pennsylvania license plates brought a flashback of the black Cherokee he had forced off the road in Canada.

'That's her. And the driver is definitely Stafford.' Kitlan pulled the van ahead, angling to cut in behind the Cherokee when the traffic began to move again. 'Damn if Cameron wasn't right. They're hunting us.'

'Not the smartest move they ever made.' Marcus reached under the dash and pulled an H&K sub-machine-gun equipped with a sound-suppressor from its mounting bracket. 'The boss wants them dead yesterday, so let's get it over with.'

Kitlan shoved the deadly weapon into Marcus's lap. 'Put that away.' He thought for a moment, then said, 'Stafford must have gotten Ramsey's ID off his body at the crash site. Ten to one he's headed the same place we are.'

'Then we take them out right now. First chance you get, pull alongside. It'll all be over in a few seconds.'

'No. Not here.'

'Why the hell not?' Marcus flipped the safety off the sub-machine-gun. 'Traffic's backed up. They can't go anywhere. They're sitting ducks.'

Kitlan grabbed the weapon from Marcus, engaged the safety, and threw it on the floor of the van at Marcus's feet. 'What's wrong with you? Huh? Did you just have a brain fart? How the hell do you think we're going to get out of here after you shoot them? We're boxed in the same way they are. And I'd give us about ten seconds before some citizen in one of these cars dials nine-one-one and has the cops blocking both ends of the street.'

'You got a better idea?'

'Christ, I hope so.'

The Cherokee was finally able to move completely off the avenue and continue east on 84th Street, only to stop halfway up the block as the traffic again came to a halt. Kitlan made the turn, following directly behind Stafford and cutting off an irate driver who stuck his contorted face out the window and screamed a long unintelligible stream of obscenities in an unrecognizable language. For a fleeting moment, Marcus entertained the thought of firing a sustained blast through the man's windshield. Teach him a lesson he'd never forget, if he survived. But he was pretty sure Kitlan would take an even dimmer view of that.

The traffic crept forward and Kitlan swung to the far side of the street, pulling even with the driver's-side door of the Cherokee. He saw Stafford lean forward to check the numbers on the buildings.

'Yeah. They're definitely headed for Ramsey's apartment. We'll take them when they leave. That'll give us plenty of time to set it up.'

'Suppose they find something they shouldn't? Then we got another problem.'

Kitlan lost his patience. 'Which part of the plan don't you understand, Pete? What goddamn difference does it make what they find in the apartment? We're going to hit them when they come out.'

Kitlan paused for a moment and softened his tone, recalling that Marcus sulked like a child when reprimanded. 'Look, Pete, I appreciate your enthusiasm. I really do. But don't forget, Stafford took out three good field operatives by himself, and the woman put two rounds in the center of Larry's chest from a distance of fifty or sixty feet. At night. You've got to show some respect for their abilities.'

'Yeah, you're probably right. It ain't like they're gonna piss their pants when the shooting starts.'

'No, it's not. And it's in our best interest to have a good, solid plan when we go at them; not any of this spur-of-the-moment shit.'

134

Traffic began to flow smoothly as the light at the Columbus Avenue intersection turned green. Kitlan dropped back and stayed with Stafford until he was certain he was right about his destination. After seeing the Cherokee enter the ramp leading to the underground parking garage for Ramsey's building, he drove the van to the end of the block, turned south on Columbus, and dialed a number on his cellular telephone.

Chapter Thirty-One

Ben Stafford and Janet Barnes had grabbed a few hours' sleep and showered and changed at her apartment before leaving for New York at four o'clock that morning. Stafford was still feeling the effects of sleeping on the too-short sofa with his head propped up on its arm.

He was rubbing the back of his neck in an attempt to work out the kinks when he pulled up and stopped at the barricade blocking the entrance ramp to the garage beneath Jeffery Ramsey's apartment building. He lowered his window and reached out to insert his Visa card in the slot on the control box for the security cards issued to the tenants of the building. He withdrew the card, and the metal bar across the ramp raised.

Janet gave him a questioning look as he drove down into the parking area. 'You put a credit card in there.'

Stafford nodded. 'Most of those systems will work off any magnetized card.'

'There's a comforting thought.'

Stafford drove slowly around the dimly lit garage, past rows of parked cars used primarily for weekend getaways as opposed to everyday transportation. He paused where a black Mercedes 500S was parked and noticed that the tenants' apartment numbers were stenciled on the wall of their allotted spaces. He continued on, again checking the makes and models of each of the cars.

'How do you know which car belongs to Ramsey?'

'His registration card was in his wallet.'

Stafford stopped directly behind a silver Mercedes CLK coupé, checked the license plate, and noted the apartment number on the wall. 32B. He pulled into an empty slot four cars up and removed a small center punch from the glove compartment as he and Janet got out of the Cherokee and walked back to where the coupé was parked.

Stafford looked around the garage, making certain they were alone, then placed the pointed tip of the center punch against the driver's side window and pressed it forcefully into the glass. The window shattered instantly, making a loud popping noise.

Stafford reached inside, opened the door, and climbed in. The alarm wailed for only a few seconds before he had the wiring harness out and the system disabled.

Janet watched and listened for any sign that the noise had drawn attention to what they were doing. Satisfied that it had not, she gestured toward the wiring harness dangling beneath the dash. 'Benefits of a misspent youth?'

'Delta Force. They taught me and Eddie a lot of neat tricks.'

Stafford saw the light in Janet's eyes dim for a moment as she was reminded of her brother. He felt the same twinge of sorrow and turned away and began searching the car. He felt under the dash and the seats, and checked the glove compartment where he removed a number of credit card receipts and put them in his pocket. He opened the center armrest console and unplugged the dockable cellular phone and handed it to Janet.

'Put this in your shoulder bag.'

'Why do we want his cell phone?'

'To see what numbers he programmed into memory dial.'

Janet feigned surprise. 'I'm impressed, Stafford. You're more than just a pretty face.'

As Stafford continued to search the interior, Janet walked around the outside of the car. she knelt on one knee and looked inside the right front and right rear wheel wells, then did the same on the left side. Pausing at the back of the car, she knelt and slid her hand behind the license plate. She smiled to herself, took a small Swiss-Army knife from her shoulder bag, removed the screws holding the plate in place, turned the plate over, and peeled off the duct tape that secured a sandwich bag containing a set of keys against the back. She took the keys from the bag, reattached the plate, and walked around to reach inside the car and jangled the keys in front of Stafford.

'I take back what I said about you being more than just a pretty face.'

Stafford glanced at the keys. 'Ramsey's?'

'Looks like spares for the car and his apartment.' She winked and smiled. 'Are you feeling properly chagrined?'

Stafford shrugged. 'My way's quicker.'

'And what do we do next? Set the building on fire so we can sneak past the doorman in the lobby during the panic?'

'If all else fails.'

'I'm beginning to believe what I've heard about bounty hunters. Kick in doors. Smash everything in sight. Hope you got the right house and shot the right people.'

'We've got a few morons who give the rest of us a bad name. But most of my time is spent on stakeouts or talking to attorneys, detectives, witnesses, victims, local snitches. Anyone who can give me a lead on the person I'm looking for.'

'And when you find them they just come along peacefully?'

'Believe it or not, less than five percent of the people I bring in resist. Occasionally I run into a bad ass who goes down hard and won't hesitate to use a gun, but it's not very often I have to kick in a door or use deadly force.'

'So how do we get past the doormen?'

'This time of the morning it shouldn't be too difficult.'

After an unproductive search of the car's trunk, Janet followed Stafford up the stairwell to the entrance to the lobby. She stayed just inside the landing as Stafford opened the door a crack to peer out. He turned back to her and smiled.

'Piece of cake.'

'This ought to be good.'

A bank of three elevators was only a short distance from the stairwell, across a broad hallway that branched off the main part of the lobby, fifty-plus feet from the reception desk at the entrance to the building. Stafford saw that one of the doormen had his back to him as he stood at the main entrance greeting the departing tenants and opening the door for them. The other doorman was at the desk, his face buried in a copy of the *Daily News*.

Stafford waited until a few seconds after he heard an elevator chime its arrival, then motioned for Janet to follow him. When he opened the door to the lobby, seven people were exiting one of the elevators as a second one arrived delivering a dog walker with six eager canines over which he exercised little or no control; two of them, a Rottweiler and a Great Dane, appeared to individually outweigh the man.

Screened from view of the doormen by the departing tenants, who, in their harried preoccupation with avoiding the unruly urban dog team unceremoniously dragging the human sled across the lobby, paid no attention to Stafford and Janet as they casually crossed from the stairwell and entered one of the elevators just as the door closed.

Stafford pressed the button for the thirty-second floor. 'Do I get back my more-than-a-pretty-face rating.'

'Maybe. If we don't end up having to shoot our way out.'

Chapter Thirty-Two

Experience and training had taught both Stafford and Janet not to walk near corners or doorways on the street, and to never enter closed spaces too quickly. Keeping that in mind, they entered Jeffery Ramsey's apartment five seconds apart, with Janet checking the hallway before closing and dead-bolting the door behind them.

They stood motionless inside the foyer, their backs against the wall, listening, guns drawn and wary eyes tracking the expensively furnished two-bedroom corner apartment. To their right a large living room, a study with a computer workstation, and a kitchen/dining area all flowed together into one bright and airy room. Two walls had been knocked out, opening up the floor space to accommodate a six-station weight machine, a treadmill, a Stair Master, and a recumbent exercycle. Chairs and sofas upholstered in white leather, and glass-topped tables with limestone bases were placed in conversational groupings on highly polished oak floors partially covered with silk Persian carpets. The seating arrangements were positioned to take advantage of the spectacular view of the Manhattan skyline and the Hudson River provided by the floor-to-ceiling privacy-glass walls that ran the length of the room.

Too far above the street for the noise of the city to intrude, the apartment was still and silent; the low hum of the refrigerator motor the only sound. After a full minute, Stafford pointed for Janet to check the living room, study and kitchen area, while he moved down the hallway to his left toward the master bedroom and guest room.

Janet quickly cleared the open, flowing rooms and sat down at the workstation. She turned on the computer and was prompted for a password. Having learned that more often than not a person's habit patterns carried over into all facets of their life, she began searching the desk, removing drawers and holding them up to look underneath. She found what she was looking for taped to the underside of the fourth drawer she examined. Like most people who occasionally forgot their passwords, Ramsey had hidden his within easy reach of his work area. Janet typed in EAGLES TALON 486 and began opening the dead man's files.

Stafford finished a search of the guest room and moved on to the large walk-in closet in the master bedroom. He checked the pockets of twenty-four designer suits, evenly divided among Brioni, Zegna, and Gucci, and found nothing of interest. He then examined a set of leather luggage, looking for used airline tickets, itineraries, credit card receipts, or anything else that could tell him where Ramsey may have traveled recently.

A carry-on bag contained a used first class ticket for flights from New York to Miami to Los Angeles to Seattle to Chicago and back to New York. The schedule allowed for only one day in each city. Stafford continued searching, emptying the built-in drawers filled with socks and underwear onto the floor, and stripping the sweaters and custom-made shirts from the shelves.

He left the closet and went to the armoire against the wall at the foot of the bed. The reproduction French antique contained a built-in wide-screen television, an 8mm video cassette recorder, a CD and DVD player, and a state-of-the-art tuner/amplifier, all wired into the speakers of a Bose home theater system strategically positioned about the room. The lower drawers of the armoire, filled with CDs and DVDs, revealed a man with eclectic taste: from Mozart to Credence Clearwater Revival and *Casablanca* to *The Wedding Singer*.

After checking the drawers in the night stands on both sides of the king-size bed, Stafford was about to leave the room when something caught his eye as he walked past the open doors of the walk-in closet. It was an anomaly he should have spotted immediately, given that he had used the same deception in his own home. At a glance, the closet appeared to run the full length of the bedroom, but as he looked inside to the far end, and then back to the outside wall, he saw the discrepancy. There was a four-foot difference between where the wall inside the walk-in closet began and where the actual wall of the room began.

He went back into the closet, removed the adjustable shelves along the back wall, and quickly found a recessed handle at the bottom of the partition dividing the hiding place from the rest of the closet. A three-foot-wide section of the false wall was designed to retract into the drop-ceiling much like a roll top desk. A light went on automatically as Stafford pulled the section up and out of the way, revealing a four-foot deep and eight-foot wide area lined with more shelves.

At eye level, on a shelf directly in front of him, he counted for semi-automatic pistols of various calibers, all fitted with sound suppressors, and a box of custom-made sub-sonic ammunition for each of them. Assassin's weapons and, like the ones used by the men he had shot at his home, they bore no manufacturer's stamp or serial number.

Other shelves held an 8mm video recorder set up to be controlled from a remote location, at least forty 8mm tapes, and a computer disk in a plastic case which he slipped into his jacket pocket. He found a large garment bag Ramsey had kept packed with clothes and necessities – a 'get-out bag' in case he had to leave in a hurry.

Stafford turned his attention to the handwriting on the video-tape labels. All but two of them had a woman's name with a date and a rating system from one to five stars, disclosing that Ramsey had apparently been secretly taping his sexual conquests, and an occasional visitor. Stafford took the two tapes with the labels that read 'Meeting With Adam Welsh 6 Sept 99' and 'Meeting With Paul Cameron 11 Sept 99' and set them aside.

The in-depth thoroughness and sophistication of what he discovered next made the hair on the back of Stafford's neck stand up and told him that whatever else these men were, they were not ordinary drug traffickers.

On the bottom shelf, neatly arranged in their own individual leather portfolios, were three 'legends', as they were known in the intelligence trade. Three complete sets of identity papers that included credit cards, insurance cards, social security cards, birth certificates, and three current passports from Great Britain, Canada, and Australia, all bearing photographs of Ramsey under three different names. In addition, the portfolios contained the equivalent of fifty thousand dollars in cash in the currency of each country, along with a bound, neatly typed life history from grade school through college and military service to places of employment for each of the legends, all thoroughly backstopped, Stafford suspected, to withstand even the most careful scrutiny and investigation.

Janet startled him when she entered the closet and suddenly appeared at his side. 'The only files on his computer are personal finances; monthly bills, stuff like that.'

'Do you know how to recover deleted files that are still on the hard drive?'

'Yes. But he's got a shredder program like the one DEA uses to delete classified files. Makes it impossible to retrieve them. He obviously put it to good use.'

Stafford reached in his pocket and handed her the floppy disk. 'Try this.'

Janet took the disk and cast a curious glance at the labels on the 8mm videotapes. 'Jeffery Ramsey was a very busy boy . . . and a kinky one.'

She saw the open portfolios on the lower shelf and flipped through the contents. 'What's all this?'

'A lot more than we bargained for.'

He told her about the legends and what he was sure they meant. 'The passports aren't forgeries, they're the real thing. And you can lay odds that the credit cards are all active with zero balances and high limits.'

'I only know one agency that operates on that level. Our friends at Langley.'

'If they're behind this, that means it was never just about money. The could have simply rolled Eddie and me up and

143

told us to give it back or suffer the consequences. They had options besides killing us.'

'Maybe you saw something you weren't supposed to see.'

'Like what?'

'Like something that's scaring the hell out of some very powerful people. The kind of thing that makes senators hold hearings and investigative reporters froth at the mouth.'

Stafford picked up the two 8mm tapes he had set aside. 'Let's see what these tell us.'

They left the closet and Stafford opened the armoire and turned on the television and the VCR, inserting the tape of the meeting with Adam Welsh. It began with the head of the CIA's Counter Narcotics Center sitting on one of the leather sofas and Jeffery Ramsey handing him a Martini and then taking a chair across from him. Stafford estimated from the angle of the shot that a sub-miniature surveillance camera and microphone were hidden in one of the wall decorations at the far end of the room.

The two men spoke in a way experienced intelligence operatives often talked, saying only what was necessary to be understood in the event they were overheard. The conversation was guarded and cryptic and at times a disjointed shorthand that only someone with prior knowledge of the subject could follow.

The non-specific terms like 'the shipment' and 'the transfer location' told Stafford nothing about Welsh, whose name and face neither he or Janet recognized, and nothing about what was in the shipment or where it was coming from or going to; although Stafford strongly suspected it concerned the twenty million dollars he and Eddie Barnes had found. Only first names were used when the two men referred to people they both obviously knew. An angry exchange near the end of the tape, however, gave Stafford one important piece of information that confirmed his suspicions about the legends he had found in the closet. Welsh clearly referred to 'the DDO' as having given detailed and specific orders. And Stafford had no doubt that DDO stood for the CIA's Deputy Director for Operations.

The second tape showed Jeffery Ramsey in a meeting with

144

Paul Cameron of Cameron & Associates. It was another guarded and cryptic conversation that revealed nothing new. Again, there was no clue to Cameron's profession, but judging from the interplay between the two men it was clear he was a superior of lesser stature than Welsh. The tape ended when two attractive women arrived dressed for an evening out.

Stafford concluded that the surreptitious taping was less about recording what was said than it was about Ramsey establishing that both men had been there for a meeting.

Janet agreed. 'They're cover-your-ass tapes. When push came to shove, Ramsey didn't trust the people he worked for.'

Stafford put the small 8mm tape cassettes into the cargo pockets of his leather jacket and followed Janet from the bedroom to the living area. He pulled up a chair beside her as she sat at the computer workstation and inserted the floppy disk and brought up the list of files it contained. Each file bore the name of a major American city: New York, Miami, Chicago, Dallas, Denver, Phoenix, Seattle, San Francisco and Los Angeles.

Janet opened the New York City file and the screen displayed a list of six names, each followed by a telephone number and a second number ending with the letter K; the numbers immediately preceding the K ranged from 100 to 600.

Janet smiled triumphantly. 'Jackpot!'

Stafford studied the list. 'Looks like a record of payments made or received, in amounts from one hundred thousand to six hundred thousand dollars.'

'I don't think the K stands for thousand. I'm pretty sure it's for kilos.'

'Why kilos?'

'Because all of the people on this list are drug dealers. The third one? Viktor Kirilenko? He's Russian mafia. And right now he's in jail here in New York City, on Rikers Island, waiting to go on trial for conspiracy to distribute.'

'You know him?'

'You could say that. I put the piece of garbage in there. He was my last bust with DEA. And I know the rest of these mutts, too.' Janet pointed to each name. 'This guy's a

145

Columbian, these two are Jamaican Posse, and the Chinese guy runs the show in Chinatown. All major players. And the last one, Jamal Jackson, AKA "Blue Gums", is my personal favorite. I put a hole in his chest when we traded shots in an alley in Brooklyn. He wounded two of our agents and his slimy thousand-dollar-an-hour-lawyer got him off on a technicality.'

Janet opened up the Los Angeles and Miami files and found the same combination of names, telephone numbers, and numbers followed by a K.

'I recognize two other names in L.A. and three in Miami. At one time or another we had all of them under surveillance when they came to New York to make deals with the Russians for heroin coming in from Eastern Europe. Again, all major players.'

'So what are we looking at here? The CIA's bringing in drugs and selling them to these guys? If you're right, and the K is for kilos, they're moving one hell of a lot of product. I've been running a mental tab on the files we've looked at so far and I'm already up to fifty-three hundred. And you've got six cities to go.'

Janet opened the rest of the files and read them as she spoke. 'I've heard old DEA hands who served in Southeast Asia tell stories about the CIA. When they needed money to fund some black operation, and wanted to avoid Congressional oversight, it made no difference to them how they got it. They had alliances with drug lords in the golden triangle then, so it's really no big stretch to believe they're up to their old tricks again.'

Stafford completed his mental tabulations when Janet opened the last file. 'I count a total of twenty thousand kilos.'

'Sounds like a lot, but it isn't. Twenty-thousand keys spread over nine major cities? A little over twenty-two hundred keys each. By the time that gets broken down and distributed to the street-level dealers, then out to the suburbs and the surrounding communities, it's maybe two weeks' supply.'

Stafford looked at the monitor. 'That's all the files on the disk?'

'Yes.'

'None for Canadian cities?'

'No. Why?'

'I was just thinking maybe they sold a major shipment of drugs somewhere in Canada and were transporting the money back to the States when the plane crashed.'

Janet turned off the computer, removed the disk, and gave it to Stafford. 'If I could get into Rikers Island and talk with Kirilenko, I might be able to get us some answers.'

'You put the guy in jail and you think he's going to help you?'

Janet flashed a mischievous smile reminiscent of her brother's. 'I'll use all my girlish charms.'

'I know someone who might be able to arrange it.'

Chapter Thirty-Three

Against his better judgement, Stafford conceded Janet's point that she knew the city better than he did and tossed her the keys to the Cherokee. She drove up the ramp from the underground garage onto 84th Street and turned right, stopping at the intersection at Columbus Avenue where she made another right turn and merged with the steady flow of traffic in the three southbound lanes.

Stafford, the memory of the last time Janet drove still vivid, had his seat belt and shoulder harness snugly in place. He took his cellular phone from his jacket and placed a call to Patrick Early, a lieutenant with the New York City Police Department. Early, an old friend who had served in Delta Force with Stafford and Eddie Barnes during the Gulf War, was now the whip of the 19th Precinct detective squad. It was Early whom Stafford thought might be able to arrange for Janet to talk with Kirilenko at Rikers Island. He was told Early was expected back shortly. He left a message that he was en route to see him.

'Where's the nineteenth precinct station house?'

'East Sixty-Seventh between Lexington and Third.'

Janet thought for a moment. 'I'll cut over to Central Park West and take 79th Street through the park to the East Side.'

She put on her left turn signal and checked the side and rear-view mirrors as she prepared to pull into the far outside traffic lane. It was then that she noticed the green BMW tailgating dangerously close, only a few feet off their bumper.

'Look at this moron. If he gets any closer we'll have to get married.'

The BMW suddenly pulled out to pass them on the right. As it came abreast of the Cherokee, Stafford saw that the driver's window was down and he was staring at them, a curious smile on his face. The BMW stayed even with them as the driver looked away for a moment to gauge the traffic in front of him. When he turned his attention back to the Cherokee the smile was gone and he had a gun in his hand. He held it out the window and aimed it at Stafford's head.

'Gun!' Stafford shouted, and in that same instant Janet saw the weapon in her peripheral vision.

She floored the accelerator and the Cherokee roared ahead a split second before the driver of the BMW fired four times in rapid succession. The shots entered at an upward angle, tearing chunks out of the window in the rear door and showering the inside of the car with shards of glass.

The driver of the car directly behind the BMW, who had seen the gun and heard the shots, had backed off, leaving an opening for Janet as she cut into the inside lane to avoid hitting the car in front of her. The driver of the BMW sped ahead through the heavy traffic. Then, four cars in front of the Cherokee, for no apparent reason, he abruptly slowed down. Janet swerved back into the center lane to avoid hitting the cars that braked in response to his sudden deceleration.

Stafford drew his pistol, took two spare magazines of ammunition from the glove compartment, put them in his jacket pocket, and lowered both front windows. Janet pulled her own pistol from the holster at the small of her back and placed it in her lap. Her shoulder bag was on the floor, tucked in against the seat. Keeping her eyes on the BMW and driving with one hand, she reached down and felt through the bag until she found the spare magazine for her weapon.

'I'll try to cut him off and run him into the curb.' Her voice was charged with adrenaline, her eyes intent on the ever shifting traffic ahead.

'No. Just stay with him and don't give him a clear shot at us. I'll call nine-one-one. Let the cops handle it.'

Stafford dialed the emergency number and got an immedi-

149

ate response. He reported the shooting to the operator, gave her their location, the license numbers of both cars, and told her they were in a black Cherokee and in pursuit of a green, late-model BMW on Columbus Avenue. The 911 operator relayed the information to the police dispatcher. Stafford stayed on the phone, keeping the line open.

The driver of the BMW continued speeding south on Columbus Avenue, weaving erratically in and out of traffic. He cut off a florist's delivery van and sent it crashing into a parked car, causing a three-car pile-up behind it.

Janet expertly avoided the accident but lost ground. She was now six cars behind the BMW. The driver again slowed and looked for the Cherokee in his rear-view mirror.

Janet passed another car and began to close the distance. 'This guy's either the world's dumbest get-away driver, or he's got a plan we don't know about.'

'He wants to keep us in the game.' Stafford looked behind them, expecting to see a shooting team in a follow-up car ready to make another attempt on their lives, but he saw nothing that aroused his suspicions.

Janet saw an opening ahead and cut back into the inside lane, passing two cars on the right. She was now only three cars behind the BMW and gaining. 'I'm beginning to get a real bad feeling about this.'

The BMW was running in excess of eighty miles per hour as it approached the intersection with West 76th Street. The driver ran the red light just as a limousine pulled out from the cross street. He hit it a glancing blow at the same time the chauffeur swerved hard to the right to avoid the collision. The momentum of the chauffeur's evasive maneuver, added to the force of the impact from the BMW, was enough to rock the limousine up and over onto its side.

The two cars immediately behind the BMW had no time to react defensively. The screeching of brakes and the crumpling and wrenching of sheet metal filled the air as the first car smashed into the undercarriage of the limousine, rolling it over onto its roof, followed by the second car slamming into the rear of the first car. The chain reaction collision blocked the inside lane entirely and part of the center lane.

Without warning, Janet cut to the left across two lanes of traffic to the only clear lane, swinging wide of the accident. A car behind her skidded out of control to keep from hitting her and caused yet another series of rear-end collisions. Traffic behind the Cherokee slowed to a crawl as all of the drivers tried to merge into the far left lane.

Janet continued to close on the BMW as it sped down the broad avenue. She glanced in the rear-view mirror at the trail of wreckage behind them.

'Looks like the remnants of a demolition derby back there. The boys in blue are not going to be amused.'

At the 74th Street intersection, the driver of the BMW braked hard, then powered into a right turn onto the narrow cross street. He was now heading west, going the wrong way on a one-way street. Janet followed close behind, rocking the Cherokee up on two wheels and bouncing it back down as she made the turn and saw the BMW halfway up the block running flat out.

Stafford reported the change of direction to the 911 operator as he watched a woman carrying a bag of groceries step from the curb near the end of the block. She was looking for traffic in the opposite direction and never saw the BMW. It struck her full force, throwing her onto the hood and up over the roof. She hit the street like a rag doll and lay motionless. Janet braked and swerved to avoid her, sideswiping two parked cars and sending an oncoming taxi up onto the sidewalk in the process.

'Send an ambulance to West Seventy-Fourth between Columbus and Amsterdam,' Stafford told the emergency operator. 'The shooter just ran down a pedestrian.'

At the end of the block, the BMW skidded into another right turn and was now heading north on Amsterdam Avenue. Janet followed close behind. Stafford saw the driver of the BMW check their position then move from the center lane into the inside lane where his brake lights flashed as he again slowed.

'Back off, Janet. This guy is definitely setting us up for something.'

Janet continued closing on the BMW. 'I know. No

problem. I'll give him plenty of room until the cops shut him down; I just don't want to lose him.'

Stafford reported their location to the 911 operator, then asked, 'Aren't there any patrol cars in the area?'

'Units are responding now, sir.' There was a brief pause and then the operator spoke again. 'The police dispatcher has instructed me to tell you to break off your pursuit. They have the description and license number of the vehicle and they will handle it from here on in.'

Eleven blocks north of where Janet was holding her position four cars behind the BMW, an NYPD blue and white, its roof lights and siren on, sped down Broadway. Fourteen blocks south of the Cherokee, a second blue and white coming off West End Avenue onto 60th Street made a left turn onto Amsterdam Avenue. The driver immediately turned on his light bar and siren and raced north. Three more units responded from the 20th Precinct station house on West 82nd Street, but they were soon caught in the snarled traffic on Columbus Avenue.

With one final look to make certain the Cherokee was still with him, the driver of the BMW braked and swung off Amsterdam onto 78th Street, now heading back toward Columbus Avenue.

Janet floored the Cherokee and made the turn just as the BMW reached the end of the block and skidded to a panic stop at the backed-up traffic on Columbus. She and Stafford watched as the driver ran from the car and disappeared around the corner. Stafford reported to the emergency operator that the man was now out of the car and running down Columbus Avenue, then he hung up and put the phone in his pocket.

Stafford slipped his pistol inside his waistband. 'I'm getting out at the corner; maybe I can catch him on foot.'

'Yeah, right. And like I'm going to wait in the car.'

Chapter Thirty-Four

Tony Kitlan sat in the driver's seat of the dark-blue van watching the street behind him through the side-view mirror. He was parked at the curb on the south side of West 78th Street with the engine running, only a short distance from the intersection with Columbus Avenue. Peter Marcus sat beside him holding a submachine-gun in his lap, flicking the safety on and off. The seats in the back of the van had been removed and three heavily armed men, wearing balaclavas to hide their faces, sat cross-legged on the floor. Marcus turned to look out the rear window and his sullen expression changed to one of eager anticipation.

'Get ready,' he told the three men in the back.

Kitlan saw the Cherokee appear in the side-view mirror as it turned the corner onto the one-way street in pursuit of the BMW. He had been certain that Stafford and Barnes would go after the man who had shot at them. Everything in the background information Cameron had provided on them indicated that was exactly what they would do.

Marcus had argued to take them as they came up the ramp from the garage. Kitlan dismissed the plan out of hand, knowing that Stafford and Janet could have simply retreated back down into the garage to an area he could not easily control, leaving open a possible escape route through the building. Marcus then offered a second plan of attack: to pull alongside the Cherokee once it was on Columbus Avenue, throw open the van's sliding side door, and have the three men in the rear open up with assault weapons.

153

Kitlan dismissed that idea as well. The broad three-lane avenue provided an excellent escape route, and with the unpredictability of the traffic flow it was possible one or both of them might survive and get away. Marcus had ridiculed the plan Kitlan finally decided on, considering it half-assed and more complicated than it needed to be.

But Kitlan held firm. Given what he now knew of the abilities, training, and experience of both Stafford and Janet Barnes, he wanted as much of an advantage as he could get, preferably to have them trapped with no way out. He believed he had accomplished just that as he sat watching the Cherokee approach. What he had not anticipated was the traffic jam on Columbus Avenue that resulted from the reckless and unprofessional way in which the driver of the BMW had carried out his part. Unless the traffic cleared quickly they would have no choice but to flee on foot after the attack on Stafford and Janet.

Kitlan timed his move perfectly, waiting until the Cherokee reached the middle of the block before pulling out from the curb. He cut the wheel hard to the left and stopped broadside across the narrow street, blocking it completely.

Janet slammed on the brakes and brought the Cherokee to an abrupt halt. 'Oh, shit! What was that you were saying about being set up?'

Stafford immediately looked for an escape route. Cars parked at the curb on both sides of the street prevented them from using the sidewalks. The back of the van still partially blocked the spot where it had been parked, and a sturdy-looking lamp-post was in the center of what little of the space wasn't obstructed. Stafford doubted that ramming the van at an angle and trying to take down the lamp-post would get them through, and if in attempting to do so they disabled the Cherokee to the point where it could no longer be driven, or the doors were damaged and they were unable to get out, they would be extremely vulnerable to an attack.

Janet's response to the situation was instinctive. She immediately put the Cherokee in reverse, but a quick look in the rear-view mirror told her that the driver of the van had sprung the ambush perfectly. Three cars had turned off Amsterdam behind her, blocking any avenue of escape in that direction.

Suddenly, the sliding side door of the van was thrown open and two men jumped out. The first man ran to the rear of the van carrying an olive-drab-colored cylinder approximately three feet long. The second man followed, firing an assault rifle from the hip as he ran. The poorly aimed rounds ricocheted harmlessly off the pavement in front of the Cherokee. A third man, armed with a sub-machine-gun, knelt in the van's open door to provide covering fire for the two men.

Stafford instantly recognized the olive-drab cylinder for what it was – a portable rocket launcher. 'Get us sideways in the street. Now!'

Janet floored the accelerator and swung the Cherokee into a wide turn that left them broadside in the street fifty feet from the van. 'Is that a LAW he's got?'

'It sure as hell is.'

The man with the light anti-tank weapon dropped to one knee facing the Cherokee and extended the cylinder to its full length. He placed the weapon on his shoulder, then looked behind him to make certain the backblast would be unobstructed.

'Get out!' Stafford shouted, just as the man kneeling at the side door of the van fired into the Cherokee. The hail of bullets passed through the open window and struck the windshield, spider-webbing the safety glass and blowing holes in it, narrowly missing Stafford and Janet as they ducked below the dash.

Stafford returned fire through the open window, driving the man back inside the van and out of sight as Janet opened the door and jumped out. Stafford quickly turned his attention back to the man with the rocket launcher who was aligning the weapon's sight.

Janet, crouched low behind the front end of the Cherokee, took a quick look over the hood. The man with the assault rifle was kneeling beside the man with the LAW. He was now taking careful aim at Stafford, who was still inside the vehicle. She popped up and fired two quick shots at him. He swung the weapon in her direction and returned fire, the rounds tearing into the hood of the Cherokee.

Stafford's eyes were riveted on the man with the LAW. His

155

finger was on the trigger mechanism that when pressed released an electrical charge that fired the deadly rocket. He was aiming at the front passenger-side door of the Cherokee, prepared to fire at any second.

With no time to get out of the vehicle and away from the effective range of the rocket blast, Stafford took careful aim and again fired through the open window. His first shot creased the side of the man's head, the second, fired a split-second later, struck him in the center of the forehead and killed him. At the same time, Janet fired at the man with the assault rifle. Both of her shots hit him in the chest and killed him as he was about to fire at Stafford.

Stafford crawled across the center console and out of the Cherokee, taking cover behind the rear of the vehicle with Janet still in position at the front end.

Kitlan cursed aloud and ignored Marcus' I-told-you-so look as both men pulled their face masks down into place. Kitlan got out of the van and fired a short burst from his sub-machine-gun at the front of the Cherokee when he saw Janet take another quick look over the hood.

Marcus got out on the other side of the van and ran around to join him. 'You wanna tell me again how stupid my plans were? Huh?' He fired at Stafford when he appeared from around the rear of the Cherokee, forcing him to retreat back behind the vehicle. 'I told you we should've just hit the fuckers with a full force drive-by on Columbus. But you had to get fancy. You get fancy; you get a cluster fuck.'

Janet again popped up over the hood and immediately ducked back down as Kitlan fired another short burst at her before she could take aim.

Marcus watched the back of the Cherokee waiting for Stafford to reappear. 'So, got any other brilliant ideas?'

Kitlan fixed Marcus with a menacing stare. 'Shut up, Peter. No operation ever goes exactly as planned. So just shut up and take care of business, or I'll shoot you in the face where you stand.'

Marcus grinned and opened fire when he saw Stafford take a quick look around the back of the Cherokee. 'Okay. But I was right.'

The sounds of the intense gun battle filled the street and echoed loudly off the surrounding buildings, causing the few pedestrians caught out in the open, and the drivers and passengers from the cars behind the Cherokee, to run panic stricken down the street and away from the scene.

The man inside the van again appeared in the open side door, his eyes on the LAW lying in the street. He leapt from the door and ran toward it.

Stafford, peering around the rear of the Cherokee, saw him and shot him in the leg as he tried to scoop it up in his stride. The man dropped to the ground and crawled between two parked cars. Marcus opened fire on Stafford just as he pulled back behind the Cherokee, the bullets shattering a rear window.

Janet saw that Kitlan was distracted by the volley of rounds fired by Marcus. She got off three quick shots at him before dropping back down behind the hood of the Cherokee. The bullets missed Kitlan's head by inches, striking the van behind him. He immediately dropped into a kneeling position behind a car parked at the curb. On the opposite side of the street, the man Stafford had wounded was lying in a prone position between two parked cars firing the assault rifle on full auto, providing covering fire for Marcus as he made an attempt to get to the rocket launcher.

Stafford stepped out from behind the Cherokee and sighted on Marcus as he ran. Before he could shoot, a bullet from a burst fired by Kitlan tore through his upper left arm. He felt a searing flash of intense pain and immediately ducked back under cover.

Janet also saw Marcus running for the LAW. Before he could get to it her shots sent him diving between two parked cars on the opposite side of the street from Kitlan.

She looked to her right and saw Stafford holding his left arm and wincing in pain. 'Are you hit?'

'Flesh wound. In and out. I'm okay.'

Stafford saw Marcus preparing to make another attempt for the LAW. He fired four rapid-fire shots to drive him back, then again took cover behind the Cherokee where he opened the rear passenger door and crawled inside. He reached into the area behind the rear seat and grabbed two Kevlar vests kept there for the occasions when he and a backup needed body armor to bring in a hard case who was a known shooter.

He came back out and tossed one of the vests to Janet. 'Better late than never.'

Janet pulled the vest on and fastened the Velcro straps in place. Stafford did the same and again took his position at the rear of the Cherokee. He spotted Marcus moving down the sidewalk in a low crouch behind the parked cars. He fired, emptying his magazine at him, stopping his advance and forcing him back under cover. Janet watched the opposite sidewalk for any signs of Kitlan as Stafford reloaded his pistol and kept a watchful eye on the rocket launcher lying in the street.

Janet noticed the blood dripping from Stafford's wound and grabbed her shoulder bag from inside the Cherokee and pulled out a scarf. She took a quick look over the hood, then jumped up and lay down suppressing fire when she caught a momentary glimpse of Kitlan on the sidewalk. Across the street, Marcus' head appeared over the roof of a car and she emptied her magazine at him, replacing it with a full one before running to Stafford's side where she expertly tied the scarf around the wound, stemming the flow of blood. 'I count three left.'

'Yeah. The two trying to outflank us and the guy I shot in the leg.'

'What do you think?'

'Cops should be here any minute. We can hold out until then.'

Janet moved back to the front of the Cherokee and took another quick look over the hood, scanning the street for a target.

Still using the cars parked at the curb for cover, Kitlan and Marcus moved in a concerted effort from opposite sides of the street toward Janet and Stafford. Kitlan was in position for a clear shot at Janet from the side when the wail of a police siren drew his attention. He looked over his shoulder toward Columbus Avenue and saw that a patrol car had somehow managed to make it through the backed-up traffic to the intersection. Two police officers, one with a shotgun, climbed out and took cover behind the open doors.

Kitlan turned his attention back to Janet and held his sights on her for a head shot. A split second before he fired a three-shot burst, she raised up from a crouch to peer over the hood of the Cherokee to see where the police car had stopped. The bullets hit low, striking her in the rib cage on the left side of the Kevlar vest. The impact knocked the wind out of her, stunning her and throwing her to the ground.

Stafford saw her go down and ran to pull her in close to the Cherokee, out of the line of fire. He then jumped up and fired at Kitlan, driving him back under cover. He immediately turned his attention to the other side of the street where Marcus appeared between two parked cars, preparing to rush them. Stafford fired five shots in quick succession. One of them creased Marcus' shoulder as he dove back to the sidewalk behind one of the cars.

More sirens pierced the air as a police car turned off Amsterdam Avenue and skidded to a stop at the abandoned cars behind the Cherokee. A few seconds later, another swung in behind the first. All four cops were quickly out of their cars and advancing.

Realizing that he had lost the day, Kitlan broke off the attack on Stafford and Janet. He signaled to Marcus, and both men began retreating toward the van, with Marcus acting as a rear guard and firing at the cops using the abandoned cars to advance on them.

A burst of fire from Marcus' sub-machine gun put one of the cops down with a leg wound. His partner ran to his side to drag him under cover and was shot in the head from a second burst. Marcus slapped a full magazine into his weapon and looked around for another target. He saw Kitlan fire at the cop with the shotgun on Columbus Avenue, forcing her back behind the open door of the patrol car.

'Cover me!' Kitlan shouted, and ran to where the rocket launcher lay in the street.

Marcus opened fire, keeping Stafford and Janet and the cops behind them pinned down. He then ran towards Columbus Avenue, firing short bursts at the cops there as Kitlan grabbed the LAW and ran behind a car parked at the curb.

Stafford peered around the rear of the Cherokee and saw the man he had shot in the leg attempting to get to his feet. As Marcus approached, the wounded man extended his hand for help. Without even pausing, Marcus calmly fired a three-shot burst into the man's head before joining Kitlan behind the car at the curb.

Kitlan rose to one knee, shouldered the rocket launcher, and took aim. He quickly aligned the sights on the patrol car and the two cops that stood between him and an escape down Columbus Avenue. By the time the cops saw the weapon being aimed at them they had no hope of getting away.

Kitlan pressed the firing mechanism and the rocket roared from the launcher. It struck the right front end of the patrol car, exploding into an orange-white fireball. The force of the blast killed both cops and blew the patrol car over onto its side and out into the avenue. A secondary explosion from the gas tank followed, causing a massive chain-reaction collision that had drivers and passengers running in panic from their cars.

Six uniform cops from the Twentieth Precinct, after running the four blocks from the station house, reached the intersection just as the rocket struck. The blast knocked them to the ground unconscious as pieces of shrapnel cut into their bodies.

Kitlan dropped the expended rocket launcher and both he and Marcus left their sub-machine-guns, drawing sound-suppressed pistols from their shoulder holsters as they ran to the intersection.

Stafford saw them disappear around the corner. He knelt beside Janet who was still breathing with difficulty. 'Are you going to be okay?'

'Yeah. In a couple of minutes.'

Stafford helped her into a sitting position and propped her against the side of the Cherokee where she began to take slow, even breaths.

'There's two left. They just took off.'

Chapter Thirty-Five

The ambush had lasted less than three minutes and left six people dead, three of them police officers, with seven other cops wounded and at least eight civilians with minor injuries from automobile collisions.

A police Emergency Services Unit truck worked its way through the traffic jam on Columbus Avenue, getting as close as it could to the intersection at 78th Street before the heavy weapons team it was transporting jumped out and ran toward the scene.

One of the six cops wounded by shrapnel from the rocket blast rose to his knees and shouted to the lieutenant in charge of the ESU team. He pointed to where Kitlan and Marcus were running through the backed-up traffic to the opposite side of Columbus Avenue. The lieutenant saw them, with Stafford in pursuit, and sent half of his men after them as the others began securing the immediate area.

Kitlan and Marcus ran east on 77th Street, along the sidewalk bordering the Museum of Natural History. They split up when they reached Central Park West, pulling their masks off and holding their pistols out of sight beneath their jackets. Kitlan vaulted the wall into Central Park and disappeared into the woods as Marcus signaled to an unsuspecting cab driver pulling away from the curb after dropping off a fare.

When working upscale neighborhoods in daylight hours, the cab driver usually left the sliding window in the bullet-proof plexiglass partition separating him from his passengers open. Marcus leaned forward from the back seat, put his hand through the opening, and placed the tip of the sound-suppressed pistol to the driver's head.

'Drive!'

The man began babbling in a high-pitched voice in a language Marcus could not understand. He tapped him on the side of the head with the pistol, then pointed through the windshield.

'Drive or die! You understand that?'

The taxi sped off, nearly colliding with oncoming traffic as the terrified driver recklessly pulled out to pass on the two-way street. He slowed down only after Marcus again tapped him on the side of the head with the pistol and motioned for him to do so.

Stafford was running flat out as he came around the corner off Columbus Avenue onto 77th Street. He was a full block behind Kitlan and Marcus, but in time to see Kitlan vault the wall and Marcus get in the taxi. He went into the park after Kitlan, dropping into a crouch in the underbrush on the other side of the wall. His pistol followed his eyes as he glanced over the network of footpaths and trails that meandered through the woods.

He caught a momentary glimpse of Kitlan, recognizing the tan suede jacket he wore. He was no more than fifty yards ahead, moving along a path through dappled patches of sun and shade. He was holding his pistol inside his jacket and had slowed to a walk to keep from drawing attention to himself. Stafford sprang to his feet and ran after him.

Kitlan walked through a pedestrian tunnel beneath the park's West Drive, then followed a path that skirted the edge of The Lake and crossed an arched stone bridge. A short distance from the bridge, he took a trail that branched off in the direction of the rocky, wooded thickets of The Ramble. As he entered the trail, he paused to look over his shoulder and was surprised to see Stafford in pursuit and closing fast.

Kitlan immediately broke into a run. Two women, deep in conversation and each with a child in a stroller, were stopped

162

in the middle of the trail. The insouciant, territorial looks they gave Kitlan when they saw him approaching said in no uncertain terms that they expected him to run into the dense underbrush to get around them.

Annoyed by their arrogance, Kitlan headed straight for them. Running full force, he lowered a shoulder and drove it squarely into the chest of one of the women. The powerful blow lifted her off her feet and slammed her to the ground flat on her back at the side of the trail. Both women screamed in outrage as Kitlan ran on.

A jogger coming from the opposite direction misread what had happened to the women, believing that Kitlan had just mugged them. He was a big, heavily muscled man with an imposing presence, which was all it usually took to bully most people he challenged into submission. With visions of himself on the six o'clock news as a 'I just did what anyone else would have done' humble hero, he ran down the middle of the trail, shouting, his face filled with indignation and bravado.

'Where the hell do you think . . . ?' was all he got out before Kitlan shot him between the eyes and killed him without breaking stride.

The terror-stricken women were pushing their strollers at breakneck speed and shouting for the police when Stafford came around a bend in the trail toward them. One of the women saw the gun in his hand and screamed. She and her friend stopped running and grabbed their babies from the strollers, clutching them frantically to their breasts as they stumbled through the thick tangle of underbrush to get away.

Stafford ignored them and leapt over the deserted strollers and the body of the dead would-be hero as he caught a momentary glimpse of Kitlan disappearing into the woods at a point where the trail intersected with a bridle path. He stopped at the edge of the trail and took cover behind a tree, his eyes searching the deeply shadowed woods.

Kitlan lay well-concealed in a dense tangle of underbrush, the sights of his pistol aligned on the small portion of Stafford's head that was visible through the trees. He kept a light pressure on the trigger, waiting until his target stepped farther out into the open.

Stafford was about to move deeper into the woods when he heard, and then saw, two mounted cops from the Central Park Precinct bearing down on him. They were cantering their horses down the bridle path, guns drawn, shouting to him to drop his weapon and to get on the ground.

Stafford looked back to the woods and saw nothing of Kitlan, then to the mounted cops whose expressions told him that unless he complied immediately they would not hesitate to shoot him. He lay his pistol on the ground, stepped away from it, dropped to his knees, and laced his fingers together behind his head. The adrenaline rush of the ambush and the chase had kept him going, but now, as he knelt in the path, he began to feel faint from the loss of blood. He wavered and nearly toppled over as the cops came to a stop and towered over him, their horses breathing heavily and dancing sideways, the powerful muscles in their haunches rippling.

From his concealed position, Kitlan assessed as good to excellent his chances of killing Stafford and both mounted cops before they knew where the sound-suppressed shots were coming from. He watched as one of the cops dismounted to handcuff Stafford while the other kept his weapon trained on him from astride his horse.

Kitlan again aligned his sights for a head shot at Stafford. He was about to squeeze the trigger when he saw four cops from the ESU team coming up the trail. They wore body armor and carried full automatic weapons, and the way they moved indicated they were well-trained and highly competent.

Kitlan removed his finger from the trigger, backed slowly out of the underbrush, and slipped quietly away through the woods.

Kitlan came out of the park on the Upper East Side at 5th Avenue and 73rd Street, walking close behind a group of men who had just finished a softball game. As the light turned green and he followed the group out into the crosswalk, he saw three patrol cars, roof lights swirling and sirens wailing, speeding down the avenue toward him. He was about to draw his pistol and run for cover when he realized the cops had not seen him. All three cars screeched to a halt at the curb and six uniformed cops, weapons drawn, got out and ran into the park.

Kitlan continued east on 73rd Street and crossed Madison Avenue. A delivery boy wearing a light-blue smock and carrying a bag of groceries from a nearby delicatessen walked ahead of him. Kitlan saw only one other person on the narrow tree-lined residential street of elegant brownstones: an elderly man walking his dog.

He waited until the old man and his dog turned the corner, then came up behind the delivery boy just as he descended the steps to the lower level entrance of a five-story brownstone. He followed him down into an entryway mostly hidden from view of passers-by, and ordered him at gunpoint to put the bag down and take off his smock.

The boy did as he was told without protest. Kitlan judged him to be no more than seventeen years old and was intrigued by his unwavering composure. When ordered to turn around and face the wall, he did not cry or plead, his only reaction was a look of sad resignation that his life was about to end. Few things earned Kitlan's respect. Grace under pressure was one of them.

'It may not seem like it right now, kid, but this is your lucky day.' He then knocked him unconscious with a blow to the base of the skull.

Kitlan climbed back up the steps to the sidewalk and continued east on 73rd Street carrying the groceries and wearing the smock. A patrol car sped by, the cops inside giving him no more than a cursory look as they raced toward the park.

Convinced that he had not been followed, Peter Marcus ordered the cab driver to pull in to the curb on Lexington Avenue at 53rd Street where he shot him twice behind the right ear, got out of the cab, and casually walked away to disappear down a nearby subway entrance.

An elegantly dressed middle-aged man carrying a hand-tooled leather attaché case came out of the Citicorp Center and rushed for the taxi Marcus had just left. He slid into the back seat and announced where he wanted to go, then took a cellular phone from his pocket and began dialing a number. When the cab didn't move, the man looked up and noticed that the

165

driver was slumped against the door. He leaned forward for a closer look and saw the blood splatter and bits of brain on the windshield.

With calm deliberation, the man put the phone back in his pocket, checked to make certain he was unobserved, then got out of the cab and quickly blended in with the steady stream of pedestrians on the busy street.

Chapter Thirty-Six

Stafford sat on an examination table in the emergency room of the Cornell Medical Center as an intern finished putting stitches in the exit wound in his upper left arm. Janet was visible through a partially drawn curtain, perched on the edge of the bed, her blouse off, talking to a detective while a doctor checked her ribs.

The trauma rooms were filled to capacity with the seriously wounded cops. Those with minor, superficial wounds had been treated by nurses and were now waiting in the hallway, along with a coterie of high-ranking brass from One Police Plaza who had descended on the hospital in force, to learn the fate of their fellow officers.

The ER doors swung open and the swarm of TV news crews outside, jostling for position behind police barricades, could be seen and heard shouting questions at Patrick Early as he flashed his lieutenant's shield to the uniformed cops manning the barricades. Ignoring the reporters, Early hung the gold shield from the chest pocket of his tweed sport coat and came through the doors, his cop eyes scanning the crowded lobby and hallway. He nodded to a deputy chief he knew from the six years he had spent with the Intelligence Division's organized crime unit, then stopped to talk with the captain of the Twentieth Precinct where the ambush had taken place.

Stafford got down from the table when the intern finished bandaging his wound. He borrowed a pair of scissors from a nearby tray and used them to cut the bloodstained sleeve from his shirt before putting it on. He spotted Early out in the hall and saw the captain he was talking with point to the exam room. Early entered the room and embraced his old friend, then held him at arm's length and searched his eyes.

'Tell me this wasn't about bringing in some bail jumper, Ben. Please tell me it wasn't about that.'

'It wasn't.'

'The captain of the two-oh says you disobeyed an order to break off your pursuit. And the woman with you impersonated a DEA agent.'

Stafford's temper flared. 'There were some pretty nervous cops out there, Paddy. She only did it to keep them from shooting me when I took off after the two guys who got away.' He jerked a thumb toward the Twentieth Precinct captain. 'And that disobeying an order is bullshit. I called nine-one-one as soon as the guy in the BMW fired at us. We were about to back off when they sprang the ambush. At that point your people weren't anywhere around. So what the hell were we supposed to do? Just sit there while they shot the shit out of us?'

Early raised a hand. 'Hey, easy. I'm on your side. The captain says you saw one of the shooters get in a cab?'

'The short stocky one.'

'A couple of uniforms found a cabbie shot to death at Lexington and Fifty-Third. Probably your guy.'

Early pointed toward Janet, who was putting on her blouse as she continued to talk to the detective. 'Who's she?'

'You don't recognize her?'

Early stared at her for a moment. 'No.'

'That's Eddie's kid sister, Janet.'

'Yeah, huh? I haven't seen her since she was maybe . . . fourteen. Eddie told me she was DEA. Working out of a task force here in the city. She's not with them anymore?'

'Long story.'

'You want to run this whole thing down for me? From the top.'

'Okay. But I've got to leave a few things out, for your own good.'

'And what's that supposed to mean?'

'It means I don't want to put you in a position where you

have to make a choice between being a cop and being my friend.'

Early nodded a tentative understanding and Stafford began. He saw the pain in his friend's eyes when he told him how Eddie Barnes had died.

Early fell silent, in his mind's eye he was taken back to when Barnes had saved his life during the Gulf War. He was wounded, and pinned down, and Barnes had run through withering enemy fire to rescue him and carry him to the extraction helicopter. Then, as now, Early carried a solid two hundred and twenty pounds on a six-foot-two-inch frame, and he smiled to himself as he recalled how Barnes had joked about how heavy he was as he ran with him over his shoulder to the helicopter. 'We get out of this? I got two words for you, you fat mick bastard. Salad bar.'

The smile faded with the reverie. 'Last time I saw him was March,' he told Stafford. 'He came into the city for Saint Patrick's day. Stayed with Ellen and me. Drove her nuts with war stories, but the kids loved it.'

Stafford completed his abridged version of events, having left out the parts about the money and the break-in at Ramsey's apartment, knowing full well that Early could easily fill in the blanks.

'Doesn't take a rocket scientist to figure out you and Eddie took something off the plane these guys want back.'

'That part doesn't matter.'

'Why not?'

'Because it's not about that anymore.'

'Then what's it about?'

'I'm not sure. Janet thinks maybe we saw something we weren't supposed to see. I think maybe she's right.'

'Saw what?'

'I haven't figured that out yet.'

'And you think the Agency's behind it?'

'One way or another.'

Janet finished talking with the detective and came over to join Stafford, her eyes fixed on Early as he turned to greet her and extended his hand.

'I'm Patrick . . .'

'I know who you are.' Janet shook the proffered hand.

Early covered her hand with both of his for a moment. 'I'm sorry for your loss. Eddie was my friend. I loved him like a brother.'

Janet nodded and lowered her eyes. 'I know. He often talked about you.'

Stafford moved closer to Early and lowered his voice. 'We need a favor.'

Early said nothing, waiting to hear what the favor was. Janet told him.

'I want to talk with a drug dealer at Rikers Island. Viktor Kirilenko. I busted him a few months ago. All I'll need is maybe ten or fifteen minutes alone in a conference room with him.'

'He's tied into this?'

'Maybe.'

Early hesitated, then locked eyes first with Janet and then with Stafford. 'No more gun play. Any problems, you back off and let us handle it. I help you, and you start up again, it's on me.'

His eyes went back to Janet. 'For Eddie.'

'For Eddie,' she repeated.

'I know a deputy warden over there I can reach out to. But I set this up, what makes you think this guy will talk to you without his attorney present?'

'He's gutter-smart, but otherwise he's a moron. He's going to wonder what I want, and he's arrogant enough to think he can get over on me.'

Stafford pulled on his leather jacket, probing the bullet hole in the sleeve with his finger. 'Can we get our guns back, and the personal stuff from my car?'

'You got concealed weapons permits, right?'

Stafford and Janet confirmed that they did.

'I'll take care of it.'

Early's attention was drawn to a woman and a young girl outside one of the trauma rooms, the wife and daughter of the cop most seriously wounded by shrapnel from the rocket blast. A cluster of uniformed cops from the same precinct, anger and concern etched on their faces, stood watch outside the room as

170

a team of doctors and nurses desperately tried to save the cop's life.

The doctor who had opened the cop's chest to massage his heart stepped back and stripped off his gloves. His expression and body language told the young girl that her father had died. Her mother embraced her and they both began to cry.

Early shook his head in anger. 'Christ! That's four dead cops.'

'They were out-gunned, Paddy. They didn't stand a chance.'

'Were you able to give the detectives who caught the case anything?'

'Nothing. I got a quick look at the one I was chasing with his mask off, but it was from a distance through the trees and in profile. No way I could ID him.'

'Then all we got is two terrified women from the park whose descriptions are so different you'd think they weren't even looking at the same guy. And a delivery boy who can't, or won't, describe anything but the gun that was stuck in his face.'

'What about the van and the BMW?'

'Van's registered to a non-existent company in Queens. BMW was stolen in midtown this morning. On top of that the weapons are untraceable, and I'll give you odds any prints we lift aren't going to be on file anywhere.'

'That's pretty much the same story with the guys who came at me at home, and the one Janet took out at Eddie's place.'

The frustration Early was feeling showed on his face. 'Is there anything else you can give me?'

'Nothing that would help you catch the shooters.'

Stafford and Janet exchanged a look that confirmed they were in agreement on keeping the videotapes and the computer disk to themselves. Stafford's fear was if they turned them over to Early, and there was CIA involvement, the Agency had a proven track record for making evidence and anyone with direct knowledge of it disappear; a police lieutenant notwithstanding.

'I promise you this,' Stafford told Early. 'Whatever we find out about the guys who killed the cops, we'll give you.'

171

'I'll hold you to that.' Early pointed to Stafford's wounded arm. 'In and out?'

'Yeah. I'm good to go.'

He looked to Janet. 'How 'bout you?'

'Bruised ribs. I've had rougher dates.'

Chapter Thirty-Seven

Two hours after leaving the hospital emergency room, Janet drove the Ford Explorer Stafford had rented at the midtown agency across the two-lane bridge that provided the only access to Rikers Island, the 415 acre prison compound in the middle of New York City's East River.

The guard at the entrance gate directed them to the visitors' parking lot, then phoned ahead as he passed them through. They locked their guns in the glove compartment and walked the short distance to the administration building where they signed in at the security checkpoint.

'We're here to see Associate Warden Daniels,' Stafford told the guard.

'He's on his way.'

No sooner had the guard spoken than a steel-reinforced door opened and a short square-built man with the countenance of a Rottweiler appeared and motioned with his head for Stafford and Janet to follow him. Without a word of introduction, Daniels led them down a long corridor to an empty conference room used for prisoners and their lawyers. He opened the door and, with the same head movement that seemed to be his primary method of communication, motioned for them to enter the room.

'You've got fifteen minutes.' Daniels went back out into the corridor, closed the door, and left.

Janet rolled her eyes. 'I thought he'd never shut up.'

She sat beside Stafford at the conference table, leaned in

close, and spoke in a whisper. 'Kirilenko probably doesn't know I'm not with DEA anymore. So follow my lead. Okay?'

Stafford nodded his consent as the door opened and two guards entered, one a tall, broad-shouldered, densely-packed black woman whom Janet estimated outweighed her male partner by at least fifty pounds. They each had a firm hold on one of the prisoner's arms as they escorted him into the room.

Kirilenko had the hooded, soulless eyes of a psychopath and looked like what he was: a street-wise drug dealer and enforcer for the Russian mafia. His ankles were shackled and his hands cuffed in front of him, yet he still managed a semblance of an arrogant swagger as he shuffled across the room and sat in a chair facing Janet and Stafford.

The female guard looked at Janet. 'You want us to stay?'

Janet shook her head.

The guard's expression suggested that Janet's choice might not be the smart one, but she simply shrugged, turned on her heel, and followed her partner from the room, closing the door behind her.

Despite the handcuffs, Kirilenko adroitly fished a cigarette and matches from the chest pocket of his gray prison jumpsuit, then fixed Janet with a menacing stare.

'You remember me, Viktor?'

Kirilenko nodded. 'I know you. I got long memory.'

Janet smiled in response to the thinly veiled threat.

Stafford sat, quietly watching the interplay between them. He felt the undercurrent of mounting tension and was curious as to how Janet planned on getting the cooperation of a man who felt such an intense hatred for her.

Kirilenko's gaze shifted to Stafford. 'Who's this?'

'My supervisor.'

'You got balls comin' to see me. DEA cunt.'

Janet's eyes flashed with anger, but she kept her composure. 'English wasn't my strongest subject, Viktor, but I'm pretty sure you've got a mixed metaphor there, or at the very least a fucked-up simile.'

Kirilenko's brow furrowed. 'The fuck you want?'

'First, I'd appreciate it if you didn't smoke in here.'

Kirilenko snorted a short, gruff laugh, and with elaborate

174

gestures, lit the cigarette. He inhaled deeply and leaned forward, his face twisted into a taunting sneer as he exhaled a forceful stream of smoke into Janet's face.

In a sudden, explosive move, Janet reached across the table, grabbed the cigarette from the corner of Kirilenko's mouth, and flicked it into his face. Chairs toppled noisily as they both sprang to their feet.

Lithe and agile, with exceptional balance and speed, Janet gracefully side-stepped the physically disadvantaged Kirilenko, avoiding his grasp as he nearly tripped over his ankle chains when he lunged for her, his cuffed hands reaching for her neck. She feinted an overhand right and threw a solid left hook that caught him in the throat. Kirilenko gagged and coughed, then lunged again.

Janet danced out of his reach and stunned him with a crescent kick to the side of his head, followed immediately by a flurry of punches to his face and a back-fist that split his lip. Blossoms of blood opened on his cheek and above his eyes as he staggered back against the wall.

His ears ringing and his vision momentarily blurred, Kirilenko paused to shake off the effects of the blows.

Stafford, surprised and caught off guard by the suddenness of the assault, grabbed the enraged Russian by the hair as he again went after Janet. Using his own momentum against him, Stafford spun him around and slammed him into the door, pinning him there and twice banging his head against the frame before he stopped struggling.

'That's enough! It's over! Understand?'

The door flew open and the two guards rushed in as Stafford, still clenching a fistful of Kirilenko's hair, dragged him back to the table, righted his chair, and sat him down.

Kirilenko, eyes wide with rage and nostrils flaring, slowly composed himself. Stafford waved the guards off. They paused in the doorway, looking at the damage done to the Russian's face, then stared in open amazement at Janet, who stood in the middle of the room in a fighting stance, taking slow even breaths, her fists balled, glaring at Kirilenko as he forcefully cleared his throat and used his sleeve to swipe at the blood trickling into the corner of his right eye.

The guards left and Janet picked up her chair and again sat at the table. She smiled contemptuously when she saw Kirilenko searching for broken teeth with the tip of his tongue; there were two, the result of the back-fist and the kick to his head.

Stafford tried the voice of reason. 'All right. Let's get down to why we're here.' He took Ramsey's driver's license from his pocket and laid it on the table for Kirilenko to see. 'Do you know this man?'

Kirilenko glanced at the photograph on the license, then went back to glaring at Janet. 'I tell you and this DEA cunt nothing.'

Janet tensed. 'Call me that again, you mouth-breathing piece of Russian shit, and I'll gouge out one of your beady little eyes.'

Stafford shook his head in exasperation. 'This is going real well.'

'Just let me handle it,' Janet snapped.

'And your plan is what? To beat it out of him?'

Kirilenko grunted. 'Fuck!' A broken tooth had cut the edge of his tongue and a small spray of blood escaped from his mouth with the word.

The look Janet gave Stafford told him she was not as angry and out of control as she wanted Kirilenko to think she was. She leaned across the table and flashed a wicked smile at the battered Russian, her voice mocking.

'Pay close attention to what I'm telling you, moron. The case the government has against you is weak as hell. Unless . . .' Janet held up a finger and used the pregnant pause effectively. 'I just happen to come up with some new evidence. You know how that works, Viktor?'

Kirilenko shrugged as though unconcerned, but Janet saw something in his eyes that told a different story.

'My lawyer says they got nothing.'

'This isn't about what they have now, you idiot fuck. It's about what I'm going to get for them if you don't give me what I want. The way things stand right now, you lose, you'll do five years, tops. There's even a chance the case could get tossed and you'll walk. But when I get finished? After I offer some of your friends who are in here facing fifty years a real

176

good deal? Like maybe change my testimony, or make a few things disappear from the evidence locker so the charges against them get dropped? What do you think they'd do for a deal like that, Viktor? Give you up in a New York minute, that's what they'd do, and you damn well know it.'

Janet flashed her evil smile again and wiggled her eyebrows. 'Maybe I can even get one of them to put me on to the gun that killed that FBI agent over in Brighton Beach. Tie it to you.'

Kirilenko's eyes flicked from Janet to Stafford and back to Janet. The FBI knew that the Russian mafia was responsible for the death of one of their undercover agents six months ago, but they had no evidence and had been unable to come up with an informant with any reliable information.

'It could happen, Viktor. One of your friends testifies they saw you kill that Feeb, and you're dead meat. It's not like any of them give a shit about you. You're sitting in here because you can't even come up with a lousy fifty grand to make bail. That's chump change to your Russian mafia buddies. But I don't see any of them reaching in their pockets to help you out.'

Kirilenko took a handkerchief from his pocket and dabbed at the cut on his cheek. Janet watched him and realized what it was she had seen in his eyes.

Kirilenko was not one of the hardened older Russian criminals who had spent years in Siberian prison camps under the communists. His mother was a drug addict and a prostitute, his father unknown, and he was raised in a state-run orphanage. He began his life of crime as a Moscow street thug after the collapse of the former Soviet Union and never had to worry about being thrown into the brutal camps run by the KGB. His only period of incarceration had been for six months in a military-style camp for juvenile offenders before coming to New York four years ago at the age of twenty-three, where he quickly established himself as someone to be feared.

But as tough and vicious as he was on the street, Kirilenko had not been tempered and tested by long periods of confinement, and he was doing hard time. After only a few short months in Rikers, he was already climbing the walls. Janet sensed his weakness and went after him with a vengeance.

'You know what they do to people who kill FBI agents, Viktor? They bury their ass in that new underground prison out in Colorado. Supermax. That's what they call it. They'd probably put you in the Bomber Wing with psychos like Kaczynski and McVeigh. Now that's some serious isolation. You'll live like a goddamn mole. Spend the rest of your worthless life in a six by nine cell with no windows. Your bed and chair bolted to the floor. Your only companion a thirteen-inch black and white TV you get to watch one hour a day. But the guards decide what you watch and when you watch it. And you know they're going to fuck with you for killing an FBI agent. Maybe pipe in reruns of the Bullwinkle show. Boris, Natasha, Moose and Squirrel. Make your pathetic Russian ass homesick.'

Kirilenko shifted his seat, his eyes on the floor as Janet closed in for the kill.

'But hey, it's not all bad. Every day they give you one hour of natural light. In your own private, ten-foot square, chain-link exercise pen. Of course there's a downside to all that privacy and isolation; it messes with your mind. In six months you'll be talking to yourself. In nine you'll be hearing voices inside your head talking to you. By the end of the second year you won't even remember what a woman feels or smells like and you'll be whacking off eight times a day for lack of anything better to do.'

Janet lowered her voice, as though she was about to disclose things too terrible to be spoken aloud. 'And by the end of the third year, Viktor? You're gone through the looking glass and never coming back. Your power of speech and your mental faculties diminish to the point where you just sit in your cell and watch insane images on the backs of your eyelids, mumbling and drooling like some demented lab animal.'

Kirilenko slammed his fists on the table and lunged forward. Stafford shoved him back in his chair. 'I didn't kill no FBI.'

Janet shrugged and again flashed the smile. 'What the fuck do I care?'

She leaned in close and locked eyes with him. 'Don't think for one second that I can't make it happen, Viktor. That would be the dumbest angle you ever played.'

Kirilenko went back to staring at the floor and dabbing at his cuts. He nodded to himself as though reaching some private decision, then looked up and tapped the photograph of Ramsey on the driver's license.

'Okay. I know him.'

'You bought drugs from him?'

Kirilenko hesitated. Janet softened her tone. 'Come on, Viktor. You know we can't use anything you say against you. Your lawyer's not here and we haven't read you your rights. And I give you my word, you help me, not only will I not do anything to hurt your case, maybe I can even do something to make your time in here a little easier.'

'He didn't sell to me. I sold to him.'

Janet exchanged a look with Stafford. 'If that's the kind of bullshit you're going to feed us, we're out of here.'

'Is not bullshit.' He tapped the photo again. 'This man bought large quantities of drugs. More than once.' He saw the skeptical look on Janet's face. 'Who's moron now? Huh? Who's idiot fuck? Why would I say I sold drugs if I bought? Selling looks better for me than buying?'

'Okay. He bought drugs from you.' Janet hesitated, then, 'What else can you tell me about him?'

'Only what I hear on street.' Kirilenko winced as he touched the handkerchief to his split lip and applied pressure to stop the bleeding.

'What? Am I supposed to guess? What did you hear?'

'He bought from Jamaicans. Columbians, too.'

'And what else?'

'A friend from Russia. He says he knows this man was CIA in Moscow.' Kirilenko sat back in his chair and folded his arms across his chest. 'That's all I know.'

Janet looked to Stafford who nodded. The last piece of information convinced them that Kirilenko was probably not holding anything back. Stafford got up from the table and opened the door, signaling for the guards to come into the room. They entered and each took Kirilenko by an arm. The

Russian paused in the doorway and turned to Janet.

'You said you can make things easy for me here, yes?'

Janet grinned. 'I lied. I'm not even with DEA anymore, you moron.'

Kirilenko bellowed like a wounded animal. 'Fuck your mother!' He struggled to free himself from the guards, dragging them across the room with him.

Janet calmly stood her ground, centered and ready for the response she had hoped to elicit. She caught the enraged Russian flush on the bottom of his nose, driving upward with the butt of her hand, then danced out of his reach.

Kirilenko howled in pain and dropped to his knees.

'That's for Anna Cernikova. You goddamn pig!'

Stafford wrapped his arms around Janet to restrain her. The guards quickly picked Kirilenko up, blood gushing from his shattered nose, and rushed him from the room.

Kirilenko shouted incomprehensible curses in Russian as they dragged him away. The female guard looked back over her shoulder at Janet with a trace of a smile on her face as she disappeared around a corner at the end of the hallway.

Stafford and Janet left the administration building and walked across the parking lot. They had not spoken since leaving the conference room. Stafford broke the long silence.

'Who's Anna Cernikova?'

'She was one of my confidential informants. Worked as a waitress in a Russian-mafia-owned nightclub in Brighton Beach. She was a good kid. Got accepted into Brooklyn College. That piece of garbage found out she was a CI and he raped her and beat her half to death.'

'That's why he's locked up?'

'No. Some of his buddies told her it was either go home or they'd finish the job. The day she got out of the hospital she went back to Moscow. No victim. No case. The only thing we could nail him on was a half-assed conspiracy charge he's probably going to beat. He's in Rikers because the state has first crack at him for intent to distribute, but he'll probably walk on that, too. It was a bad search.'

'At least you got in a few good shots.'

'I did, didn't I?' Janet smiled. 'I rarely get mad, Stafford. But I always get even.'

Stafford changed the subject. 'Look, I'm out of my depth here, but I don't get it. Even with the discounts the Agency would get for buying volume wouldn't they need one hell of a distribution network to put the stuff on the street?'

'Yes. And that's what doesn't make any sense. The profits wouldn't be worth the organizational headaches, the risk, or the fallout if the press ever got wind of it. Now if they were bringing drugs into the country and using cutouts to sell to these people, that would make sense. They could have eliminated the middle man and gotten even bigger discounts by buying at the source in Mexico, Columbia, Sicily, Lebanon, Thailand. Then the profits would be enormous.' Janet shook her head emphatically. 'No. There's something drastically wrong with this picture.'

They reached the car and Janet pressed the remote entry button on the key to open the doors. 'So where do we go from here?'

'I know a place we can stay until we decide what to do next.'

Janet drove out of the lot and off the island as Stafford consulted a road map. 'Looks like the quickest way from here is over the George Washington Bridge to New Jersey.'

'Where are we going?'

'Pocono Mountains of Pennsylvania. I've got a small fishing cabin on a lake up there. My father built it when I was a kid. It's a little rustic, but nobody knows about it.'

Janet feigned an exaggerated look of relief. 'You creeped me out there for a second. I thought you might be thinking of checking us into one of those honeymoon places. Pocono Paradise. Round-the-clock room service. Suites decorated all in pink and white with a heart-shaped, king-sized waterbed.'

Stafford looked at Janet and smiled. The more time he spent with her, the more she reminded him of her brother.

'So when you mentioned earlier about using all your girlish charms on Kirilenko. That was them? What you did back there?'

'Pretty much. What do you think?'

181

'I think you need professional help. And if I were you, I wouldn't make a habit of trading punches with two-hundred-pound psycho cons with twenty-inch arms. That definitely wasn't one of the smartest things you ever did.'

Janet flashed a playful smile and winked. 'I figured I could take him in shackles.'

Stafford laughed and tuned the radio to a country music station. 'Your supervisor, huh? I like that.'

'In your dreams.'

Chapter Thirty-Eight

Adam Welsh pulled his car into the parking lot at the Great Falls Park visitor's center just before sunrise. He turned up the collar of his windbreaker and wished he had worn his hiking boots instead of loafers as he set out on a fog-shrouded footpath along the banks of the Potomac River that took him deep into the surrounding woods.

He reached the designated meeting site on a rock ledge overlooking the river just as the first rays of the morning sun rose above the horizon. He stood quietly watching the fast-flowing water cascade over and around huge boulders as he thought back on the conversation he had with Paul Cameron the previous evening.

John Galloway, the CIA's Deputy Director for Operations, kept to his exercise regimen without fail. His five-mile run began in the pale predawn light each morning and followed a network of crisscrossing bridle paths and trails that took him over some of the roughest terrain in the park at a pace that would wear down most men half his age.

Welsh heard the DDO approaching before he saw him; the staccato beat of his footsteps rising above the sound of the river as they slapped the well-worn surface of the nearby trail.

Galloway appeared out of the fog like a ghostly specter, his breath visible in the cold, crisp morning air. His fashion sense intact even when exercising, he wore a gray and white micro-fiber jogging suit with a scarlet accent stripe running diagonally down the front of the jacket. His running shoes were a matching gray and white, and the Sea Island cotton mock turtleneck he wore under the jacket was the exact shade of the scarlet stripe. His salt and pepper hair was combed straight back and perfectly in place, and only a light dew of perspiration glistened on his forehead as he stopped at the side of the trail to check his heart rate monitor before joining Welsh on the ledge.

A man in a kayak went by, bobbing and weaving through the boulders as he struggled to stay upright in the churning water. Both men watched until he was out of sight, then Galloway, well aware of what had happened on the streets of New York the previous day, got straight to the point with Welsh.

'Where is Cameron getting the incompetent fools he's sending after Stafford and the Barnes woman?'

'They're his best people, sir. You know Tony Kitlan and Pete Marcus, and their capabilities. They've handled difficult assignments for us in the past. But as I've told you, we're not dealing with inexperienced civilians. They have good instincts, they're aware of their surroundings, and they don't panic in tight situations.'

'I don't need a testimonial, Adam. I need results. And I need to know what Cameron intends to do to put an end to this fiasco before it gets completely out of hand.'

'He's doing everything he can. Sooner or later Stafford and Barnes are going to make a mistake.'

'And where are they now?'

'I don't know. If they're still intent on coming after us, they'll surface again soon enough.' Welsh stared out across the river for a moment, then broached the next subject reluctantly. 'But I'm afraid we have an even bigger problem. They may have something in their possession that can compromise our entire operation. Something they can bargain with if the Secret Service finds out they have the supernotes and gets to them first.'

'What are you talking about?'

'They searched Ramsey's apartment before Kitlan and Marcus could sanitize it. They found the legends. The port-folios were opened and we have to assume read and recognized for what they are and where they had to have come from.'

'The legends in and of themselves only point the finger, they prove nothing.'

'Unfortunately, that's not the worst of it. Kitlan found a video-recording system Ramsey used for secretly taping people in the apartment. One of the cameras was hidden in the bedroom; the other was in the living room.'

'So he was a deviate who liked to watch himself perform.'

'Not in the living room. The microphones were strategically placed to pick up conversations in the seating areas. I had meetings in that room with Ramsey. If he has me on tape, that connects the Counter Narcotics Center to him in the same time frame in which he ended up dead in a plane that crashed while transporting twenty million in counterfeit money.'

'Did Kitlan find any incriminating tapes?'

'No, but he said there were gaps where the tapes of Ramsey's sexual conquests were lined up on the shelf. The dust outlines indicated two were missing. I can't imagine Stafford and Barnes walked off with part of his porno collection.'

Welsh's expression told Galloway that the other shoe was still to drop. 'Let's hear the rest of it.'

'There's reason to believe Ramsey kept some sort of personal record of the people we bought drugs from.'

'What reason?'

'Kitlan had Stafford and Barnes under surveillance after they left the hospital. They went to see someone at Rikers Island. Cameron found out through a source that it was Viktor Kirilenko; one of the dealers we've been buying from. I don't know any other way they could have tied Kirilenko to Ramsey.'

Galloway shook his head in disgust. 'Then they have enough information to piece most of it together, if they haven't already. And more than enough, if the Secret Service gets their hands on it, to unravel our entire operation.'

'I haven't heard anything from Quinn, our Secret Service liaison. Which doesn't necessarily mean he isn't on to Stafford and Barnes.'

'If Kitlan had them under surveillance why doesn't he know where they are now?'

'After they left Rikers they took surveillance detection measures. They timed their move through a construction site on the Cross-Bronx Expressway perfectly. If Kitlan had tried to get around the flag man they would have made him.'

'And you have no idea where they might have gone?'

'If I had to guess, with their backgrounds and experience? I'd say they've gone to ground to mull over what they've learned and to consider their next move.'

Galloway heard something behind him and his hand went immediately inside the jacket of his jogging suit to the compact nine millimeter Glock pistol in the cross-draw holster strapped snugly to his waist. He turned to see a young couple on mountain bikes coming down the trail. He watched them with suspicion as they whooshed by and disappeared around a bend, then turned back to Welsh and jabbed a finger into his chest.

'Finish it, Adam. Finish it or they're going to finish us.'

Galloway turned and abruptly left the ledge. What had begun as a simple matter of tidying up to cover his tracks, following the crash of the Lear jet, had grown into something far more complicated and convoluted. The gut instincts that had served the DDO well throughout his life now told him the situation with Stafford and Janet Barnes was fast approaching the point where it would no longer be containable by any damage control operation.

John Galloway never left anything to chance, attributing much of his success as a career intelligence officer, as in everything else he did, to never being without a fall-back position and a contingency plan. He began to formulate just such a plan as he picked up his pace and continued his run along the wooded trail in the direction the bikers had gone.

Chapter Thirty-Nine

Tom Quinn and Steve Jacoby, the Special-Agent-In-Charge of the Counterfeit Division, entered the operations center at Secret Service headquarters in Washington, DC shortly after eight o'clock. Nicole Grant, the agent awaiting their arrival, had just finished loading the mapping software for the northeastern section of Pennsylvania into the classified and ultra-sophisticated piece of electronics equipment on the table before her. She nodded a greeting to the two men, then pointed to the equipment's monitor with a triumphant smile.

'I found your boy.'

Quinn and Jacoby approached and watched a steadily blinking indicator move across a map displayed on a sixteen-inch active matrix LCD screen built into the fold-down top of an aluminum case that contained a portable tracking device called Triggerfish.

With the aid of a person's cellular telephone service, Triggerfish was capable of pinpointing that person's exact location and monitoring their movements by homing in on the signal emitted by their cellular telephone, whether installed in a vehicle, or carried around in a briefcase or a coat pocket. The person being tracked did not have to be using the phone at the time; the unit only had to be left on in the mode to receive calls for Triggerfish to find and track its signal. When operated from a surveillance vehicle, the device allowed the agents to stay well behind their targets to avoid being seen without fear of losing them.

The signal Triggerfish was locked on to and tracking at the moment was originating from Ben Stafford's Star Tac cellular phone. It was being picked up and relayed to Secret Service headquarters by his cellular service in Philadelphia, who, after receiving an official request by Special Agent Nicole Grant, had provided her with the electronic serial number and the mobile identification number necessary for Triggerfish to locate Stafford's specific cellular phone.

Quinn and Jacoby watched as the indicator moved along a road that followed the shoreline of a small lake in a remote, heavily forested area of the Pocono Mountains of Pennsylvania.

Jacoby studied the terrain displayed on the map. 'Looks like the place is in the middle of nowhere. What are they doing up there?'

'My guess is staying out of harm's way until they figure out who their enemies are and how they can get to them.' Quinn pointed to the map. 'Look at the place. Densely wooded terrain. Only one road in and out. Real easy to spot someone approaching. Great place to go to ground, or to set up an ambush.'

Agent Grant looked up from the screen. 'The name of the immediate area is Mystic Lake. Just before you came in I hung up from a call with a local sheriff's deputy; not the sharpest knife in the drawer.'

'Does Stafford or Barnes have a place up there?'

'I asked, but he didn't know. I tried calling the county records office, but they don't open until nine. But it makes sense that either Stafford or Barnes would have some connection to the place, otherwise why would they choose it; it's not exactly one of your major garden spots.'

'Did you get anything useful out of the deputy?'

'Just general stuff. It's a low-key, out of the way, mediocre vacation area. Couple of state-run camp grounds. There's a small village at one end of the lake with a mom and pop grocery store, a clapboard church he thought belonged to a holy roller sect that talked in tongues and fooled around with snakes, and four bars. He was real sure about the number of bars. And that's about it.'

'How big is the lake?'

'Not very. A little over 400 acres with maybe fifty or sixty places built along the shore; mostly small weekend fishing cabins. He said the area's pretty much deserted after the Labor Day weekend until the first week of June.'

Jacoby looked to Quinn. 'It's your call, we can send a couple of agents from the Scranton field office to pick Stafford and Barnes up. Can't be more than an hour's drive.'

'No. I'd rather try to get them to come in. Besides, we really don't have anything solid to tie them to the money. And I guarantee you they're both smart enough to know that. Plus, if they lawyer-up, and we've got no reason to hold them, then we've shown our hand for nothing and lost any chance of them telling us what they know.'

'If you don't want them picked up, then at least let the agents sit on them until you work something out.'

'That area looks too isolated and restricted for an effective close-up surveillance. And I don't want to take the chance of Stafford or Barnes spotting them. As wired as they've got to be after the past two days, they're likely to start shooting before our guys have a chance to identify themselves. If Stafford keeps his cellular phone on, we'll know where they are anyway.'

Jacoby conceded the point. 'What makes you think they'll come in voluntarily?'

'I've read their background reports. They've both played by the rules all of their lives. Given the opportunity I think they'll cooperate.'

'Have you come up with anything on the shooters in New York?'

'No. But that in itself tells us something. It's the same story for the three men Stafford took out at his home, the one Janet Barnes killed in Reston, and the three left dead in the street in New York. Not one of them had any ID, their fingerprints weren't on file anywhere, their weapons had no serial numbers or manufacturer's stamp, and the Range Rover used in Pennsylvania, and the van used in New York were registered to virtually untraceable shell companies. And we both know who specializes in putting ghosts like that in the field.

Well organized. Well equipped. And cold-blooded enough to kill their wounded without hesitation, let alone anyone who gets in their way.'

'If it is the boys from Langley, we'd better tread lightly. Because if we're wrong ... Well, let's just be absolutely certain before we open that can of worms.' Jacoby watched the progress of the indicator on the screen for a moment, then turned back to Quinn. 'How do you want to proceed with this?'

'Straight up. I'll call Stafford and try to convince him we're not connected to the people trying to kill them, then see if I can arrange a meeting some place where they'll both feel comfortable.'

Agent Grant zoomed the Triggerfish map in to its full magnification as the indicator left the road around the lake and veered toward the shoreline. It continued to blink steadily and began to move faster as it reached the symbol for a footbridge that spanned a narrow channel of water to a small island. The island had one path, depicted on the map as a thin brown line. The path followed a meandering course along the shoreline and through the woods before making its way back to the footbridge.

Jacoby watched the indicator picking up more speed as it left the bridge and began to follow the path around the island. 'Is he in a vehicle?'

Grant shook her head. 'I don't think so. Probably running; seems to have picked up the pace when he left the road around the lake.'

Jacoby voiced his concern. 'Not running away from someone, I hope.'

Quinn shook his head when he saw that the indicator was keeping to the thin brown line that coursed its way around the island.

'No. He wouldn't stay out in the open on that path if someone was chasing him. He's too smart for that. He'd be in the woods in a heartbeat.'

190

Chapter Forty

Stafford and Janet ran side by side as they came off the footbridge onto Conservation Island. They were into their sixth mile and Stafford's arm ached, as did Janet's bruised ribs, but the run had turned into a contest of wills and neither of them wanted to be the first to back off the grueling pace Janet had set.

The tiny island, just over one half mile long and a few hundred yards wide, had a state-maintained nature trail with markers identifying the various trees and wild flowers and lichens and mushrooms that grew on the forest floor and along the shoreline. Drawn to vacation spots with a lot more diversions, Janet was less than impressed with her surroundings, and voiced her opinions as they ran.

'We've run all around this lake, Stafford, and I don't get it. There's nothing here. This half-assed nature trail and that's it. Like anybody cares about the name of some mushroom. So what's the attraction?'

'The attraction is there aren't any attractions. Even at the height of the summer season it's not crowded.'

'That's not too difficult to understand. I mean what's an evening's entertainment around here? Swatting mosquitos and picking deer ticks off your legs? Waiting for Lyme's Disease to kick in?'

Stafford laughed. 'That's only when the place really rocks.'

'I believe you. And look at that lake. It's full of stumps.'

'Those stumps keep the power boats and jet skis off the

water. Rowboats and canoes only, which makes for good fishing and peace and quiet.'

'Whatever lights your fire.'

'This place holds a lot of good memories for me. I taught my daughter how to fish up here. How to read a map and compass. We used to take long hikes through the woods. Camp out. Annie really loved . . .' Stafford's voice trailed off.

It was then that Janet recalled her brother telling her about the automobile accident involving Stafford's wife and daughter. 'I'm sorry, Stafford.' She offered an apologetic smile. 'Sometimes I don't know when to shut up.'

'It's okay.'

'How's your daughter doing?'

Stafford simply shook his head as they continued along the trail where it left the woods and followed the shoreline. Janet let the subject drop.

They were breathing heavily and fading fast when Stafford was both surprised and relieved to hear the cellular phone chirp from the pocket of his pullover nylon shell. They stopped running and Stafford unzipped the side pocket and removed the phone, suspecting that the call was from Tony Nardini, the bail bondsman in Philadelphia; the only person other than Annie's doctor who had the cellular number.

'Ben Stafford.'

'Good morning, Ben Stafford. You don't know me, but that's something I think we should remedy, and fast.'

Stafford tensed. 'Who is this?'

'Special Agent Tom Quinn of the United States Secret Service. We need to talk, and my guess is you don't need to be told why.'

'Guess again. What do you want?'

'Like I said, we need to talk.'

'And like you also said, I don't know you. Maybe you're Secret Service and maybe you're not. And even if you are I still don't know why you want to talk to me.'

Janet stared at Stafford, her brow knit. 'Secret Service?' She mouthed the words.

Stafford nodded to her as Quinn continued. 'As far as my credentials are concerned, hang up and call Secret Service

192

headquarters in Washington, ask to be connected to the Counterfeit Division, and then ask for me. And as far as why I want to talk with you, as I told you, I think you already know that.'

'And as I told you, I don't.'

Stafford hung up, called information for Washington, and got the number for Secret Service headquarters. He dialed and was soon connected to the counterfeit division. Quinn came on the line, his tone casual and friendly.

'Do I have your undivided attention now?'

'All right. You are who you say you are. But unless you've got something else to tell me, this conversation is over.'

'I'll tell you this, I've got nothing to do with the people who've been trying to kill you and Janet Barnes for the past two days.'

'And how do I know that?'

'What reason would the Secret Service have to kill you?'

'What reason would anyone have?'

'Tell you what; don't treat me like a fool and I'll pay you the same respect. Deal?'

'You still haven't told me what you want.'

'I'm the Secret Service liaison to the CIA's Counter Narcotics Center. Does that tell you anything?'

'It sure does. It tells me not to believe a goddamn thing you say.'

Quinn considered his next move carefully, then decided to take the chance. 'Right now I'm watching you run around the shoreline of an island on Mystic Lake in the Pocono Mountains of Pennsylvania. Correction. You were running. At the moment you're standing still.'

Quinn paused to let the revelation sink in. 'Yesterday afternoon you bought two hundred and fifteen dollars' worth of men's and women's exercise clothing and running shoes from a Foot Locker store in Teaneck, New Jersey. One hour and ten minutes later you stopped in a gun shop in Port Jervis, Pennsylvania and bought a used Benelli twelve gauge semi-automatic combat shotgun, a used semi-automatic CAR-15 assault rifle and three thirty-round magazines, plus ten boxes of shotgun shells and ten boxes of hollow point ammo for the

193

CAR-15, along with a few other accessories. Sounds like you and Barnes plan on going to war.'

'What's your point?'

'My point is the bad guys wouldn't call to tell you they know where you are, or that they're tracking you through credit card purchases and your cellular phone signal. They'd just close in for the kill.'

Stafford looked to Janet, who had a peculiar knowing look on her face as she whispered to him. 'I think we should talk to him.'

'Why?'

'Just set it up. I'll tell you when you're off the phone.'

Quinn's voice came over the speaker. 'You still there?'

'I'm here.'

'So are we going to meet?'

After a long silence Quinn spoke again. 'Come on, Stafford. Cooperate with me and we'll make this all go away.'

'My terms.'

'No problem. Where and when?'

'How soon can you get here?'

'Is there an airport nearby.'

'No. Got a helicopter?'

'I can get one.'

'I'll give you the coordinates for my place. It's on the lake. Get a chopper with floats and you can land on the water in front of the cabin. Otherwise you'll have to set it down on the road.'

Quinn studied the map spread out on the table before him. 'Looks like you're about one hundred and ninety miles north-east of DC. Probably an hour and a half flight. It'll take me at least a few hours to line up the helicopter and get things organized.' He glanced at his watch. 'It's eight forty-five. Rough estimate . . . I can be there around two this afternoon.'

'You, a pilot, and a co-pilot, that's it.'

'And a security detail. Six agents. Just in case we run into any bad guys.'

'All right. But that's it. Are you ready to copy?'

'Ready.' Quinn wrote down the coordinates as Stafford recited them from memory.

'And don't even think about putting a surveillance team on us like your CIA buddies did. We see anyone sniffing around before you arrive, we're out of here.'

'You sure about that CIA tail?'

'Positive. They had a transmitter on my car.'

'No kidding,' was all Quinn said in response, then added, 'Keep your head down until I get there, huh?'

Stafford hung up. 'They're tracking the cellular signal,' he told Janet as he turned off the phone and put it back in his pocket. 'If they can do it, so can the Agency.'

Quinn saw the blinking indicator disappear from the screen as Triggerfish lost the signal. Special Agent Nicole Grant looked up and cocked an eyebrow.

'I sure hope you know what you're doing.'

'You and me both.'

Janet and Stafford continued their run at a slower pace as they left the island and headed back along the lake road in the direction of the cabin.

Janet slapped her forehead with the palm of her hand in comic fashion. 'I must be losing it. I should have figured out what was going on long before this.'

'Figured what out?'

'Why the CIA would be buying drugs. You were right about the figures in Ramsey's files. The "K" was for thousands. Not kilos. And you counted twenty thousand "K". Right? Twenty thousand times one thousand is twenty million. The exact amount you and Eddie got off the plane. They were going to lay off the entire twenty million on the drug dealers in that file.'

'So where do the Secret Service enter into the equation? Their primary job is to protect the President and catch counterfeiters?'

'You just said the magic word.'

'What? The money's counterfeit? Bullshit. That's the first thing Eddie and I checked when we got back. There wasn't any difference between the bills we got off that plane and the ones I had at home.'

'And the ten grand Eddie left at my apartment looked fine, too. It even felt right. But we're not talking about bills run off on some copying machine, or scanned into a computer and printed on crappy paper. Drug dealers aren't rocket scientists, but there's no way anyone could pass low grade funny money off on them without them finding out as soon as they tried to launder it. And Kirilenko said he'd sold to Ramsey more than once. Which means Ramsey had to be real confident in the quality of what he was passing. And that means he was passing stuff so good you'd have to put it under a microscope to tell the difference. In other words supernotes. You familiar with them?'

'Only what I've heard. They're above average counterfeit of the new one hundred dollar bill. Started turning up in Europe a couple of years ago.'

'Calling them above average is like calling a Ferrari basic transportation.'

'They're that good?'

'Don't get any better. About six months before I left DEA we busted a heavyweight Jamaican Posse dealer. Confiscated about three hundred keys of cocaine and four hundred thousand dollars in one hundred dollar bills. The next day a couple of Secret Service agents showed up to examine the money. That seemed a little strange to me at the time. I mean why would they think it was counterfeit? But it makes sense now. Some of the supernotes Ramsey was passing probably showed up somewhere, they traced them back to a drug dealer, so they started checking all the hundreds confiscated in drug busts.'

Janet smiled and shook her head. 'You gotta hand it to those spooks. The diabolical bastards are probably making the stuff themselves. Which means they're getting millions of dollars' worth of drugs for printing costs. And at a discount for volume, so they can turn right around and sell them at the going price to dealers in Europe or Asia or anywhere else and make a real killing.'

'And all this leaves us where? We turn the money over and say a *mea culpa*?'

Janet shrugged. 'Let's hear what this guy Quinn has to say.

Or better yet, let's see how much of what he knows he can prove.'

'You're thinking about keeping Eddie's share?'

'Like I said before. We can burn that bridge when we get to it.'

'But if it's counterfeit . . . ?' Stafford let the question hang.

'What can I tell you? It's an imperfect world.'

Janet once again picked up the pace. They ran in silence until they reached a narrow gravel driveway that cut through the woods for a few hundred yards and ended at Stafford's cabin in a private, sheltered cove at the north end of the lake. The nearest neighbor in any direction was at least one half mile away.

The rustic-looking log cabin sat in a small clearing in the woods fifty feet from the water's edge. A lopsided wooden dock extended ten feet out from shore and an aluminum rowboat, pulled out of the water two years earlier and overturned, lay on the ground beneath the trees.

The cabin was overhung with towering pines and hardwood trees ablaze with autumn color, the leaves just past their peak but still magnificent. A wooden swing hung from rusty chains at one end of a screened-in porch that sagged in the middle, and the chimney, made from stones hand-picked by Stafford's father, was crooked.

The interior was cozy and inviting. There was no television. No radio. And no telephone. It was intended as a place to get completely away from the assault on the senses by everyday life. It had two small bedrooms, a kitchen with an old wood-burning stove that kept the entire cabin warm on even the coldest days during deer hunting season, and a large picnic-bench-style table handcrafted of oak. A swing-out window with a stick to prop it open looked out on the colorful woods behind the cabin. A cupboard shelf held blue tin cups passed down by some ancient relative, while others were stocked with cans of soup and packets of hot chocolate mix long out of date. The bags of groceries Stafford and Janet purchased in the village sat unpacked on the table.

197

The living room had random-width pine floors, a fieldstone fireplace, and a large picture window overlooking the lake. It was furnished with a comfortable and well-worn overstuffed sofa and four similar chairs that had been there since the place was built. An old corduroy shirt and a pair of jeans faded by wear hung on a nail near the front door. Stafford had put them there to dry after he and Annie were caught out on the lake in a thunderstorm during their last visit, eight months before the accident that took her mother's life.

Stafford had left the windows and doors open when he and Janet went for their run, and the stale, musty odor that greeted them on arrival was gone, replaced by cool, fresh air redolent with the scent of autumn. The screen door banged behind them as they came in off the porch and Stafford pointed toward the bathroom.

'You can have the shower first. I'll put on some coffee.'

Janet looked out the window toward the lake. 'I think I'll play nature girl. How deep is it off the end of the dock?'

'Ten or twelve feet.'

Janet got a towel and a bar of soap from the bathroom and went back outside. She took off her nylon running jacket and removed the cummerbund-style elasticized waistband she had purchased at the gun store. The broad waistband had a leather insert sewn into it that fit her pistol perfectly, and Velcro fasteners allowed her to adjust it as needed to hold the gun snugly at her side as she ran.

She removed the pistol, concealed it inside the towel, and placed it on the dock. Then, without hesitation or inhibition, she stripped off her clothes. Stafford stood at the window watching her, admiring her figure and muscle tone and noticing the black and blue marks on her rib cage. Completely naked, she launched herself into a graceful dive off the end of the dock into the clear, cold water. Stafford turned to go into the kitchen and heard her let out a loud hoot as she came to the surface and swam out into the cove.

Chapter Forty-One

Before leaving Secret Service headquarters, Tom Quinn made arrangements to borrow a Counter Assault Team from the Presidential Protection Division. The six-man CAT team, armed with fully automatic M-16s and shotguns, was expert in tactics for suppressing ambushes and traveled as part of the presidential motorcade for that specific purpose. Having just completed a training exercise at the Secret Service training center in Beltsville, Maryland when Quinn called, the team was en route to meet him at the United States Customs Department hangar at Dulles International Airport.

The Customs Department provided the Secret Service with air assets when needed, and Quinn had made further arrangements to have a Bell 206 Long Ranger helicopter fitted with lightweight floats for the flight to Pennsylvania. He was still angry over the fact that the CIA had lied to him and kept him out of the loop, and as he pulled out of the headquarters underground parking garage, he placed a call to Lou Burruss, Adam Welsh's second-in-command at the Counter Narcotics Center.

'Nothing new here,' Burruss told him. 'We're still trying to locate the crash site.'

Despite his best intentions to remain composed, Quinn lost his temper. 'Don't piss on my boots and tell me it's raining, Lou. I know you had Stafford under surveillance when he got back from Canada. Which means you knew where the site was and that he and Barnes found it.'

There was a brief silence before Burruss replied. 'I apologize for not leveling with you, but it wasn't my decision. I don't run the show around here.'

'I'm aware of that. I'm just calling to tell you that if you have any surveillance on Ben Stafford and Janet Barnes, pull it off. Now.'

'To the best of my knowledge there is no surveillance on them at the present time.'

'With bullshit statements like that you could run for President. Do I need to have you define the word "is"?'

'What I meant was, I don't know what anyone else is doing, but they are not under surveillance by the Counter Narcotics Center.'

'Then keep it that way. They've agreed to talk with me and I've set up a meeting. I don't want any of your people screwing it up.'

'Where's the meeting?'

'That's need to know. A concept I'm sure you're more than familiar with. And you don't need to know.'

'I was only going to suggest we could provide some additional security. Judging from the heat those two have been drawing you might need it.'

'Pay attention, Lou. From this point on this is a Secret Service case. So back off.'

'I'll pass that along.'

'You do that. And Lou, if you or Adam Welsh withhold information or interfere with my investigation again, I will personally arrest both of you for obstruction. You got that?'

Quinn hung up before Burruss could reply and headed out of the city in the direction of the airport.

Burruss dialed the number for Adam Welsh's cell phone and reached him shortly after he had pulled out of the driveway of his home in suburban Rockville, Maryland.

'Quinn found Stafford and Barnes and set up a meeting.'

'Where?'

'He wouldn't say. And he's pissed. He knows we lied to him.'

'Why did he call?'

'To make sure we didn't have any surveillance on them.'

Welsh thought for a moment, then decided the time had come to initiate a preliminary damage control operation.

'I want you to get rid of the satellite tapes of the crash site, and all cables, faxes, reports, computer files, or any other documents, no matter how insignficant, that concern this operation from the time the plane went down.'

'I don't understand.'

'It's quite simple. The operation never happened. Clear enough?'

'There are other people here who know we were tracking that plane. And Sunnyvale has a record of moving the satellites for us.'

'That's right. The Secret Service informed us about the transmitter. We tracked the plane from St John's, Newfoundland until we lost the signal somewhere over the Quebec wilderness. We looked for it. We found nothing.'

'What about Carole Fisher? She recorded all the satellite passes.'

'You leave Carole to me. I'll make certain she has a clear understanding of what she did and did not see. You handle the physical evidence.'

'Aren't you forgetting the report from the Ottawa station about the dead bush pilot, and the surveillance team I had on Stafford?'

'I haven't forgotten anything. We were looking into the possibility of the bush pilot helping us to determine if the plane went down in that area. He was found dead. We put Stafford under surveillance because his name turned up in the bush pilot's records. Stafford made our surveillance and we lost him. End of story. Now do what I told you to do and don't waste any time doing it.'

Welsh hung up and slowed to ease his way into the heavy flow of traffic where Route 270 merged with the Capital Beltway. He thought for a moment, then dialed Paul Cameron's office at Cameron & Associates in New York City.

Cameron unlocked the desk cabinet where he kept the telephone for the secure private line used only for calls from Welsh. He picked up the receiver and heard the distinctive static hiss and crackle caused by Welsh's scrambler. He activated his own scrambler and the line cleared immediately.

Welsh started talking without preamble. 'Do you have Quinn under surveillance?'

'I've had a team on him ever since you called following your conversation with the DDO this morning. They just checked in to report that he left Secret Service headquarters five minutes ago.'

'He's set up a meeting with Stafford and Barnes. Find out where.'

'I'll get on it right away.'

'I don't want whatever it is they got from Ramsey's apartment falling into Quinn's hands. If they manage to turn anything over to him before Kitlan gets to them, you tell him he's to take whatever measures are necessary to get it back.'

Welsh hesitated and then added. 'And Paul, there's a distinct possibility this could all go south on us. The prudent course of action would be to make some preparatory arrangements in the event that happens.'

Chapter Forty-Two

Quinn dialed the number for the Customs Department hangar as he came off the ramp and merged with the steady stream of fast moving traffic on the Dulles Toll Road.

Two car lengths behind him and to his left, a white van with Premier Carpet Cleaners stenciled on the doors paced him in an outside lane. The van was purposely in Quinn's blind spot, allowing the driver and the passenger in the front seat an unobstructed view into his car without revealing their presence.

The driver saw Quinn put the cellular phone to his ear. 'He's making a call,' he announced loudly.

The man seated at an electronics console built into the back of the van pulled on his headset and watched the monitor before him. In a matter of seconds a mountain of blue peaks appeared on the screen as the state-of-the-art high-speed scanner found and locked on to Quinn's cellular phone.

'I need to speak to Doug Henning,' the man heard Quinn tell the person who answered the phone in the small office off the hangar bay.

'Got him,' the man at the console said, and switched on the reel-to-reel tape recorder.

Quinn heard a door open and someone shout Henning's name above the noise in the hangar. A few moments later he heard the door close and the pilot came on the line.

'Henning.'

'Tom Quinn. Secret Service. Operations said you're my pilot.'

'That's me.'

'What's the status on the floats for the helicopter?'

'They're putting them on now.'

'Were you informed about the six agents coming with me?'

'No. But it's no problem. The cabin holds seven. And you'll be traveling in style. Tufted leather seats, individual headsets for the stereo system. And a bar.'

'This is a Customs Department chopper we're talking about?'

'Got it off a Mexican drug lord we busted with a hundred keys at the Phoenix airport. By the way, nobody told me where we're going either. I have to file a flight plan.'

Quinn had purposely limited the number of people who knew his destination to as few as possible. He took a slip of paper from his shirt pocket and read the coordinates for Stafford's cabin to Henning.

'The name of the place is Mystic Lake. The coordinates put us at the subject's cabin. We'll have to land on the water.'

'Thus the reason for the floats.'

'How long to get there?'

'Give me a second.'

Quinn heard Henning put down the phone and unfold an aeronautical chart before coming back on the line.

'The chopper cruises at one sixty. It's one hundred and eighty-two miles to Mystic Lake. So we're looking at an hour and ten minutes, give or take. We should have a pretty good wind with us. Could make it in an hour.'

'I'd like to get airborne as soon as possible.'

'Another half hour, tops.'

Quinn hung up and drove in silence, going over in his mind the sequence of events following the plane crash. There were things that seemed too convenient, and others that did not fit at all, which led him to believe that everything that happened since Stafford and Barnes returned from Canada was in some way connected to the Counter Narcotics Center, though its origins, he was certain, were to be found on a much higher level.

When he reached the entrance to Dulles International, Quinn turned onto an access road that took him away from the

204

commercial airline terminals toward a private corner of the airport allocated for government hangars. He glanced in his rear-view mirror and saw a Chevy Suburban with blacked out windows make the same turn he did and speed toward him. The Counter Assault Team had made good time.

The driver of the van, having obtained the information Paul Cameron wanted, broke off the surveillance when Quinn ended his call with the pilot. He took an exit ramp off the toll road as the man at the console dialed the number where Cameron had told him he could reach Tony Kitlan.

Kitlan was in his office above the floor of a warehouse in Long Island City when the call came in. He wrote down the name of the lake and the coordinates as he listened to the recording of Quinn's conversation with Henning being played over the phone to him.

When he hung up, Peter Marcus leaned across the desk and looked at what Kitlan had written. 'Where's Mystic Lake?'

'Let's find out.'

Kitlan turned on his notebook computer and inserted the DVD for the navigational software. He entered the coordinates in the 'Locate by Longitude/Latitude' dialog box and clicked on 'OK'. The screen quickly displayed a map of the lake centered on the precise location of Stafford's cabin. Kitlan backed off on the magnification until the map showed the entire area from New York City to Mystic Lake. He entered Long Island City as the starting point and Mystic Lake as the destination, then instructed the mapping program to select and highlight the quickest route and to calculate the time and distance for the trip. Within seconds the information was displayed.

'Easy hour and a half drive,' he told Marcus.

'It's in the middle of the boonies. What's there?'

'A cabin on a lake.' Kitlan looked at Marcus and smiled. 'How would you like to take along that little toy you've been looking for an excuse to use?'

Marcus' face brightened, losing its perpetual scowl. 'Sure. What do we need it for?'

'Seven Secret Service agents will be leaving Dulles airport

by helicopter in about a half hour for the same place we're going. If they leave on schedule, they should get there around the same time we do.'

'Helicopter, huh? I like that. How many men are we taking?'

Kitlan got up from behind his desk and walked out of the office onto the catwalk overlooking the floor of the warehouse. A dozen men were busy sealing crates and loading them on a truck. The crates contained fully automatic AK-47 assault rifles and Claymore antipersonnel mines being readied for shipment to a radical survivalist group in northern Idaho. The weapons had cost Cameron virtually nothing, having traded for them with drugs purchased with supernotes; the five hundred thousand dollars they would receive from the survivalist group was pure profit.

'We'll go in heavy this time. Ten of us. And your new toy.'

Marcus grinned like a child on Christmas morning.

Chapter Forty-Three

Janet Barnes sat cross-legged on a rag rug in front of the field-stone fireplace, warming herself before the cheerful blaze she found waiting for her upon returning from her swim in the lake. She finished the cup of green tea Stafford had made for her and got up to go out to the kitchen to join him. She had on jeans and a cotton turtleneck, and before leaving the room, she pulled on an old corduroy shirt she found hanging on a nail by the door, wearing it open with the shirt-tails tied at her waist.

Stafford immediately noticed the shirt and stared at her for a long uncomfortable moment. He had a particularly vivid image of his wife and daughter on an autumn night two years ago when they had taken a moonlight boat ride. His wife had borrowed the thick, warm shirt and wrapped herself and Annie in it as they sat drifting on the shimmering surface of the lake and listening to Stafford point out and name the constellations. It had been their last visit to the cabin.

Janet saw the look in his eyes and understood. 'I did it again, didn't I? I'm sorry.'

'No, it's all right.'

'I'll put something else on.'

'No. I promise you, it's okay. It looks good on you.'

Janet did not want to make the moment more awkward than it already was and accepted his compliment with a smile.

Stafford went into the living room and got the small nylon day-pack he had purchased to hold the boxes of twelve gauge shells, the assault rifle ammunition, and the thirty-round magazines. He slung the compact Benelli semi-automatic combat shotgun over his shoulder, along with the bandolier the owner of the gun store had thrown in at Janet's insistence. He then picked up the CAR-15 he had gotten for himself and went back into the kitchen and placed everything at the far end of the table.

He had no reason to believe the Secret Service had a hidden agenda, but he was not going to be caught off guard in the event someone managed to find the cabin, with or without their help. As an afterthought, he held up the shotgun and asked Janet. 'Are you any good with this?'

'No. I was planning on using it as a club.'

'You never let up, do you? I've used it before. I thought maybe I could give you some pointers, that's all.'

Janet smiled. 'Eddie had one just like it. He gave me a pretty extensive course in instinctive shooting with it. Plus I shot skeet competitively for about six years.'

'That answers that question.' Stafford looked at his watch and estimated they had at least forty-five minutes until Quinn arrived. 'You hungry?'

'Starved.'

He took some celery and a jar of mayonnaise from among the groceries in the refrigerator and put them on the counter next to the cutting board along with an onion. He then opened a can of tuna fish and handed it to Janet.

'What's this?'

'Tuna fish. What does it look like?'

'I know *what* it is. What I meant was, what do you expect me to do with it?'

Stafford pointed to the things he had placed on the counter. 'Make tuna fish salad while I load the ammo in the magazines.'

'What, I look like Martha Stewart to you?'

'You don't know how to make tuna salad?'

'I can mix protein shakes in a blender, and I can take the tops off those plastic trays filled with tossed salad I get at the supermarket. Anything more complicated than that, I eat out or have it delivered.'

'You're kidding, right?'

'Let me put it this way, Stafford. I have a revolving charge account at the Chinese restaurant two blocks from my apartment. They send me birthday cards. Their delivery van knows its way to my place by itself. The Wongs are thinking of adopting me.'

Stafford raised his hands in mock surrender. 'Okay. I get the point. I'll make the tuna salad. You load the magazines.'

'That I can do.'

'You're going to be a real catch for some guy, you know?'

'Yeah. Right. As if I'd marry some asshole who expects me to cook for him.'

'Do you eat with that mouth?'

Janet laughed and took a bottle of Evian and a raw carrot from the refrigerator. She got the Kevlar vest she had worn in New York City from the living room and sat at the far end of the table munching on the carrot and using a pair of needle-nose pliers to remove the three slugs imbedded in the vest.

After extracting the slugs and putting them in her pocket as keepsakes, she picked up the Benelli shotgun, loaded one of the twelve gauge double-ought buckshot shells in the chamber, then slipped seven more into the magazine and another twenty into the bandolier.

She paused for a moment before loading the magazines for the CAR-15, and watched Stafford finish chopping the onion and celery. He put them in a large bowl with the tuna fish and added a few heaping tablespoons of mayonnaise. Janet laughed softly to herself as he began to stir the contents of the bowl.

Stafford heard her and looked up. 'What's so funny?'

Janet affected a dramatic tone and used sweeping hand gestures as she spoke. 'Outside, a clear mountain lake sparkles in the afternoon sun. The crisp late September air carries a hint of the coming winter. Smoke drifts lazily from the chimney of a rustic cabin nestled in the autumn woods. Inside a cozy fire crackles in the fireplace. You're making lunch. I'm loading ammo and digging slugs out of my Kevlar vest. I'm telling you, Stafford, this is a Kodak fuckin' moment if there ever was one.'

'You're incorrigible.'

The Toyota Land Cruiser moved slowly along the road that followed the shoreline of the lake. Tony Kitlan was behind the wheel, his eyes carefully watching the woods leading down to the water's edge. Peter Marcus was in the front passenger seat while three men sat shoulder to shoulder in the back. The van carrying the other five men Kitlan had chosen to bring with him followed close behind.

Marcus had Kitlan's notebook computer on his lap. A Global Positioning System receiver the size of his hand was attached to the computer's serial port and placed on top of the dashboard. The notebook's screen displayed a map of the immediate area with the GPS position icon at the center indicating their exact location.

Upon leaving Long Island City, Kitlan had entered the longitude and latitude for Stafford's cabin into the navigation program as his destination. The GPS had done the rest. The position icon had moved across the map as the car moved, reporting speed, direction of travel, and giving spoken directions, announcing each way point and turn on the selected route.

Kitlan continued along the lake road until he spotted an overgrown driveway that cut through the woods to the shoreline. He pulled the Land Cruiser onto the shoulder and the van pulled in behind him. The map display showed that he was a little more than one half mile from Stafford's cabin, at a point where the road curved around the far end of a secluded cove.

He did not want to drive any closer and chance being seen, and his eyes followed the deeply rutted driveway to where it ended beside a barely visible rundown cabin at the water's edge. He could see that the rear window of the cabin was boarded up, and that the colorful carpet of leaves covering the driveway was undisturbed, indicating no one had been there recently.

Kitlan put the Land Cruiser in gear and drove through the woods toward the deserted cabin. The van followed close behind. The overhanging trees and thick underbrush encroaching on the narrow passage scraped against the sides of both vehicles and they were soon enveloped by the forest.

Chapter Forty-Four

Stafford stood at the kitchen sink washing dishes and looking out the window into the woods behind the cabin. He was admiring the brilliant colors and myriad shadings of a huge red maple tree and recalling how he had climbed it as a boy, and how thirty years later, when Annie was just eight, he had to rescue her from its uppermost branches. He turned away for a moment to rinse one of the dishes and, as he did, a sudden flicker of motion in the woods registered in his peripheral vision.

He looked outside and the only movement he could see was a stand of white birches swaying gently in a breeze coming in off the lake. He was about to attribute the quick, darting motion he had seen to an animal or a bird when he saw it again; this time in the waist-high underbrush. A shadowy figure moving in a low crouch. Then another, and another. All three now clearly recognizable as human. They were carrying assault rifles and taking up positions at the rear of the cabin.

Janet was at the kitchen table eating a small box of raisins for dessert and putting the last of the now fully loaded thirty-round magazines back in the day-pack. She looked over and saw the strange expression on Stafford's face.

'What is it?'

Stafford continued washing the dishes as though nothing had happened. He spoke to Janet in a low, urgent voice without looking at her.

'Take your vest, the pack, and the shotgun, and go into the

living room. Do it in a casual way. And stay away from the windows.'

Janet restrained herself from turning to look outside. 'Company?'

'Yeah.'

'How many?'

'Three so far.'

She got up from the table, put her arms above her head in an exaggerated stretch, then took the things into the living room and placed them at her feet as she stood in a corner, well out of view of anyone watching through the picture window. She put on her Kevlar vest, leaving her pistol tucked inside the waistband at the front of her jeans, then took her spare magazines from the day-pack and stuffed them in her pockets. She next slipped an arm through the bandolier she had loaded with twenty double-ought buckshot shells and slung it around her neck. The shells hung diagonally across her chest within easy reach.

Stafford entered the room carrying his CAR-15. He immediately put on his Kevlar vest and leather jacket, then took the thirty-round magazines from the pack and slapped one into the weapon and put the other two in the front cargo pockets of his jacket.

'Let's see how many we're up against.'

He led Janet into the front bedroom and over to the window. The curtains were drawn, and he stood off to the side and parted them just enough to see into the woods at the south side of the cabin. He quickly spotted two men kneeling in the underbrush approximately ten feet apart. One of them was smoking a cigarette. They were both armed with AK-47 assault rifles.

Janet followed Stafford back into the living room where he moved along the wall until he was close enough to the picture window to peer around the edge. He saw two more men run through the woods, past the front porch, and take up positions on the north side of the cabin. Another three men, all armed with AK-47s, moved at a dog trot along the shore of the lake. One of them had his weapon slung across his back, and before he disappeared into the dense woods and waist-high underbrush on the far side of the dock, Stafford caught a momentary

212

glimpse of the five-foot-long, olive-drab, high-impact plastic container he was carrying. The size and configuration of the container looked all too familiar.

'I count ten. Three in back. Three more out front. And two on each side.'

'If they have any LAWs with them and we stay in here, we're as good as dead.'

'I didn't see any LAWs. What I did see was a container for a Stinger missile.'

Janet's eyes widened. 'A Stinger?'

'They're going to take out the Secret Service chopper before they come after us. That's what they're waiting for.'

'How did they find out the Secret Service was flying in here?'

Stafford shrugged. 'Nothing about these guys surprises me anymore.'

He peered around the corner of the window again, then pulled back. 'There's no one directly in front of the cabin. The one with the Stinger and the two with him are off to the left on the other side of the dock. They're probably watching the lake for the chopper.'

'What do you have in mind?'

'There are some decent-sized boulders down at the shore-line, almost a complete semi-circle of them. They're just inside the tree line, a little off to the right of the cabin. They're surrounded by some pretty thick underbrush. If we can make it there we've got good natural cover, and a good defensive position. The water cuts off one avenue of escape, but with our backs to the lake we won't have to worry about anyone approaching from the rear.'

'We just run out the front door shooting?'

'Unless you have a better idea.'

'Sounds like a plan to me.'

'When we break for it, the one with the Stinger and the two with him have no shot at us at all; the woods are too thick. They won't even see us. The three at the back of the cabin are out of play, and the two on our left have a bad angle and the ground slopes off a lot steeper on that side; they won't see us until we're halfway to the lake.'

'And the two on the right?'

'They'll have a clear field of fire from the moment we're off the porch. It's only about sixty feet to the shoreline and the boulders, so if we go out the door at a dead run we'll have a pretty good head start before they realize what's going on and can respond.'

Janet held up the shotgun. 'If you keep the two on our left and the ones in the woods on the other side of the dock out of the picture, I'll take care of the two on the right.'

Stafford extended the telescoping stock of the CAR-15 and jacked a round into the chamber. He flipped off the safety, put his hand on the door handle, and took a deep, calming breath. 'Ready?'

Janet clicked off the Benelli's safety and nodded. 'Ready.'

Just as Stafford was about to open the door, Janet grabbed his arm. 'Listen.'

Stafford paused and stood motionless but heard nothing.

'Don't you hear it?'

A moment later the sound reached him. The faint throbbing beat of a helicopter off in the distance.

Chapter Forty-Five

Doug Henning was flying the helicopter nap-of-the-earth as he barely cleared the trees over Conservation Island before dropping down to again cruise ten feet above the surface of the lake. He glanced at the display for his GPS receiver, then looked to his right into a secluded cove that dog-legged off the main body of water and spotted a dock jutting out into the lake.

'Right on target,' he shouted to the men in the cabin behind him. 'Two minutes.' He cut back on the power and swung toward the dock for a straight-in approach. He studied the water along the shore, looking for the best spot to land, immediately eliminating a waterlily bed off to the left of the dock, and a rocky shoal in the shallows on the right.

As the helicopter slowed, Quinn pulled the rear door open and the cool mountain air rushed in. The six-man Counter Assault Team released their seat belts and cradled their weapons in their laps as they prepared to disembark the moment the aircraft touched down.

Stafford threw open the front door of the cabin and came across the porch like a runner out of the starting blocks. He ran straight at the screen door, lowering a shoulder and driving it ahead of him as he tore it from its hinges. Janet was directly behind him as they jumped the short span of steps and hit the ground in an all-out sprint for the shoreline.

At the sound of the screen door crashing to the ground, the two men on the right side of the cabin jumped to their feet and opened fire before acquiring a target. The bullets zipped harmlessly through the woods and into the side of the cabin.

Janet saw the two men and stopped running. She swung to her right just as they turned to face her. With her left hand on the forestock and her right hand on the pistol grip, she held the shotgun at her hip and, before they could train their weapons on her, she fired four rapid-fire blasts that tore limbs from saplings and sent a storm of colorful leaves fluttering into the air. One of the men screamed in pain as a half dozen steel pellets shattered his knee. The second man dove to ground when two of the blasts ripped through the brush beside him. Janet resumed running toward the shore, repeatedly glancing over her shoulder to make certain the men were still down.

The two men on the opposite side of the cabin were up and running toward the front at the first sound of gunfire. As they appeared around the corner, Stafford saw them and took aim. He fired on the run, forcing one of the men to take cover while the other stood his ground and got off a sustained burst that sent tiny fountains of soil and leaves erupting at Stafford's heels. The man made no attempt to lower his profile as he adjusted his aim. He missed again, this time overcompensating and firing into the trees in front of Stafford.

Stafford's training and experience in instinctive shooting served him well as he pointed his weapon at the man, elevated the barrel, and returned fire as he continued to run toward the lake. Two rounds struck the man in the chest. The third entered his head just above the ear and killed him outright.

The man Janet had hit in the knee was still down, posing no immediate threat. The man who had dived for cover was now up and taking aim from behind a tree. Janet slowed and shortened her stride as she turned and fired three times in quick succession. A storm of pellets tore chunks of bark from the tree and again sent the man diving to the ground.

Kitlan and the man with him left Marcus' side and ran through the dense woods on the far side of the dock in response to the shooting. They reached the cabin clearing just as Stafford and Janet ducked into the underbrush and out of sight behind the cluster of boulders.

Kitlan stopped at the very edge of the tree line and turned to his companion. 'Stay here. Cover Peter and me until the chopper gets here.'

The man dropped into a prone position in the underbrush, facing toward the boulders, as Kitlan turned and ran back into the woods to where Marcus waited thirty yards away at the water's edge.

Stafford and Janet peered over the boulders, the barrels of their weapons following their eyes as they searched for targets. Stafford saw Kitlan disappear into the woods, but he did not see the man who remained behind and was hiding in the underbrush at the edge of the clearing, forty yards from where he and Janet had taken cover.

'I'm going after the guy with the Stinger,' he told Janet. 'Cover me until I get into the woods on the other side of the dock.'

Janet quickly loaded another seven shells into the shotgun and tucked it snugly into her shoulder as she rose to one knee and began scanning the surrounding woods. 'Ready when you are.'

Stafford bolted from behind the boulders and ran through the woods along the shore of the lake in a low crouch.

The man who had fired at Janet from behind the tree saw Stafford and broke from cover to give chase. He had not seen Janet run behind the boulders, and he passed within a few feet of her position as he raced after Stafford.

Janet heard him crashing through the woods and waited until he was directly in front of her, then stood up and fired a shot into his chest at near point-blank range. The force of the blast knocked him off his feet and threw him backwards. He was dead before he landed sprawled on the forest floor.

The man in the underbrush on the far side of the dock spotted Stafford running through the woods along the shore. He took careful aim, but could not get a clear shot at him as he moved in and out of the trees. The man low-crawled, using his elbows to pull himself to a better vantage point, and again took aim. This time he found an opening for a clear shot and slowly squeezed the trigger. He felt the searing pain of the steel pellets tearing into his shoulder at the same moment he heard the shotgun blast.

Stafford looked back to see Janet still aiming the Benelli at the man who had been about to shoot him. He swung toward the wounded man and killed him just as he fired without effect at Janet, the bullets hitting the ground ten feet in front of the boulders.

Stafford ran past the dock and continued on into the woods. The trees and underbrush were so thick that he could not see more than a few yards ahead. He moved slowly and cautiously over the rocky, uneven ground in the direction he had seen Kitlan go. He entered a stand of pines, carefully parting the drooping boughs as he worked his way along the shore ten feet in from the water's edge.

The sounds of the gun battle carried out across the lake, and Quinn and the six-man Counter Assault Team heard the sharp staccato reports over the noise of the rotors and the wind rushing into the cabin.

'AK-47s,' one of the CAT team members said, having recognized the distinctive sound of the Russian-made assault rifle. 'And a semi-auto shotgun, too, unless somebody's real good with a pump action.'

The pilot and co-pilot had not heard the shooting, and Quinn alerted them to the fact that they were going into a hot landing zone.

'How hot?' Henning shouted above the rotors and the wind noise.

'Don't know. Multiple weapons. Some of them full auto from the sound of it.'

Believing that his men had Stafford and Janet contained for the moment, Tony Kitlan stood at Peter Marcus' side, providing security for him as he placed the Stinger missile on his right shoulder and pulled open the antenna array and sight assembly.

He watched as Marcus pressed a rectangular switch at the front of the launch tube to activate the infrared tracker and to prepare the missile for firing. The deadly weapon was designed to detect the heat from the exhaust of an aircraft and follow it to its source, and Marcus heard a steady tone that changed in pitch and intensity as the tracker quickly locked on to the incoming helicopter's exhaust.

Henning was less than fifty yards from shore when he again slowed the helicopter. He and the co-pilot were continuously scanning the rocky shoreline for any signs of a threat. Had the situation not been so deadly serious, the double-take Henning did would have been comical. He was turning his head slowly, following the shoreline, when he suddenly jerked it back to a spot he had just passed over. In the dense woods thirty yards to the right of the dock, at the edge of the tree line, he saw two men standing on the shore of the lake. One of them appeared to be armed with an assault rifle, but it was the other man who drew Henning's full attention; he had a Stinger missile on his shoulder and was aiming it directly at the helicopter.

'Stinger!' Henning shouted at the top of his lungs. 'Nobody said anything about Stingers! What, are you guys, nuts?'

Marcus was familiar with the relatively uncomplicated process of sighting a Stinger missile to bring down an aircraft under most circumstances; a simple matter of properly leading his target as a duck hunter leads a duck. It was, however, the technique for shooting down a helicopter that was hovering or flying directly toward him with which Marcus was unfamiliar. A technique that was the one exception to the otherwise uncomplicated process.

As he stared down the launcher at the incoming helicopter, Marcus failed to align the Stinger's sights in the precise manner required for the missile to turn toward its target with enough centrifugal force to arm its warhead. He sighted the only way he knew and pulled the trigger, holding it in for the three seconds required to ignite the booster. He felt a weight go off his shoulder as the booster charge propelled the missile from the tube, and then, seconds later, a safe distance away, the main solid-fuel rocket motor kicked in and the Stinger was on the way to its target.

The helicopter was less than thirty yards from shore, slowed almost to the point of hovering, when Henning saw the bright orange flash from the backblast as the missile left the launcher, followed by the thin white contrail from the rocket engine as it sped upward.

Henning knew he had absolutely no hope of completely avoiding the missile, and only a slim chance of limiting the damage to the helicopter with a precisely timed evasive maneuver. His eyes were riveted on the sleek projectile streaking toward him. At the last possible moment, he broke hard to the left and dove to within a few feet of the surface of the lake. The missile followed the helicopter's exhaust trail, but because of the mistake Marcus had made in the sighting, the warhead did not arm itself and Henning's evasive maneuver caused it to strike the tail rotor, shattering it without exploding.

Henning fought for control of the crippled aircraft, but without its tail rotor it began to rotate wildly. Its forward momentum carried it to the shoreline where it crashed into the woods a short distance from where Janet had taken cover behind the boulders.

Janet had seen the missile hit, and she had watched as five men armed with M-16s jumped clear of the helicopter and into the lake near the shore only seconds before it struck the trees and crashed to the ground where it landed on its side.

She saw two injured men, one of them Tom Quinn, and the other the sixth member of the CAT team, crawl from the wreckage. The CAT team member dragged his legs behind him as he moved away from the helicopter. Quinn, who was bleeding from a puncture wound in his right side and was favoring what Janet judged to be a dislocated left shoulder, went back inside the helicopter and pulled out the badly injured and barely conscious Henning, and then returned for the co-pilot who appeared to be dead.

Janet looked behind her and saw the five men who had jumped into the lake coming ashore. They drained the water from their weapons and took up defensive positions in the woods to her right. Quinn spotted Janet and acknowledged with a nod that he knew who she was. The CAT team member with the broken legs stayed behind to cover the pilot and co-pilot and Quinn drew his pistol and stayed low as he made his way over to Janet and crouched next to her behind the boulders.

'Where's Stafford?'

'He went after the guy with the Stinger.'

Three men appeared from behind the cabin and began to move through the woods in the direction of the crash site. Quinn saw them and, at his hand signal, the five members of the CAT team moved out in short rushes.

The three men saw the team closing in on them, but before they could get off a shot they were cut down with a withering barrage of full automatic fire from the M-16s.

The CAT team moved expertly through the woods around the south side of the cabin, sweeping the area for targets of opportunity. The man Janet had wounded in the knee saw them coming and threw down his weapon and shouted for them not to shoot. One of the team members handcuffed him to a tree before they continued on to the rear of the cabin.

As they came around the north side and approached the body of the man Stafford had killed when he ran off the porch, another man, wanting only to cover his escape through the woods, stepped from behind a large oak tree. He emptied his magazine with a poorly aimed burst that went high over the heads of the team. They reacted as one and sent a hail of bullets into the man's body and killed him. They returned to the front of the cabin where Quinn caught their attention and used a hand signal to direct them toward the area where he had seen the Stinger launched.

Chapter Forty-Six

Kitlan and Marcus had watched as the five men armed with M-16s leapt from the helicopter into the lake. Their line of fire from where they knelt at the tree line fifty yards away was partially obscured by limbs overhanging the rocky, uneven shoreline, allowing them no clear shot at any of the men as they surfaced. And after seeing the obviously well-trained and highly disciplined unit move ashore and immediately drop into defensive positions in the woods, they thought better of engaging them.

They heard the exchange of gunfire coming from the direction of the cabin; the CAT team's M-16s clearly the dominant sound. When Kitlan heard no more answering shots from the AK-47s, he realized it was time to cut his losses and run. He led the way as he and Marcus retreated through the woods toward the far end of the cove and the deserted cabin where they had left the Land Cruiser.

Stafford reached the spot where the expended missile launcher lay at the water's edge. He heard someone running through the woods ahead of him and dropped to one knee, his eyes moving along the shoreline in the direction of the sound. The loud snap of a branch drew his attention to a thickly wooded area near the limits of his vision where he saw Kitlan and Marcus emerge from the deep shadows beneath a stand of pines into a section where the trees thinned. They were glancing over their shoulders as they ran.

Stafford got to his feet and ran after them. Marcus saw him coming and stopped to take aim. Stafford closed fast, firing short bursts as he darted through the trees, adjusting his aim with each burst. Before Marcus could get his assault rifle to his shoulder, Stafford found his mark. The bullets first struck the ground at Marcus' feet, then his legs, and finally the center of his chest and his neck. Marcus dropped his weapon and staggered backward, toppling into the lake where he lay motionless in a shallow weed-bed.

Kitlan looked back to see Marcus floating face down in the water. He ran faster, following the path of least resistance in an effort to put enough distance between him and Stafford to get under cover and set up an ambush. He cut deeper into the woods and disappeared into another stand of pines.

Stafford lost sight of Kitlan and stopped running. He inserted a full magazine in his weapon and began to move slowly in the direction he had last seen him. He paused every ten feet to listen, and to check his back trail in the event he was being followed or someone had circled around behind him.

Kitlan reached the far side of the pines and stopped to watch and listen. Certain that Stafford could no longer see him, he dropped into a prone position behind a large dead fall, rested the barrel of his assault rifle on top of the rotted log, stared down the sights and waited.

Janet had helped Quinn remove his suit coat and used it to fashion a makeshift sling for his dislocated shoulder. The gash in his side was bleeding heavily, and she took off Stafford's old corduroy shirt and folded it for him to use as a compress.

She handed him the cellular phone she had taken from his jacket pocket. 'You might want to call nine-one-one and get an ambulance or two in here. Not to mention a semi to haul the bodies out.'

Quinn took the phone as Janet stood up and scanned the woods around her; the only person she saw was the man hand-cuffed to the tree, his face etched with pain.

Quinn watched as she took two shotgun shells from the bandolier across her chest and insert them in the Bennelli's magazine.

223

'Relax. The CAT team's got things under control. Besides, we need to talk.'

'Later.' Janet walked out from behind the boulders and started toward the driveway.

Quinn called out to her. 'Where are you going?'

'Hunting.' She looked over her shoulder as she reached the driveway. 'Keep some pressure on that wound.'

She had listened to the sporadic gunfire from the woods on the other side of the dock. The shots had seemed to be moving farther away from the cabin, and she believed she knew why. At the top of the driveway, she turned and ran down the main road, following it to where it curved around the far end of the cove.

She remembered the overgrown driveway she and Stafford had passed on their run, and when she reached it, she slowed and proceeded cautiously along its edge, staying just inside the tree line until she saw the van and the Land Cruiser parked at the deserted cabin.

She veered off into the woods, bypassing the cabin as she moved forward with even greater caution, holding the shotgun at the ready. She heard something in the underbrush, ahead and to her right. She stopped and froze in position. The only sound was an errant breeze rattling the leaves of a nearby white birch tree, but she knew that was not what she had heard.

She continued on, placing each step toe to heel, lowering her foot gently onto the forest floor as she shifted her weight forward. She paused when she heard the sound again, and slowly moved her eyes over the densely wooded area before her. Her pulse quickened when she spotted something on the ground in the underbrush near a stand of pines. She moved to her right for a better view.

Thirty feet in front of her, she saw Kitlan lying behind a large dead fall, shifting his position to get comfortable. He was facing away from her and staring down the barrel of his weapon. Janet put the shotgun to her shoulder and advanced through the trees, pausing after each step as she silently closed in on him.

Kitlan was so focused and intent on the woods in front of

him that he was completely unaware of Janet's approach. He heard someone off to his left, and looked to see Stafford twenty yards away, studying the ground, tracking him through the trees along the shore. He watched as Stafford found his trail at the point where he had cut deeper into the woods, and then saw him turn and head straight through the pines toward the dead fall.

Kitlan adjusted his position to his left, put his cheek to the assault rifle's stock, and took aim. He saw the Kevlar vest Stafford wore, and he aligned his sights on his head. As he was about to squeeze the trigger, a soft rustling in the brush directly behind him sent a chill down his spine.

Janet stood a few yards away with the Benelli to her shoulder, a light pressure on the trigger. 'Put the gun down.' She spoke just above a whisper with no urgency in her tone.

Kitlan's body stiffened. He lay completely still, watching Stafford approach through the trees, unaware of the deadly drama unfolding ahead of him.

Janet spoke again in the same quiet, emotionless voice. 'You have two choices. Put the gun down, or die. Makes no difference to me either way.'

Kitlan took what he saw as his only chance of escape. Considering Stafford the lesser threat for the moment, he concentrated on Janet, and in a sudden, fluid move, flipped over onto his back to fire at her. It was a desperate and ill-conceived decision.

Before he could swing the barrel of his weapon in Janet's direction, she fired two blasts from the Benelli, sending the equivalent of eighteen thirty-eight caliber slugs into Kitlan's head and chest.

At the sound of the shots, Stafford ran through the deep shadows beneath the towering pines, the barrel of his rifle tracking where he looked. He reached the dead fall to see Janet standing over Kitlan's lifeless body.

She turned to Stafford, her eyes as flat as her voice. 'Do you think he's one of those who killed Eddie?'

'Probably. But he's just a soldier. Not the one who ordered it.'

Stafford looked at the angle of fire Kitlan had from his

ambush position behind the dead fall and understood immediately that he would have been killed were it not for Janet. 'Thanks. I would have walked right into it.'

They both heard something in the woods ahead and quickly swung their weapons in that direction, immediately lowering them to their sides when they saw the CAT team appear out of nowhere.

The team leader came forward as the rest of his men continued to watch the surrounding woods. He looked down at Kitlan's body.

'With him and the guy we saw face down in the lake, we get a count of ten; nine dead, one wounded. Are there any more?'

Stafford shook his head. 'No, that's all I saw.'

'You don't mind if we escort you back to the cabin, just in case you counted wrong?'

'Absolutely not.'

The team leader returned to his men and led them back the way they had come, with Stafford and Janet in the center of the formation as they moved through the woods.

By the time they reached the cabin, the sirens were fast approaching on the lake road. Stafford and Janet helped the CAT team carry the badly injured pilot, and their teammate with the broken legs, out of the woods and lay them on the dock. They went back for the dead co-pilot and placed him a short distance away from the others. Stafford covered him with one of the blankets Janet got from the cabin to keep the injured men warm until help arrived.

Quinn was still on his feet, talking with the leader of the CAT ream, instructing him to call the Scranton field office and arrange for transportation. He appeared to be going into shock from his loss of blood, and Janet convinced him to lie down on the dock, placed a thick wool blanket over him and elevated his feet.

They had completely forgotten about the man handcuffed to the tree until he shouted for help. One of the CAT team members uncuffed him and carried him over his shoulder to the dock where he handcuffed him to piling.

Three rescue squad ambulances from nearby communities arrived within minutes of each other and the EMTs quickly went into action, removing their stretchers and equipment from their vehicles. The scene took on a carnival atmosphere when four state police cruisers, followed by three county sheriff's department vehicles, and two township cop cars arrived almost as a caravan and filled the area cleared of trees at the front and sides of the cabin. Amid dueling radios squawking in the background and flashing roof lights, the various law enforcement factions began arguing over crime-scene protocol.

Quinn was placed on a stretcher and an EMT immediately applied a trauma dressing to the puncture wound in his side to stop the bleeding. He then hooked up an IV, running normal saline wide open, while his partner removed Quinn's suit coat from his dislocated shoulder and replaced it with a proper sling.

Stafford went into the cabin and returned as the EMTs were about to load Quinn's stretcher into the ambulance. His suit coat lay across his legs, and Stafford slipped the computer disk and the two eight millimeter videotapes taken from Ramsey's apartment into an inside pocket.

Quinn watched him do it. 'What's that?'

'If I'm right, the answers to all your questions.'

'We still need to have our conversation.'

'And you still haven't given me one good reason why.'

Quinn smiled through his pain. 'I could give you twenty million reasons why.'

Stafford gave him his best blank stare.

Janet heard the exchange from where she stood a short distance away. She came over and quickly changed the subject. 'You arrived with the cavalry just in the nick of time, Quinn. Thanks.'

'You're welcome. Now I'm going to tell you both one more time; we need to talk, and we're going to talk.'

Janet smiled and winked. 'Absolutely. When you're feeling better.'

'Count on it. And I'm also telling you to back away from this right now. The Secret Service will take it from here on in. Don't go looking for any more trouble.'

Stafford gestured toward the man handcuffed to the dock. 'They came looking for us.'

'Just stay off the horizon until I get this sorted out.' He made direct eye contact with Janet. 'We'll find whoever it was that gave the order to kill your brother.'

Janet's expression clouded. 'Nothing personal, Quinn, but you won't be offended if I don't hold my breath.'

The EMTs loaded Quinn's stretcher and closed the doors. As the ambulance drove away, Stafford looked around to make certain he would not be overheard and turned to Janet. 'He's not going to quit, you know.'

'He can't prove we have the money.'

'But he knows we have it. And he's going to want it back.'

'Like I said—'

'I know,' Stafford interrupted. 'We'll burn that bridge when we come to it.'

They saw another state police cruiser pull in and watched as the driver squeezed past the vehicles already crowded into every available open space. He parked partway into the woods on the north side of the cabin, and Janet smiled to herself as she watched him climb out of the car. He wore lieutenant's bars on his uniform, and the other troopers, who appeared to have been waiting for his arrival, quickly gathered around. After a brief discussion, one of his men pointed toward Stafford and Janet, and the lieutenant marched in their direction, shoulders squared and back braced.

The military creases in his shirt were razor-sharp and perfectly aligned, and the brim of his Smokey Bear hat touched the top of his mirrored sunglasses just so. His black leather belt and pistol holster gleamed bright in the afternoon sun.

Janet turned to Stafford and rolled her eyes. 'Give him a baton and he could lead a parade.'

Stafford stifled a laugh. He thought of Eddie's reaction to the Customs officer at the Canadian border, and was again reminded of how much brother and sister were alike.

'Don't do it, Janet.'

'What? I was just making an observation.' She paused for a moment, then, 'Ten to one if we pants this sucker we find he's wearing starched shorts.'

'Please. I'm begging you. Do not do this. You mess with this guy and we're going to be here all night. Just let me do the talking. I'll tell him what happened and we'll be on our way in no time.'

'Stafford, you hurt my feelings. Do you honestly believe that I, a former DEA agent, would in any way antagonize a fellow member of the brotherhood of law enforcement while in the performance of his duties?'

Stafford simply shook his head, knowing from past experiences with Eddie that once set in motion there was no way to head it off.

The trooper stopped in front of them, and before he could so much as introduce himself, Janet unnerved him by putting an arm around his shoulder, buddy to buddy fashion, and leaned in close as she spoke.

'How are ya doin'?'

'I'm fine, thank you, mam.'

The trooper tried to politely ease his way out of Janet's grasp, but she pulled him in even closer and flashed a wicked smile as she patted his shoulder.

'Good. Glad to hear that. So let me ask you something, Lieutenant. You guys are real sticklers about preserving the integrity of a crime scene. Right?'

'Yes, mam. We certainly are.' The trooper's eyes grew suspicious.

With one arm still around his shoulder, Janet reached across his chest with the other and pointed to where his cruiser was parked on the north side of the cabin, the front end pulled into the woods beneath the trees. 'Is that your cruiser over there?'

The trooper looked where she was pointing. 'Yes it is.'

'Well, this is just a suggestion, you understand, but I was thinking you might want to move it.'

'And why is that, mam?'

'Oh, I don't know, Smokey. Maybe because there's a body under your right front tire.'

Chapter Forty-Seven

The television screen in the fifth floor office at Secret Service headquarters went to static as Tom Quinn pressed the rewind button on the VCR remote. After a few moments, he switched to fast forward and advanced the tape until he found the part in Adam Welsh's meeting at Jeffery Ramsey's apartment where Ramsey had questioned Welsh's instructions. Welsh's response was what Steve Jacoby, the Special-Agent-In-Charge of the Counterfeit Division, wanted to hear again: the one slip, divulged in anger, in an otherwise guarded conversation.

Welsh jabbed a finger in Ramsey's chest as he spoke. He was well within range of the concealed microphone and his words were clear and easily understood.

'I don't care what you think would be best, Jeffery. The DDO's orders to me were detailed and specific. There will be no deviations from the plan. Is that clear?

Quinn stopped the tape, ejected it from the VCR, and handed it to Jacoby. 'We can tie the survivor from the attack at Stafford's cabin to Cameron & Associates. We can tie Ramsey to Paul Cameron and Adam Welsh. And we can tie Welsh to John Galloway. We've got enough to take them all down.'

The SAIC of the Counterfeit Division got up from behind his desk and turned the tape over in his hand as he stood at the window watching the Washington traffic stream by five floors below.

'Galloway is a very influential and politically dangerous

man, Tom. You can't just drag him out of his house in hand-cuffs with a raincoat over his head on what you've got at this point. And there's no way in hell he's going to come in and talk with us voluntarily.'

'Any way you cut it, he's ultimately responsible for the murder of Eddie Barnes. And from all indications, he's not only been running a criminal enterprise involved in selling drugs and passing hundreds of millions of dollars in super-notes, in all probability he set up and controls the apparatus that prints them.'

'You can't prove that.'

'Not yet. But give me some time and I will. I have all the loose threads I need to unravel his entire operation.'

'What about Stafford and the Barnes woman?'

'They're at his place in Chadds Ford, Pennsylvania. I put round-the-clock surveillance on them. Mostly for their own protection.'

'Have they admitted to having the money from the crash site?'

'No. But they have it. In the end they'll listen to reason.'

'And if they don't?'

'We can always play hardball. But as I said before, I think this stopped being about the money when Eddie Barnes was killed. They want to see whoever was responsible brought to justice.'

'You'll never connect Galloway or Welsh, or for that matter even Paul Cameron, to the death of Eddie Barnes. Not unless one of them points a finger at the others. And I can't see that happening.'

'Maybe not. But even if I can't, I can still bury them on the counterfeiting charges. I have evidence that ties Galloway and Welsh to everything Cameron's men were doing.'

'All circumstantial.'

'There are witnesses who can connect the dots.'

'Drug dealers and convicted felons.'

'I have phone records to establish their relationship, and that they were in contact with each other at critical times when large shipments of supernotes were coming into this country.'

'With no recordings of what was said.'

231

'I have the tapes from Ramsey's apartment.'

'Subject to interpretation.'

'Preponderance of evidence. We've gotten convictions with a lot less.'

'Not against men like these. They'll have the best lawyers from the best law firms.'

'So what are you saying? We do nothing?'

'No. I'm not arguing with you about what should be done. Only about the best way to do it. Keep in mind that you're talking about bringing down one of the most powerful men in the CIA, along with the head of their Counter Narcotics Center. When this gets out the media will go into a feeding frenzy. The political fallout will be enormous. And we still don't know how high up this goes. What if it doesn't stop with Galloway?'

'Then we go where it leads us; no one's above the law. Just tell me how you want me to proceed.'

'With the stakes being what they are, I'm afraid that decision's a little above my pay grade. I have a meeting set up with the Director and the Assistant Director for Investigations at ten fifteen. I'll get back to you after we've talked.'

'Let me take a run at Welsh and Cameron. We've got them on tape. That's our strongest evidence. If I can convince them they're looking at a minimum of fifty years on the counterfeiting charges alone, I guarantee you I'll get one of them to flip.'

'I'll let you know what the Director says.'

Chapter Forty-Eight

Sam Wilson, the President's national security advisor, arrived unrecognized and unattended at the sidewalk café in the Georgetown section of Washington as the last of the evening light faded on what had been a perfect fall day in the nation's capital. The meeting with Lloyd Dixon, the Director of the Secret Service, had been hastily arranged only one hour earlier, at a location removed from the ever-vigilant eyes of the White House press corps. Wilson had come directly from the Oval Office to personally inform Dixon of the President's decision regarding what was at best a potential political disaster for his administration.

Wilson spotted the Secret Service Director at a table in a darkened, candle-lit corner of the quiet café and eased into a chair beside him. He waved off an approaching waiter and leaned in close to avoid being overheard. The two men spoke in hushed tones for only a few moments, then Wilson reached across the table, shook Dixon's hand, and left.

Dixon stared after him as he disappeared among the Friday evening crowd of shoppers and college students that filled the sidewalks. He was angered over the decision handed down, but it had not surprised him; in the detached and analytical corner of his mind he had suspected that it might end this way.

During his twenty-eight years with the Secret Service, he had been assigned to protection details for two Presidents, and eventually risen to become Special-Agent-In-Charge of the Presidential Protection Division, and later the Assistant

Director for Protection Operations. Having spent that much concentrated time in close proximity to the machinations of White House politics, he knew all too well that difficult situations with the potential for embarrassing or damaging the administration and the President, when no other solution was at hand, often got conveniently resolved and covered up by being classified top secret for 'reasons of national security'.

Dixon nursed the drink he had ordered on arriving at the café and glanced at his watch for the third time in as many minutes, eager to have the evening over with. If the man with whom the President wanted him to meet and work out their differences was on time, Dixon estimated that he could still get to see most of his daughter Maggie's performance in the fall play at Madison High School in nearby Vienna, Virginia.

At six thirty sharp Dixon's pager beeped. He looked at the display and read the message 'Six fifty', telling him that the man he was to meet was en route to the prearranged meeting site and would be there in twenty minutes. He left the money for his drink on the table and walked back to where he had parked his car in a small lot across the street from the Georgetown Club.

Dixon drove east on M Street to Pennsylvania Avenue, where he turned right and continued on to Washington Circle. He then headed south on Twenty-Third Street, and for the first time in he did not remember how long, he checked to see if he was being followed.

When he reached the intersection at Constitution Avenue, he turned left and parked at the curb just beyond Henry Bacon Drive, near the Vietnam Memorial. He got out of the car and stood beneath the trees, watching for anyone who had pulled over in response to his stopping. Satisfied that he was not followed, he left the sidewalk, stepped over the railing, and walked across the grass toward the Reflecting Pool.

Off in the distance, approaching from the opposite direction, he saw a tall, shadowy figure backlit by the Lincoln Memorial. As the figure drew closer, Dixon recognized Earl Lockwood, a reclusive man who shunned publicity and had spent his entire adult life in the intelligence community. He was well-liked and respected by anyone who had ever dealt with him, and he had served the current President as Director of the Central Intelligence Agency for the past six years.

Dixon first met Lockwood fourteen years ago, when he was on the protection detail of a former President and Lockwood was then the national security advisor. Dixon recalled hearing at the time that Lockwood's nickname, for reasons never divulged, was Frosty, and that no one other than his closest friends dared call him that.

Dixon looked around and saw no sign of the security detail that always accompanied the DCI wherever he went, but he knew they were somewhere nearby keeping a watchful eye on the nation's spymaster.

As the two men came abreast of each other, Lockwood motioned for Dixon to walk with him around the Reflecting Pool.

'I don't get as much exercise as I should these days,' he told the Secret Service Director, his voice a soft Kentucky drawl. 'I used to run three miles every morning. Now I'm lucky if I can walk the same distance without stopping to rest.'

Dixon, who exercised regularly and was in excellent physical condition, simply nodded, waiting for the DCI to get to the point of the meeting, which he promptly did.

'First let me apologize for this godforsaken mess. I should have been on top of it, and I wasn't. No excuses. All the signs were there for anyone who took the time to look.'

'Does it go any higher than John Galloway?'

'No. He and Adam Welsh were the only two active CIA employees knowingly involved. It was a rogue operation from start to finish. You have my word on that.'

'I want some guarantees that the counterfeiting part of Galloway's operations will be completely destroyed, along with the ability to start it up again.'

'I understand. Let me tell you what's been done so far. As of this morning we secured the presses he used to print the supernotes in a warehouse on the outskirts of Paris. They are being dismantled and will be shipped back to the Bureau of Engraving and Printing, along with the hand-engraved plates. The remaining stock of currency paper on which the money was printed will be destroyed, along with the pallets of the most recently printed supernotes we found packaged and ready for shipment.'

'How much?'

'Four hundred million. Galloway was nothing if not enterprising.'

'I want agents from our Paris office present while the currency paper and the counterfeit notes are destroyed, and I want the plates turned over to them.'

'Done and done.'

'I was told that Galloway and Welsh are being allowed to resign.'

'With forfeiture of all pensions and privileges,' Lockwood added with emphasis.

Dixon smiled at the notion that loss of their pensions would hold any significance for Galloway and Welsh. 'Something tells me they'll manage without them.'

'I suspect you're right. But under the circumstances it was all we could do. No one wanted any of this to see the light of day, let alone drag it through the courts.'

'And Paul Cameron?'

'He's out of business as of today. We've shut down his offices worldwide and confiscated his files. There are some other highly classified matters involved, so I can't turn all of the files over to you, but if we find anything in them pertaining to the counterfeiting operation I will personally see that they are hand-delivered to you.'

'Cameron gets a walk, too?'

'I'm afraid so. All part of the deal.'

Dixon tried but failed to hide the anger in his voice. 'They're murderers and thieves.'

'No one is more aware of that than I am. And if there was any other way of balancing the scales without jeopardizing the President and his administration, I would be the first to order it done.'

Dixon read the subtext. 'Galloway took precautions against retaliation in the event he was caught?'

'Let's just say he was a very resourceful and cautious man with highly developed instincts for self preservation.'

Lockwood stopped walking and looked casually over his shoulder. It was a prearranged signal that brought two of his security guards out of the shadows to accompany him back to his chauffeured car.

'Again, I sincerely apologize for this. And I'm especially regretful of the inadequate resolution. I can only tell you that I will do everything I can to see that nothing like it happens again on my watch.'

'Let's hope not on anyone's watch.'

The two men shook hands and Lockwood turned and walked back toward the Lincoln Memorial. His security detail immediately moved from their stand-off positions and came forward and flanked him, escorting him back to his world of secrets and intrigue.

Dixon looked at his watch. If he hurried, he could still make the opening of his daughter's play. As he walked back to his car, he considered calling the head of his counterfeit division, and the agent who had been in charge of the investigation. But they were not calls he relished making, and he decided to wait until the following morning when he could speak to Jacoby and Quinn in person.

Chapter Forty-Nine

Following an early morning cross-country run through the rolling farmland of Chester County, Pennsylvania, Ben Stafford and Janet Barnes continued their workout in the gym on the upper level of the bank barn at Stafford's home in Chadds Ford. The gym was fully equipped with a complete circuit of weight machines, and a heavy bag that hung from a rafter on a thick chain in one corner.

Janet pulled on a pair of workout gloves as Stafford began with four sets of ten repetitions each on the incline press. A television sat on a stand near the door; the volume was up and it was tuned to the ABC News Sunday morning talk show, *This Week*.

Janet started her workout with a series of combination punches that struck the heavy bag with authority, rocking it and sending it swinging. The blows came harder and faster as she established a rhythm, occasionally dancing gracefully back to launch a kick with amazing quickness that landed high up on the bag.

The rapid-fire thuds of her workout drew Stafford's attention. He stopped his exercises to watch her bob and weave as she delivered the solid punches and kicks non-stop, her face tense, her eyes on fire as though the bag was more than an inanimate object.

'Anybody I know?'

'My former boss at DEA.'

Janet's expression suddenly changed. She stopped punching

238

and turned her attention to the television, staring at the screen in disbelief.

The five regulars on the panel were engaged in the round-table discussion part of the show, touching briefly on a variety of topics from the week's events in and around the nation's capital. Janet had heard the mention of Adam Welsh along with the CIA's Deputy Director for Operations. She remembered Welsh's name on the label of the videotape from the meeting in Ramsey's apartment, and that the DDO had been referred to during the conversation on the tape.

Stafford heard Janet repeatedly mutter the word 'no', and he got up from the incline-press machine and came over and stood by her side.

They listened as George Will commented on the speculation among Washington insiders concerning the two high-level resignations at the Central Intelligence Agency. Sam Donaldson added that the word around town was that the Deputy Director for Operations had left after thirty-three years of service to take an exceptionally lucrative job in the private sector, and that Adam Welsh was the latest casualty in the failure of the war on drugs, adding that the Counter Narcotics Center was for the most part ineffectual in its efforts and needed new leadership.

Cokie Roberts was skeptical of Donaldson's explanation, offering the opinion that the CIA were past-masters of spin and with them one never knew what was smoke and mirrors and what was reality. Having no further information they could sink their teeth into, the panel moved on to the next topic.

'Son of a bitch!' Janet shouted. 'Son of a bitch!' She stripped off the heavy bag gloves and threw them across the room. 'They let them resign. The rotten, lying bastards covered it up and let them resign.'

Stafford said nothing and went back to the incline press. He continued his exercises as Janet paced back and forth across the gym.

'So what do we do now? Huh? Those slimy murdering bastards had my brother killed and they get away with it?'

Stafford did another set of repetitions, his face a silent mask of anger and frustration.

'Answer me, Stafford. What do we do now? Say something, goddamn it.'

Stafford stopped exercising and got up and walked toward the door without comment.

'What? That's it? You're quitting? Eddie's death means nothing to you?'

Stafford's temper erupted from the rage that was building inside him. He turned and shouted at Janet, startling her and causing her to take a step back.

'This is not how it ends! Do you understand? This is not how it ends? They do not kill Eddie and then walk away with a slap on the wrist! The system may have failed to set things right, but I will not.'

Janet recovered her composure and softened her tone. 'So what do we do?'

Stafford's voice held its hard edge. 'I don't know. But there is no way in hell I let it end like this.'

Janet came forward and took both his hands in hers. 'I'm sorry. I didn't mean what I said. I know you loved Eddie. I'm just so damn angry I can't think straight.'

'I'm taking you back to Washington this morning.'

Janet released his hands. 'Taking me back? What is that supposed to mean?'

'I don't want you involved in anything I might have to do.'

'You're dumping me?'

'I'm not dumping you. I have to do this part alone.'

'Why? You think I'm some incompetent moron incapable of helping you?'

'You know better than that. I just don't want both of us in jail if things go wrong.'

Janet calmed down and lowered her voice. 'How long is this going to take?'

'Two or three days.'

'Okay. But I want to be included in whatever action you take against Galloway and Welsh; you owe me that. And if I don't hear from you within seventy-two hours, I'm going after them on my own.'

'Fair enough.'

*

Stafford and Janet showered and changed and ate breakfast before packing for the trip to Washington. As he was about to leave the house, Stafford stopped to check his answering unit to make certain there were no calls from his daughter's doctor; he was in the habit of checking whenever he was away from the telephone for any length of time, sometimes calling in to retrieve his messages as often as every hour, depending on how heavily Annie weighed on his thoughts that day.

Besides the usual messages from Nardini, the bail bonds-man in Philadelphia, there was a message from Tom Quinn asking Stafford and Janet to contact him. Quinn left his home, office, and cellular numbers. The message was time-stamped within minutes after the *This Week* television show ended.

'Do you want to call him?'

Janet shook her head. 'What's the point? And how did he know I was here with you?'

As Stafford drove out of his driveway, Janet immediately spotted the dark-blue Mercury sedan with two men in the front seat that pulled out from a side road and began to follow them.

'Secret Service?'

'That would explain how Quinn knew you were here.'

Janet turned and looked out the rear window. 'I always thought of the Secret Service as the elite of the federal law enforcement agencies. You would think they'd be a little better at their jobs, wouldn't you?'

'They are. This is probably their way of letting us know they haven't forgotten about us, or the twenty million.'

'It's not the brightest goddamn thing they've ever done. I mean if I were them, I would take into serious consideration our recent experiences with people sneaking up on us, and also that we don't really know who they are. Which presents the distinct possibility that we might start shooting at them.'

Still not entirely comfortable with the presence of the car behind them, Janet took her pistol from her shoulder bag and tucked it into the waistband at the front of her slacks. Stafford unzipped his leather jacket for quick access to the pistol in the shoulder holster he was wearing beneath it, and continued down the narrow country road, watching in the rear-view mirror as the car paced them from a distance of only a few hundred yards.

'Hang on.'

Stafford cut the wheel hard and drove the rented Ford Explorer off the road and into a neighbor's field, bouncing and swaying across the uneven pasture land. Janet looked back to see the Mercury stop at the side of the road, unable to follow. The man in the front passenger seat talked into a two-way radio.

'They probably have a second car watching the road leading out the back of your property.'

'For all the good it'll do them.'

Stafford left the field at the top of a rise and turned onto a farm track that led through a thick stand of woods. At that point, the agents in the surveillance car at the side of the road lost visual contact with the Explorer. Stafford emerged from the woods at the far side of his house onto the same road he had left. He was behind the Secret Service car now, but around a sharp bend and well out of sight. He drove in the opposite direction, following a circuitous route over back country roads, eventually taking Route 202 to where it intersected with I-95, then heading south on the heavily traveled interstate highway toward Washington.

'Don't take this the wrong way, Stafford; it's not that I think you're a slow learner or anything, but you do have your cellular phone turned off, right?

'Bite me, Barnes.'

'In your dreams maybe.'

Chapter Fifty

The cellular phone in Janet's shoulder bag rang as she was unlocking her car in the parking lot of the Delaney Funeral Home in Fairfax, Virginia. She placed the cloisonné urn containing her brother's remains on the front seat and answered the call, breathing a silent sigh of relief at the sound of Stafford's voice.

'You just made it under the wire, Stafford. You had two hours left out of the seventy-two we agreed on.'

'Pack a bag for the islands.'

'Which islands?'

'The Leeward Islands. Get down here immediately. I'm not sure how much longer the window of opportunity is going to last.'

'What window?'

'I'll tell you when you get here.'

'I'll get there a lot faster if you tell me which Leeward Island.'

'Saint Martin. I already booked a flight for you. I prepaid the ticket in cash, so don't use your credit cards for anything that will leave a trail down here.'

'Which airline and which flight?'

'American Airlines. Leaves Dulles at eleven fifteen with a connection in San Juan that puts you in here around five thirty. It's eight forty now, that gives you less than two hours to pack and get out to the airport an hour before your flight leaves.'

'No problem.'

'Are you under surveillance?'

'They've been watching me round the clock for the past two days.'

'Can you shake them?'

'Oh, I'll think of something.'

Stafford hung up the payphone at the ferry dock and walked back to his table at the sidewalk café overlooking Marigot Harbor. It was the off-season, and the picturesque old town was quiet and peaceful with few tourists at the cafés or shopping in the expensive boutiques. Palm trees swayed in a gentle island breeze and the tropical sun sparked off the blue-green waters of the Caribbean, but the ambiance of the place was lost on Stafford. He sat drinking beer from a long-necked bottle and using the binoculars he had purchased in a camera shop to look out across the harbor to where the two-hundred-foot luxury motor yacht *Invincible* was anchored fifty yards offshore.

Stafford had begun his search three days ago by calling in a favor from a Washington, DC detective who got him Adam Welsh's unlisted telephone number and home address. Later that night, Stafford established that the split-level house on a cul-de-sac in Rockville, Maryland was deserted and that it had a rudimentary security system. The heavily landscaped lot had a six-foot-high hedge that concealed the rear terrace from the neighbor's view and gave him all the cover he needed to bypass the security system and gain entrance through a terrace door in the early morning hours.

He found what he was looking for on a desk in a small study off the master bedroom: the name of an airline and two flight numbers scribbled on the back of an envelope by the telephone. A call to the airline later that morning told him that the first flight was to Miami and the second a connecting flight to Saint Martin.

Among the array of photographs on the shelves above the built-in desk, Stafford found one showing Cameron and Welsh, whom he recognized from the tapes in Ramsey's apartment, with Galloway, whom he identified from a photo he had pulled

244

up during a Nexis-Lexis search for information about him. The three men were standing on the aft deck of a large motor yacht. The picture had been taken by someone on the dock, and the name *Invincible* was clearly visible on the fantail.

Later that same morning, Stafford placed a call to a member of the New York Yacht Club, a criminal defense attorney for whom he had done some work in the past, and asked him if he could find out who owned the yacht *Invincible*. After consulting Wood's International Yacht Registry, the attorney called back to tell him that the yacht was registered to Cameron & Associates. The registry also provided former names of the yacht under previous owners, and revealed that the *Invincible* was once called the *Wayward Wind*. The always thorough attorney had located a brochure prepared by the former owner when the *Wayward Wind* was for sale. He faxed the photographs and schematics to Stafford at his hotel room, noting that Cameron & Associates had purchased the yacht for forty-seven million dollars.

Stafford next called the Port Captain in Philipsburg, Sint Maarten, on the Dutch side of the island, who informed him that the *Invincible* was not in port at present. A call to the Port Captain in Marigot, Saint Martin, on the French side, confirmed Stafford's hunch; the *Invincible* was at anchor in Marigot Harbor.

Stafford dropped the Ford Explorer off at the rental agency's lot at Washington's Reagan Airport and paid cash for a ticket to Miami, where three hours later he rented another car and went to see Charlie Dardas, an old friend with whom he had served in Special Forces before joining Delta Force, and who now ran an import-export firm.

Dardas had always been an edge-walker, and Stafford had never asked him precisely what it was he imported and exported, and the information was never volunteered. But his old friend also asked no questions when Stafford told him what he needed, getting the items for him within one hour of his arrival.

After leaving Dardas' waterfront office with the items carefully packaged and disguised in a manner that would not draw the attention of a customs officer at his destination, Stafford took elaborate measures to make certain he was not being followed. He then stopped at a luggage store and purchased two identical black nylon duffle bags of the type seen in abundance at any airport. At a Good Will store in Fort Lauderdale, he bought a selection of used men's clothing and filled one of the bags with clothes in his proper size and the other with clothes that were far too small for him.

He next dropped his car off at the rental agency's location in Miami, and changed taxis three times, again filtering out any possible surveillance, before buying a ticket to Saint Martin at a Boca Raton travel agency. He arrived at the airport two hours early for his flight and promptly stored the identical duffle bags in separate lockers before going to the boarding gate to wait for other early arrivals to check in.

Twenty minutes later, a man traveling alone took a seat in the boarding area. Stafford got up and purposely tripped over the man's carry-on bag, then picked it up and apologized for his clumsiness. He made a mental note of the man's name and address on the luggage tag, and after a brief conversation that established the man was in fact going to Saint Martin, Stafford excused himself and left the area.

He went to the bank of lockers where he had stored the two identical bags and filled out and attached a luggage tag bearing the stranger's name and address to the duffle bag containing the too-small clothing and the items he had gotten from Dardas. He put an identical handwritten luggage tag with his own name and address on the second bag.

Stafford then took the duffle bags outside the terminal and waited until the porters checking luggage at the curb were inundated with passengers hurrying to catch their flights. He showed the porter his ticket and his passport photo for identification and handed him the bags. The harried porter took no notice that the name tags on the bags were different. He gave Stafford two luggage claim stubs and sent the bags on their way. Stafford had noted which claim check went on which bag, and once back inside the terminal, he threw away the claim check stub for the bag containing the items from Dardas, then boarded the flight with a carry-on bag he had packed for the trip.

The ruse was an old one, but like many tried and true methods, when done properly and under the right circumstances it still worked. Stafford knew that bags leaving Miami for Caribbean resorts, unless in response to a specific threat alert, were seldom, if ever, X-rayed for content or scanned with sensors, there were too many high-risk routes placing priority demands on the security personnel in the busy airport. But in the event the bags were X-rayed or scanned, and the contents discovered, the man whose name was on the luggage tag would be the one questioned. Considering the commonality of the black duffle bag, there was virtually no chance that the busy porter would recall that Stafford had checked it in.

If the bag made it to Saint Martin, and the items Dardas had provided were examined and recognized for what they were when Stafford attempted to get them through customs, he could simply claim that he had picked up the wrong bag. The too-small clothing would add weight to his argument, along with the identical suitcase with his own name tag. Though far from foolproof, any half-decent defense attorney could get the case against him thrown out of court as a matter of course.

Upon arriving in Saint Martin, Stafford retrieved the 'wrong' duffle bag, removed the name tag bearing the fellow passenger's name and address and tossed it into a trash receptacle. The luggage claim stub he had kept was within one digit of being the same as the one he had thrown away in Miami, and he twisted and tore the claim check attached to the bag so that the one number that did not match was unreadable.

He held up the bag with the defaced claim check attached and presented the stub for the second bag to a disinterested woman who was doing little more than glancing at the luggage as the passengers left the claim area. She barely looked at either the claim check on the bag or the stub in Stafford's hand, and he continued on through a cursory customs inspection without incident.

With the duffle bag locked in the trunk of the car he rented, Stafford went back inside the terminal. He showed his airline ticket and the claim check for the second duffle bag and explained that he had forgotten one of his bags. He then returned to the luggage claim section and pretended to look for it.

A noisy, milling crowd who had just deplaned from another flight and were intent on finding their own luggage, made it easy for Stafford to conceal what he was about to do. He pulled the second bag aside and removed his own name tag and the luggage claim check from the handle and placed them in his pocket before putting the bag back and leaving the terminal.

Janet was back in her apartment in Fairfax within fifteen minutes of Stafford's call. She quickly showered and dressed, then packed what she was taking in a carry-on bag and the small day-pack she had used at the cabin, tossing in her passport and leaving out her gun. She called Beth Cooper, a close friend who worked out with her at the gym and ran with her on most days, and asked her to come over immediately. Cooper, who lived in a nearby apartment complex, arrived ten minutes later.

Janet had chosen her because they were the same size and build, and at a glance looked somewhat alike. By the time Cooper left the apartment wearing Janet's workout clothes and distinctive wraparound sunglasses and cap, there was no telling them apart at a distance.

Janet looked down on the parking area from behind her third floor window and saw Cooper drive away in her vintage Volkswagen Beetle. The dark-blue sedan with two men in it she had spotted earlier on her way to the funeral home immediately pulled out from where they were parked across the street and began to follow Janet's car.

Janet grabbed her carry-on bag and the day-pack and quickly left the apartment. She took Cooper's Saab convertible as planned, and drove directly to Dulles airport where she parked in the short term lot and put the key and the parking stub in a sandwich bag and taped them under the right front fender.

Stafford watched Janet get off the airplane at Queen Juliana airport and waited outside the terminal until she cleared customs. She came out into the late afternoon sun dressed for

248

the tropics in an emerald-green silk T-shirt and an off-white jacket and slacks that had more wrinkles than a Sharpei.

'You take a sauna in those clothes?'

'They're linen, you philistine. It's a look.'

'What look is that, bag lady?' Stafford helped her with her luggage, taking the day-pack from her shoulder.

Janet held on to one of the straps. 'Careful with that.'

'What's in it?'

'Eddie. He once told me if anything ever happened to him he wanted his ashes scattered on the ocean. I was going to do it at Rehoboth Beach, but this place is even better. He used to talk about coming down here to go diving.'

'Yeah, I remember.'

'Well now he's here.' She released her grip on the day-pack and Stafford held it firmly in both hands. 'I take it you've found Galloway and Welsh.'

'And Cameron.'

'I'm impressed.'

'Don't be. I track people for a living.'

As Janet climbed in the rental car, Stafford put her carry-on bag and the day-pack with the urn holding Eddie's remains on the back seat, securing the day-pack in place with a seat belt before getting behind the wheel.

'So what's the plan?'

'I have it worked out, but after you hear what I have to say, I want you to give it some careful consideration before you commit to getting involved. I'm going through with it either way, but I want you to be certain. If you're not, then it's going to be best if you put some distance between us.'

Stafford talked and Janet listened as he drove to the French side of the island over a narrow winding road that took them through low rolling hills and picturesque seaside valleys. He told her in detail what he had learned and what he planned to do. When he finished, Janet's response came without the slightest hesitation.

'Count me in.'

Chapter Fifty-One

John Galloway and Adam Welsh were having a drink on the aft deck of the *Invincible* when Paul Cameron came out of the air-conditioned main salon carrying a mahogany case the approximate size of a cigar box. All three men were dressed for dinner on shore, and Galloway, his salt and pepper hair combed straight back, was resplendent in an orange silk shirt worn under a white linen and silk suit by Armani, and black, sueded leather Ferragamo deck shoes.

Galloway had taken one of the yacht's tenders to a secluded beach on the nearby island of Anguilla that morning, where he had spent the day lying in the sun and snorkeling; after only three days his tan was already deep and golden. He had the thousand-yard stare that often comes after a day in the tropical sun and salt air, and he sat completely relaxed, watching a pelican dive for fish near the edge of the breakwater as the sun dropped below the horizon.

Cameron made himself a drink and joined Galloway and Welsh at the octagon-shaped table in the center of the aft deck, placing the mahogany case before them.

Galloway turned his attention to the case. 'This is them?'

'Yes. One of my men brought them from Brussels this morning.'

'Have you examined them?'

'They're as good, if not better, than the ones we were using.'

Galloway opened the case and smiled. Inside the custom-fitted, thickly padded interior was a duplicate set of hand-engraved plates for the one hundred dollar bill. He removed one of the plates, then the other, admiring the workmanship, then addressed Welsh.

'And the engraver?'

'Run down by a truck as he stepped off a curb in Brussels yesterday morning. Killed instantly.'

Galloway simply nodded and placed the engraved plates back in the case before turning to Cameron.

'You talked to our friends in Aruba?'

'Paulo already has things set in motion.'

Since receiving the Director of the Central Intelligence Agency's ultimatum, Galloway's only concern, other than the contents of the mahogany case, were the proceeds from their drug sales deposited in numbered bank accounts in Europe.

'How much were you able to transfer out of our Austrian and Liechtenstein accounts before the DCI had our assets frozen?'

'All but seventy-two million.'

'Which leaves us . . . ?'

'Three hundred and forty-seven million and change. I divided it among our accounts in the Cayman and Curacao banks.'

'You took precautions?'

'I wired it in and out of so many different shell company accounts and banks that they'll never be able to trace it.'

The sound of a motor launch disturbed the calm of the velvet Caribbean evening as two of the crew brought one of the yacht's tenders around to the steps on the starboard side of the yacht. Called the Med ladder, the steps were used exclusively for boarding tenders and were usually left in place while at anchor.

The three men finished their drinks and, joined by the captain, descended the ladder and boarded the waiting tender.

Stafford and Janet sat on a bench in the shadows beneath a palm tree at the edge of the quay, looking out across the harbor. They had been taking turns observing the activity on board the *Invincible*. Janet had the binoculars and zoomed in

251

on Galloway as the tender roared away from the huge yacht and headed for shore.

'I'll say one thing for the murdering bastard, he sure knows how to dress.'

Stafford watched the tender draw closer and pull into the dock a hundred yards from where he and Janet sat hidden in the shadows. All four men, accompanied by the two crew members who, judging from their actions, were serving as bodyguards, got out and walked to the far end of the street, where they entered a restaurant.

'I counted ten crew not including the captain,' Stafford said. 'Five who came ashore fifteen minutes ago and went to the bar around the corner. Two with the captain and our guys. Which leaves a three-man security detail still on board.'

'An all-male crew's a little out of the ordinary, isn't it? I remember seeing some of the tapes of the drug baron's yachts DEA had under surveillance in Florida. They always had at least a few women on the crew to do the housekeeping and serve the food and drinks.'

'Which maybe tells us something about what we're dealing with.'

Stafford picked up the small waterproof dive bag he had purchased earlier and slung it over his shoulder as he and Janet got up and walked across the quay to where a narrow cobbled side street led away from the waterfront. Halfway up the block the sound of calypso music blared from a brightly lit bar whose rowdy patrons were spilling out into the street.

The bar was called the Winch Ape, a hole-in-the-wall where more than thirty customers inside required standing shoulder to shoulder. It was a popular gathering place for the crews from the luxury motor yachts and sailboats that anchored in Marigot Harbor; a place where they could drink and catch up on all the latest gossip about friends working on other yachts around the world, and the peccadilloes and activities of their wealthy owners. Most of the clientele wore knit polo shirts embroidered with the name of the yachts on which they worked, and the accents heard were predominantly English, with a few Irish and Scots thrown in the mix.

Stafford gestured toward the lively scene outside the bar.

'You're on, Barnes. All I need to know is how much longer the *Invincible* is going to be in port, so don't get anyone's antenna up by pressing for information we don't need. And remember, we've got a time element.'

Janet had changed in the room Stafford reserved for her in the beachfront resort he checked into on arrival. She was now dressed provocatively in shorts and a light cotton top revealing a bare midriff. She started up the narrow side street and Stafford reached out and held her arm.

'Be careful, huh? These guys are not the normal yacht crew. They look like hard cases, and they probably work for Cameron in other capacities as well.'

Janet smiled and winked. 'Not to worry, Stafford. I'll use all my girlish charms.'

'Now I am worried.'

Janet continued up the street, moving to the calypso beat emanating from the bar as she walked. Stafford's eyes followed her, and he recalled a story Eddie had told him; that he had honest-to-God once seen a man walk into a pole and knock himself out staring at her. Stafford had no difficulty understanding how that might have happened. His thoughts quickly returned to the task ahead as he walked back to the quay to keep watch on the *Invincible* and the restaurant where Galloway, Welsh and Cameron had gone for dinner.

A raw-boned Irishman, the engineer off a motor yacht anchored on the Dutch side of the island, stood outside the door of the Winch Ape drinking Killian's Irish Red straight from a pitcher and holding up the wall. His bleary eyes fell on Janet as she approached the entrance, but all he could manage of the charming smile that usually won the ladies' hearts was a silly grin that spread slowly across his blissful face. He mumbled something incoherent, then laughed to himself and attempted to put a proprietary arm around Janet's waist as she reached the open door. Janet sidestepped him and smiled at the harmless gesture, shaking an admonishing finger as she continued to move to the calypso beat and went inside the noisy, crowded bar.

She caught the immediate attention of every man inside,

and she spotted her target in less than a minute: a tall, ruggedly handsome blond sitting at a corner table and sharing a pitcher of beer with two of his crew mates from the *Invincible*.

Janet saw him staring at her, undressing her with his eyes, and making no effort to hide his open admiration. She heard him comment to his friends in a loud voice and distinct English accent as he jerked a thumb toward her.

'Now there's a lovely bird if there ever was one.'

Janet smiled broadly and danced over to the table where the three men sat. Pretending to have had a few drinks too many, she plopped herself into the lap of the tall, handsome Englishman.

'I love a man with an English accent. It's sooooo sexy.'

'That's me, love. Sexy Harry.'

Janet did a passable imitation of a cockney accent. 'Well, 'arry, if you're a real gent and pour me a beer, I just may let you tickle me fancy.'

Harry beamed and poured as his friends stared dumbfounded, more than a little envious of his good fortune.

Fifteen minutes later, Janet left with the information she came for and returned to the quay to find Stafford seated on the bench beneath the palm tree, alternately watching the yacht and the restaurant at the far end of the street. He lowered the binoculars when he heard her approaching.

'They leave for Aruba at two o'clock tomorrow afternoon.'

'You're positive.'

'The guy I zeroed in on was more than a little interested in me. I told him I already had plans for tonight, but I could meet him tomorrow. That's when he told me when they were leaving.'

'And he definitely said it was tomorrow at two?'

'Absolutely. I gave him my best disappointed look and told him I'd be at the nude beach at three o'clock tomorrow afternoon. So trust me on this one, Stafford. If there was any possibility of Harry making it to that beach, he would have told me.'

Stafford smiled. 'Okay. My guess is we have at least an hour to an hour and a half before any of them return to the yacht.'

'One more thing. You were right about them not being your run-of-the-mill yacht crew. I checked out Harry and the two at the table with him, then the other two on my way out. They were all wearing ankle holsters. If I had to guess I'd say they were packing small automatics, probably three-eighties.'

'And you can bet they've got a lot heavier stuff than that on board.'

Stafford made one last sweep of the *Invincible*'s decks with the binoculars then put them in the waterproof dive bag.

'How does it look?'

'Two of them are at the stern, having a beer and a cigarette on the swim platform. I haven't been able to locate the third one.'

'So is it a go?'

'It's a go.'

Stafford picked up the dive bag and walked toward the finger piers near the ferry dock with Janet at his side. He paused and gave her a long thoughtful look. 'You know I could probably make it to that nude beach at three tomorrow.'

It was the first time he had heard Janet truly laugh, and it relieved some of the tension they were both feeling as they walked out onto the pier.

Chapter Fifty-Two

The lights of the sailboats and yachts anchored in the harbor sparkled like diamonds off the dark water as Stafford, barefoot and wearing only shorts and a T-shirt, rowed the rubber dinghy away from the pier. He used the other boats whenever possible to screen his approach to the *Invincible*, while Janet alternately trained the binoculars on the two men on the swim platform and scanned the decks for the third man, looking for any indications they were being observed.

The dinghy belonged to a young couple whom Janet had seen coming ashore from a small sailboat earlier that evening. As they waited for a taxi, she had heard them talking about going to one of the casinos on the Dutch side of the island, and rightly reasoned that they would not be back until late that night.

The dinghy served two purposes: rather than Stafford having to swim out to the yacht and drip water on the decks that would reveal his presence, it allowed him to stay dry, and it gave Janet a means to approach the swim platform at the stern and engage the two men in conversation, keeping them from going back inside the yacht unexpectedly until Stafford was finished and ready to swim back to shore.

The water in the harbor was calm as they came up on the *Invincible*'s bow, and Stafford stayed in close to her starboard side to lessen the chances of being seen by anyone on deck as he rowed up to the Med ladder and climbed silently out of the boat. Without a word, Janet took over the oars and continued rowing toward the stern where the voices of the two men on the swim platform could be heard.

The *Invincible* was anchored farther out in the harbor than any of the other boats, her port side to shore, with only the moonlit water of the bay and, off in the distance, the island of Angulla visible from her starboard side. Consequently, Stafford did not have to worry about anyone from another boat seeing him as he slung the small dive bag across his back and climbed the Med ladder.

Once on board, he stood flat against the outside bulkhead and looked forward and aft, seeing no one and hearing only Janet calling out to the two men on the swim platform as she rowed around to the stern.

'What a beautiful yacht.'

'That she is,' one of the men answered, and Stafford knew Janet would have their undivided attention for as long as he needed.

He opened the door across from the ladder and stepped into the entrance lobby between the dining salon and the owner's study. He had memorized the layout of the main deck and lower deck from the schematics in the brochure the lawyer in New York had faxed him, and he immediately located the stairwell to the left of the lobby. He stood motionless for a few moments, tuned to the background noises of the yacht, listening for anything that would indicate his entrance had been noticed.

Stafford was still concerned with the whereabouts of the third crew member on board, but hearing nothing to alarm him, he descended the stairwell to the lower deck, amidships, just forward of the engine room, where he paused for a moment to orient himself before moving along the passageway toward the crew's quarters. He stopped at the point between the crew's mess and the engineer's cabin where the schematics indicated he would find a hatch cover in the deck, and he quickly found it beneath a small oriental rug put there to cover it.

He rolled up the rug and placed it to one side in the hope that anyone who happened by while he was at work would assume another crew member had put it there for a purpose.

He then opened the hatch and lowered himself into the pipe alley, closing the hatch behind him. He was now precisely where he wanted to be, between the two fuel tanks located just aft of the forward watertight bulkhead.

Stafford immediately zipped open the dive bag and removed the items he had got from his friend in Miami: a nine-volt battery, a digital countdown timer, a pencil-thin detonator containing a small primer charge, and two one-pound bricks of Semtex plastic explosives. When he finished with the careful and meticulous wiring of the components, he set the timer so that the circuit between the battery and the detonator would be completed twenty-four hours later, setting off the powerful bomb when the yacht was out in the open ocean and en route to Aruba.

Stafford was counting on Janet's source at the crew bar being right about the *Invincible*'s scheduled departure time, and that nothing would delay it. He wanted the yacht at sea and well away from Marigot Harbor when the explosion occurred, where there was no possibility of any innocent bystanders being killed or injured. To that end he and Janet had agreed that in the event the yacht had not left the harbor at least three hours before the bomb was set to go off, Stafford would make an anonymous phone call to the Port Captain and tell him where to find the bomb and how to disarm it.

Stafford carefully checked and rechecked the timer and his connections before inserting the detonator into the Semtex. He then placed the bomb between the forward watertight bulkhead and the fuel tanks, well out of sight of anyone who wasn't specifically searching for it.

He looked at his watch. He had been on board for seventeen minutes. He zipped the bag closed and slung it across his back and calmly, but quickly, began to retrace his steps. He climbed back out of the hatch, replaced the cover, and put the rug back in place. He then hurried down the passageway and paused at the bottom of the stairwell, listening before going back up to the entrance lobby, still uncomfortable that he had not located the third crew member.

At the top of the stairwell, Stafford stopped dead in his tracks. Through the window in the door leading outside from the entrance lobby, not ten feet away, he saw the third crew member. He was standing at the top of the Med ladder smoking a cigarette and staring off toward the distant lights of Anguilla. Stafford slowly lowered his body into a crouch, avoiding any quick movement that might register in the man's peripheral vision, then carefully backed down the stairwell, stopping at a point where only his head was partially visible and he could just see through the door to where the man stood.

Stafford saw him look toward the stern and then begin to walk in that direction. When he could no longer see him, Stafford moved cautiously up the stairwell until he reached the lobby where he stood beside the door and pressed himself flat against the bulkhead as he peered out the window. The man's back was to him now. He was still walking toward the stern and had reached the lounge on the aft deck.

Stafford eased open the door and heard what had drawn the man's attention as Janet's laugh carried across the water. The man was now completely out of view, at the far end of the aft deck standing at the top of the steps leading down to the swim platform. Stafford slipped out the door and over to the Med ladder and began his descent. As he neared the bottom, his left foot caught on the edge of a step. A sudden move to regain his balance caused the dive bag slung across his back to swing out and strike the side of the yacht.

The man on the aft deck heard the soft thud. He turned and moved quickly in the direction of the sound, drawing a pistol from a holster beneath his shirt at the small of his back. He stood at the top of the Med ladder, looking down and scanning the length of the yacht and listening for a full two minutes before finally flicking his cigarette over the side and returning to the aft deck and the sound of his crew mate's laughter.

Stafford came to the surface gasping for breath. He was directly under the bow, no longer visible to anyone on board, and he immediately swam to the port side of the yacht and headed for the nearest point of land. With a sailboat between him and the *Invincible*, he paused to tread water and heard Janet calling out to the men on the swim platform.

'You be sure to tell Harry I'll look forward to seeing him the next time he's in port.'

Stafford smiled, once again impressed with how cool-headed and calculating Janet could be in tight situations. Just like Eddie, he thought, and began side-stroking toward a small boat landing away from the main dock.

Chapter Fifty-Three

Stafford and Janet watched the *Invincible* set sail a few minutes before two o'clock the following afternoon. They clearly saw John Galloway, Adam Welsh and Paul Cameron on board, standing on the aft deck as the huge yacht, glistening white in the tropical sun, left Marigot Harbor and headed out to sea.

At Janet's request, Stafford rented a fifteen-foot Boston Whaler with twin outboard motors from the marina at their hotel and they set out to cruise the island's coastline. Three hours later, as the sun was about to set, they sat in solemn silence, anchored in the secluded, picture-perfect cove that Janet had chosen for her brother's final resting place.

The sunset was a magnificent palate of ever-deepening shades of red and gold, darkening the sea from aquamarine to deep blue as Janet stood in the bow holding the urn with Eddie's ashes and waiting for the precise moment when the sun sank below the horizon.

Stafford sat in the stern, staring out to sea and listening to the surf breaking on a distant reef. His thoughts were of Eddie and of all the good times they had together and of the terror and triumphs they had shared. Then Janet's voice, with an almost childlike glee, abruptly brought him from his reverie.

'Look! Look!'

Stafford looked up, and just as the sun disappeared from sight, he saw a bright green flash on the horizon.

It lasted for only a second or two, and it was then that Janet poured Eddie's ashes over the side. An ocean breeze carried some of them away in a gossamer cloud, and the gentle swells and outgoing tide took the rest down into the purple depths of the sea. Tears welled in Janet's eyes as she sat down and spoke to Stafford.

'Have you seen the green flash before?'

'Never even heard of it.'

'Scientists explain it as an atmospheric phenomenon. An optical effect. But there are others who believe there's something mystical and mysterious about it; that it can be a sign, or a premonition, or a prophecy. People can spend a liftetime watching for it and never see it. I can't believe I saw it here. Today.'

She looked toward the horizon as the tears began to flow. 'Maybe Eddie's here with us, Stafford. Maybe that's what it means. Why we saw it. Maybe in some strange way he brought us here because this is where he wanted to be. And he's telling us that everything's all right. That he's in a better place.'

Stafford smiled and touched Janet's face with the back of his hand, gently brushing away her tears.

'Janet?'

'What?'

'If Eddie was here, we both know what he'd say.'

'What?'

Stafford did his best imitation of the New Jersey accent from Eddie's childhood that he never managed to lose. 'I got your green flash. Gimme another beer.'

Janet laughed through her tears and Stafford put an arm around her and held her close.

'Oh, God, I miss him so much. He was so good to me.'

She lay her head on Stafford's shoulder and he felt her trembling. He held her tighter and kissed her on the forehead. 'I know. I miss him, too.'

When she had stopped crying and told him she wanted to leave, Stafford started the engine and swung the boat around and drove out of the cove.

Stafford bought a ticket for the last flight off the island that

262

evening; a direct flight to San Juan with a connection to Philadelphia that would get him home late that night.

Janet stood with him in the boarding area. 'Are you sure you don't want to hang out here for a couple of days? Do a little fishing? Some diving?'

'Sounds great, but I want to get back to see Annie.'

'I understand.'

'So, it's about time to burn that bridge you've been talking about, isn't it?'

'What bridge is that? I don't see any bridge? Do you see a bridge?'

Stafford smiled. 'Are you going to turn the money in?'

Janet smiled back. 'Not a chance. And you?'

'Probably not.'

'How much do you know about laundering money?'

'Either enough to pull it off, or enough to screw it up and get caught. I guess I'll find out which it is pretty soon.'

Janet took three neatly folded sheets of hotel stationery from her shoulder bag and handed them to Stafford.

'What's this?'

'A little information I picked up from a training course at DEA. Money laundering one-oh-one. It's how the big boys do it. Follow the instructions to the letter and you won't even leave a ripple.'

The final boarding call for Stafford's flight was announced over the public address system. He put the three pages of handwritten instructions in his jacket pocket and picked up his carry-on bag. 'So this is it, huh?'

'I guess so.'

'What will you do?'

'Kick back for a few days. Catch some rays. After that . . . I don't know. I've got some unfinished business to take care of, then I'll give it some serious thought. What about you?'

'There's a private clinic in Ireland. They've been making some real progress with post-traumatic-stress cases like Annie's. I couldn't afford it before. Now I can.'

'I hope it works out.'

'I'll drop you a line. Let you know where we are.'

'Sure.'

'Maybe if you get a chance you'll come over for a visit.'

'Yeah. Maybe.'

Stafford gave her a quick hug and kissed her on the cheek. 'Thanks. I couldn't have asked for a better partner.'

'Me neither.'

The woman checking the tickets at the boarding gate gave Stafford a look as the last of the passengers left the terminal and crossed the tarmac to the plane.

'Guess I better go.'

'Sounds like a plan to me.'

Their eyes met and held for an awkward moment, then Stafford simply nodded, slung the carry-on bag over his shoulder, and walked toward the gate. He stopped at the door and turned back to say something, but Janet called out to him first.

'Just get on the goddamn plane, Stafford, before this turns into some sappy fuckin' Hallmark card come to life.'

Stafford laughed and went out onto the tarmac. Janet could still hear him laughing as he climbed the steps to board the plane.

Chapter Fifty-Four

Six hours out of Saint Martin, under a tropical night sky twinkling with the pin lights of countless stars, the motor yacht *Invincible* cruised just below her top speed of 15 knots in 13,000 feet of water. The nearest land was Saint Croix to the north and Saba to the east, neither closer than seventy miles.

Following seas from the port aft quarter gave the *Invincible* a gentle rolling motion, and a warm trade wind breeze blew across her boat deck where Galloway, Welsh, and Cameron were having a late dinner and enjoying the spectacular evening at sea. Classical guitar music played softly through hidden speakers as the three men dined and discussed their plans to acquire an intaglio press and a typographic press from Galloway's contacts in Venezuela, two pieces of equipment necessary for the printing of high-quality counterfeit notes.

Two decks below where the three men sat sipping their wine and eating their dinner of lobster salad, the bomb Stafford had placed in the pipe alley between the forward watertight bulkhead and the fuel tanks was in the last seconds of its countdown. At the same instant the face of the digital timer showed four zeroes, the bomb exploded with a force multiplied five-fold by the simultaneous explosion of the fuel tanks.

The powerful blast literally blew the *Invincible* in half, leaving no watertight integrity, quickly flooding her and sinking her in less than three minutes. The only survivor among the crew or passengers was the chef, who had been standing on the foredeck having a cigarette when the explosion picked him up and threw him over the bow. He clung to a piece of wreckage, barely conscious, stunned from the concussive force of the blast, his nose and ears and eyes bleeding.

Four miles off the *Invincible*'s starboard bow, the Watch Officer on a Liberian-flagged container ship en route to Venezuela left the radio room after getting a cup of coffee. He stepped onto the deck to see a brilliant flash of orange-yellow light on the horizon. A moment later the sound rumbled out across the ocean and reached him. He trained his binoculars on the spot where he had seen the explosion and saw pieces of burning wreckage floating on the surface of the ocean. He alerted the Deck Officer, who called the Captain, and the 400-foot container ship immediately changed course to investigate and look for survivors.

Chapter Fifty-Five

Stafford held his daughter's hand as he watched the Gulfstream V he had chartered taxi into position on the tarmac outside the Atlantic Aviation terminal at the Philadelphia airport. He checked the straps that secured Annie in her wheelchair, and when he saw the pilot open the aircraft door and lower the steps, he wheeled her across the lobby toward the exit. It was then that he saw Tom Quinn enter the terminal and walk toward them.

Quinn's eyes briefly studied Annie as she sat motionless, slumped in the wheelchair and staring unseeing at the floor. He greeted Stafford with a friendly smile. 'She's beautiful. I take it she strongly resembles her mother.'

'Very much so.'

Quinn gestured toward the private jet waiting outside on the tarmac. 'The bounty hunting business must be pretty good.'

'Can't complain.'

Stafford stroked Annie's hair to comfort her as he locked eyes with Quinn. 'I'm not having any conversation with you right now. I'm taking my daughter to a hospital in Ireland. When I get her settled, you give me a time and a place and I'll be there. But I don't want anything said here that could upset her.'

'Relax, Stafford. I just stopped by to pass along some information I thought you might find interesting.'

'What information?'

'It seems that even though the system failed in dealing with the people responsible for Eddie Barnes' death, there were other forces at work.'

Stafford gave nothing away. 'Meaning?'

'John Galloway, Adam Welsh, and Paul Cameron were all on a yacht that went down in the middle of the ocean four days ago. Someone on a nearby ship saw the explosion. They picked up the only survivor; a crew member who has no idea what happened.'

'There is a God.'

'And apparently a vengeful one.'

'Who moves in mysterious ways His wonders to perform. Isn't that how it goes?'

A wry smile crossed Quinn's face. 'By the way, how was your trip to Saint Martin?'

Stafford played the game. 'In a word? Rewarding.'

'Quite a coincidence that you and Janet Barnes were there at the same time as Cameron's yacht.'

Stafford said nothing, his expression blank.

'Funny thing about coincidences though. I've found they usually aren't.'

'I'll have to take your word on that.'

'And then there's a coincidence on top of a coincidence. Your military service record shows that before you went into Delta Force, your primary MOS in Special Forces was demolitions, with cross-training in operations and intelligence.'

'Actually it isn't called demolitions. It's called engineering.'

'So you built things instead of blowing them up?'

'No. I pretty much blew things up, we just called it engineering.'

Quinn smiled and extended his hand. 'Have a safe journey.'

Stafford shook the proffered hand. 'I'll be in touch. And like I said, when you want to have that conversation, just tell me where and when.'

'I thought we just had it.'

'That's it then?'

'Unless there's something else you want to tell me.'

'Me? No. Not a thing.'

'I didn't think so. I'm guessing you already tied up whatever loose ends there were. Which would make pursuing this

268

any further an exercise in futility. And I don't know about you, but I've got better things to do. You know how it goes. So many bad guys, so little time.'

Stafford smiled but made no response.

Quinn gestured toward the waiting plane. 'Ireland, huh?'

'Dublin.'

'There are a lot of Quinns in Ireland. If you happen to run into any of my relatives be sure to give them my best.'

'I'll do that.'

Quinn looked again at Annie and smiled. As he turned to leave, he threw Stafford a choppy salute and affected an Irish brogue.

'Top of the mornin' to you, Mister Stafford.'

Stafford returned the salute and the proper reply to the old Irish saying. 'And the rest of the day to you, Special Agent Quinn.'

Twenty minutes after Stafford's chartered Gulfstream V lifted off the runway at the Philadelphia airport, Patrick Early entered the detective squad room at the Nineteenth Precinct in New York City, and as he did every morning, he booted up the personal laptop computer he kept in his office and checked his e-mail. He had six messages, but it was the third one, from bdstafford@cstone.net with the subject of 'Retribution' that drew his immediate attention.

Early opened the message and read the brief, but welcome note:

The men who killed the cops and those who sent them are dead. Ask me no questions and I'll tell you no lies.
S.

Chapter Fifty-Six

New York City's Spanish Harlem is a world apart from the luxury apartments, fashionable boutiques and glittering skyscrapers of the wealthy and prosperous Upper East Side adjoining its southern border. Tenements in various states of disrepair line the streets; some abandoned as unprofitable by landlords, some torched by crackheads, others demolished by the city as hazards and replaced with filthy vacant lots littered with empty crack phials and used hypodermic needles that crunch under foot. One in seven adults who live there are unemployed. One in three receive public assistance. Its schools have the city's highest dropout rate; its streets some of the city's worst crime.

To survive those streets there are basic rules. The way you carry yourself being of the utmost importance. Look up and ahead. Never down. Walk with purpose and never stare, but watch everyone. The right body language often being the only thing separating the victims from those who pass without incident.

Janet Barnes knew the rules of the barrio streets, and their rhythm and ebb and flow, having worked the area as a DEA undercover. Shortly after dark, she pulled into the curb near the corner of Third Avenue and 110th Street, a place she remembered as a bad corner. She slung the designer book pack she had purchased at Bloomingdales across her back as she got out of the car, her eyes quickly and calmly sizing up the street.

Latin music throbbed from an open third floor window. The smell of strong coffee came from somewhere else. Across the street from where she had parked a line formed in front of an abandoned building. Jittery people with anxious eyes waited to buy drugs from someone standing in the darkened entryway. One of the dealer's lookouts, a young boy, no older than ten, spotted Janet and whistled three times. The people in line quickly scattered and the shadowy figure inside the doorway receded into the building.

Janet took it all in, but focused her attention on the opposite end of the block and the half-dozen or so young Hispanic males standing in front of a corner bodega with duct tape across a crack in its plate glass window. Their arms were folded across their chests, their heads held high – arrogant high – as they talked among themselves. Like wary forest animals, their quick, feral eyes never left Janet, appraising her, assessing any inherent dangers in her approach.

They accepted the lookout's assessment that she was a cop; her walk and her hard, unyielding eyes and street attitude told them that. The beat-up old Volkswagen Beetle said undercover car. They were further convinced when Janet unbuttoned her black leather blazer to reveal the butt of the .40 caliber semi-automatic pistol tucked into the waistband at the front of her jeans in a cross-draw position. And they had not missed that she had walked away from her car without locking it. They smelled a trap. They were unsure of where her backup was, but their instincts told them someone was nearby. Maybe more than one; a tactical narcotics team ready to swoop down the moment she whispered into a hidden microphone.

But Janet's only backup was the .38 caliber Smith & Wesson Bodyguard Airweight revolver she carried in an ankle holster beneath her jeans. It was a bold move in a dangerous part of the city, but she was relying on the fact that no one who lived in that neighborhood would believe for one second that an unescorted white woman from outside the barrio, unless she was a decoy cop or a lost tourist, would walk their streets at night. And there was no mistaking Janet for a lost tourist.

With all eyes on her, she stopped in the middle of the block and turned into the entrance of a ten-story tenement apartment building. The door had three locks, all broken, and double-glass panels with two of the panels kicked out and replaced with plywood. She went inside to a lobby that reeked of urine and walked toward the stairs. The elevator descended with a thud and startled her. The dented door squeaked and rattled open. Three hard-looking teenage girls stepped out and stared at her with bold, suspicious eyes. They laughed as they passed by, one of them calling her an asshole in Cuban Spanish.

The apartment Janet was looking for was on the sixth floor, but she bypassed the elevator, recalling a drug bust early in her assignment to the joint task force. One of the dealer's lookouts was riding the top of an elevator car in a building the task force had targeted for a raid. Two NYPD cops took the elevator while others took the stairs. The lookout riding the top of the car, strung out on speed and giggling maniacally, stuck a sawed-off shotgun down through the trap door and shot the faces off the two cops.

Janet looked back as the elevator door shuttered closed and caught a glimpse of a fresh pile of human feces inside the car. She took the stairs two at a time, her hand on the grip of her pistol, watching the shadows on the landings. She found the apartment at the rear of the building and pounded on the door with her fist. She heard someone moving around inside and pounded again.

'Give it a fuckin' rest. I'm comin'.'

Janet recognized the voice and heard footsteps reach the other side of the door.

'Yeah. Who the fuck is it?'

'Janet Barnes, Pedro. Open up.'

'No shit!'

Janet heard two chains slide and two dead-bolts click, then the door opened a crack and she saw a piece of Pedro's face grinning at her.

'No shit!'

'You already said that.' Janet pushed the door open and stepped inside, quickly closing and locking it behind her.

Pedro Davila was barely twenty-nine years old, but his drug habit had added ten years to his once smooth, handsome face. He and Janet had a history. A highly accomplished car thief, small-time dealer, and full-time junkie, she had busted him on an intent to distribute charge shortly after coming to the DEA's New York office. Finding that he was intelligent, articulate, and knew the street, she had brokered a deal with the federal prosecutor to plead him out to two years probation, putting him back on the streets where for the next two years, until Janet left the DEA, he was her most productive snitch.

She and Pedro had one other bond; they both hated Jack Burns, Janet's former DEA boss who had sexually harassed her, set her up, and forced her to resign. In Pedro Davila's case, Burns had beaten him in an alley, breaking his nose and two ribs, partly because he wasn't satisfied with the quality of the information Pedro was producing, but mostly because he enjoyed doing it.

Janet looked around the shabby one-room apartment, taking in the peeling walls and cardboard window panes. A platform bed with a bare mattress partially covered by a grimy quilt that was either multi-colored or badly stained was pushed against one wall. An empty refrigerator with the door open, and a stove with the burners missing, stood against another. An upholstered chair, filthy and threadbare, faced a corner where there had once been a television set before it was either stolen or sold to buy drugs. Unwashed clothing lay in piles around the bare floor, along with the scattered debris from countless fast food meals. A wobbly three-legged sofa with one arm missing and pocked with cigarette burns completed the decor.

'Before I leave, you've got to give me the name of your decorator.'

Davila laughed, revealing stained and chipped teeth. A liquid cough rattled somewhere deep in his chest. 'He's doin' somethin' for Trump at the moment, but I'll have him give you a call.'

Janet searched Davila's expressive liquid brown eyes. They seemed bright and clear. 'Are you straight?'

273

'Right now I am. But I was just about to go out and address that situation.'

'That'll have to wait.'

'Yo, Janet. Not for nothin', but unless I heard wrong, you ain't DEA no more.'

'You heard right.'

'Like you was caught dippin' into the evidence locker.'

Janet's eyes hardened. 'Don't go there, Pedro.'

Davila quickly changed the subject. 'So what's up then?'

'I've got a proposition for you.'

Davila wiggled his hips and flashed an exaggerated grin. 'We gonna parrr-teee. I always wanted to get next to you, Janet.'

'Shut up, you moron.'

Janet slipped the book pack off her back and tossed it to Davila. 'Open it.'

Davila zipped open the top and looked inside. His eyes widened as he pulled out a shrink-wrapped packet of money containing ten thousand dollars in one hundred dollar bills. 'How much is in here.'

'Fifty thousand.'

'For me?'

'No. For Jack Burns.'

Davila saw something beneath the packets of money and pulled out one of the two kilos of cocaine in the bottom of the pack.

The cash was all supernotes and the cocaine had come from a wealthy Wall Street broker with a wife and three kids in Scarsdale. Ten months ago Janet had been working an undercover operation that targeted a nightclub frequented by the Wall Street crowd. The club's owners were dealing significant amounts of cocaine and heroin, and Janet had cut the broker a break by warning him of an impending drug bust. An infrequent customer, he was a recreational user, not a dealer, and not dirty enough that she wanted to see him and his family destroyed. He came to the club with his buddies, not with other women, and what convinced Janet that he was worth salvaging were the times she heard him on his cell phone, calling his kids to say goodnight and to tell them how much he loved them before he started putting Bolivian marching powder up his nose.

The broker was forever grateful, and Janet had called in her marker that evening. She had given him fifty thousand dollars in supernotes to buy the two kilos from the dealer who supplied him and more than a few of the traders in his firm.

The keen intelligence and quick mind Janet recognized in Davila when their paths first crossed quickly led him to the right conclusion. He smiled as he held up one of the kilos of uncut cocaine.

'You're gonna set that rotten fucker up.'

'No. You are.'

Davila's eyes narrowed. 'And how am I gonna do that?'

'You're going to do what you do best. Steal a car.'

'And give it to you?'

'No. Get the cops to chase you. Make sure you don't lose them. Ditch the car and run away.'

'And leave the pack on the floor behind the front seat. Right? Kind of in plain sight where the cops can see the coke and the money peeking out at them?'

'You got it.'

'What's in this for me? Besides the satisfaction of thinkin' that cocksucker could end up in the joint gettin' his fudge packed and tossin' somebody's salad.'

'Two hundred and fifty thousand dollars. Cash. If you pull it off.'

'Two hundred and fifty grand?'

'Cash.'

'Don't fuck with me, Janet.'

'I'm not.'

'How do you know I won't just take the money and the coke and disappear.'

'Because I'll hunt you down and kill you if you do.'

Davila looked for humor in her eyes and saw none. 'Hey, I was just kiddin'. Like I'm gonna settle for fifty grand cash and maybe another fifty in coke when I can get a quarter mill for a joy ride. What am I, nuts?'

'For your sake, I hope not.'

'You'll show me the two fifty before this goes down?'

'Absolutely. But remember, the key to this is you've got to get away. If the cops catch you when you ditch the car, they'll make the connection and smell a set-up. So you've got to get away clean.'

Davila smiled. 'I ditch it in the right place, they'll never catch me. Won't be too interested in runnin' into the places I go neither.'

'Do you remember the parking garage on ninety-fourth, between Lexington and Third, where we used to meet when you had something for me?'

'Yeah.'

'When you're sure you've lost them, meet me there and I'll give you your money. Then if I were you, I'd go down to Florida or someplace and start my life over.'

'I'm thinkin' maybe L.A., but that's just off the top of my head.'

'Whatever.' Janet took the book pack and unlocked the door. 'Are you ready?'

'Does the Pope wear a stupid hat?'

Jack Burns' car was parked at the curb on the north side of East 51st Street, between First and Second Avenue, almost directly in front of a tiny sublet apartment in the basement of a five-story brownstone. Janet gave Davila the book pack and dropped him off at the corner of Second Avenue, then pulled into the curb to watch him walk back down the block to where the dark-blue Ford sedan was parked.

True to his reputation, Davila had the door open, the alarm disabled, and the car started all within twelve seconds. He sped away from the curb and across Second to Third Avenue where he skidded around the corner and headed north.

As Janet pulled away from the curb at the end of the block, she saw Burns run from the basement apartment, bare-chested and wearing sweat pants, nothing on his feet and cell phone in his hand.

Davila drove up Third Avenue with wild abandon, weaving his way erratically through traffic, pausing only briefly at intersections before running the red lights. Seventeen blocks later, when he reached 78th Street, he drew the attention he

276

wanted. An NYPD patrol car from the 19th Precinct pulled out from the cross street, turned on its roof lights and siren, and sped up the avenue in pursuit.

Davila whooped and laughed as he floored the accelerator, getting all the speed the Ford had to offer. Caught up in the chase, he flashed through intersections without even looking for cross traffic, causing two rear-end collisions when cars slammed on their brakes to avoid broadsiding him. When he crossed 96th Street, he was in the barrio and on familiar ground. The two uniformed cops in the blue and white were two blocks behind him, their progress hampered by the requirement of not running down and killing any of the citizens they were sworn to serve and protect.

When Davila reached 112th Street, he made the move he had planned in his head. He hit the brakes and swerved the stolen Ford into the curb and up onto the sidewalk. He hadn't planned on putting the front end through the window of a Dominican grocery, but thought it added a nice touch, making it look like losing control of the car was the reason he had stopped and fled on foot.

Davila threw open the door, jumped out, and ran across the street and around the corner before cutting through a vacant lot and into an abandoned building. He scampered up the stairwell to the roof of the eight-story tenement, where he often came to shoot up on warm summer nights. From here he could see back across the street to the swirling lights of the three patrol cars that had converged on the stolen Ford.

Two more cars arrived and began to cruise the neighborhood, but Davila knew the cops in the chase car had not seen him, and even if they happened upon his rooftop lookout, without a description they could not possibly identify him.

He smiled to himself when he saw one of the uniform cops take the book pack from the back of the car and hand it to the patrol sergeant, who began speaking into his portable radio. Twenty minutes later all that remained at the scene was one patrol car waiting for the tow truck to come and take the damaged Ford to the police garage. With the other cars no longer patrolling the immediate neighborhood, Davila left the rooftop and headed back downtown with a spring to his step and an anticipatory grin on his face.

Janet was parked across the street from the entrance to the garage on 94th Street when Davila came around the corner. He stopped in front of the garage and looked around, not noticing the Volkswagen Beetle on the opposite side of the darkened street. Janet leaned across the seat, opened the passenger side door, set her lips and let out a sharp piercing whistle.

Davila almost bolted for the corner before he saw it was Janet who had whistled. He quickly ran across the street and climbed into the car.

'You tryin' to give me a goddamn heart attack?'

'How did it go?'

'Exactly like you wanted. They found the pack and everything.'

Davila looked over his shoulder, his eyes settling on a gym bag on the back seat. His face brightened. 'Is that it?'

'That's it.'

Davila reached over the seat and brought the bag forward into his lap. He opened it and looked inside at the neatly wrapped packets of money. 'So I could go now?'

'You can go.'

Davila opened the door and got out, clutching the gym bag to his chest. He leaned in the window as Janet started the car.

'You ever got anything else along these lines you want me to do, you call me right away, huh?'

'This is a one-off deal, Pedro. Make it last, huh?'

As Janet watched him disappear around the corner, she wondered if he would take advantage of the best opportunity he was ever going to have to leave a life that was sure to kill him, or get him killed, before he was thirty. She seriously doubted he would. Lack of brains didn't make him a junkie, and his keen intelligence wouldn't overrule whatever it was that had.

As Janet pulled away from the curb, she thought about what she had set in motion that night. Burns would scream set-up, and finding the money and cocaine in his car would not be enough to put him in prison, or even get him fired, but the

278

incident would taint his career. It would be there in his file for all to read when he was considered for promotion.

Janet might have left it at that had Burns not treated her with such blatant disrespect and complete disdain for how hard she had worked to get where she was, and for her love of the work she was doing, and for the effect being forced to leave in disgrace would have on the rest of her life.

Burns had few friends on the joint task force, and none among the New York City detectives assigned to it, whom he treated as inferiors and incompetents, when in fact they produced most of the worthwhile results. Those same cops would view the drugs and money found in Burns' car as a golden opportunity, and they would sink their teeth into the case and not let go.

Within the next week, they would receive an anonymous call from an angry woman claiming Burns got her pregnant and refused to even pay for the abortion and she was going to fix the bastard. The information she would give the detectives would lead them to five bank accounts in five separate suburban branch banks, each account containing twenty thousand dollars. Further investigation would show that the money in those accounts had been wired from a numbered account in a Bahamian bank. Upon being informed there was evidence to indicate the funds in that account were derived from criminal activities, the Bahamian bank, in compliance with international banking laws, would be forced to reveal that the account contained four hundred thousand dollars and was held in the name of John Edward Burns.

Janet estimated that within three weeks, Burns would be facing indictment on a criminal conspiracy charge. The DEA, to save itself the embarrassment of arresting one of its own, would give him the option of resigning, or risk being convicted and receiving a lengthy prison sentence. Either way, his career was over.

The thought of Burns suffering the same fate he had meted out to her gave Janet some sense of satisfaction, but it did not make her feel any better about what she had lost, although it did, she believed, close a chapter in her life she would never feel the need to revisit.

As she emerged from the Lincoln Tunnel and drove over the Pulaski Skyway, Janet tuned the radio to an oldies-but-goodies station and cranked up the volume to the sound of Elvis singing 'Suspicious Minds'. An appropriate song for Jack Burns, she thought, especially the part about 'caught in a trap, can't walk out'.

Coming down off the Skyway onto I–95 South, she looked over her shoulder and saw the spectacular Manhattan skyline sparkling in the distance. She felt a sudden and profound sense of loss for all the things she had loved about her job. Then she recalled one of Eddie's favorite sayings: all you ever get looking back is a stiff neck.

She tapped her hands on the wheel to the beat of the music as she drove on through the night, singing along with the King, and wondering what life held in store for her now, but not particularly worried about it.

Nowhere to Hide
James Elliot

Genero pulled the trigger twice in rapid succession. Onorati rocked back on his knees, then slumped over onto his side. A significant portion of the back of his head was blown away. . . Genero stared down at him for a long moment, then walked back into the living room.

Nicole Bass saw it all.

Witnessing a Mafia hit is no recipe for a long and healthy life. High-class call girl Nicole Bass is nobody's fool, and she's a woman with good reason not to trust lawman Jack Kirby. So she disappears. And now the Mob and the cops are looking for her.

But Nicole has eighteen million, five hundred and eighty-six thousand dollars worth of reason to stay hidden. . .

The chase is on, in a heart-hammering action thriller by a master storyteller.

"Elliott's prose glides over the page. . .a deeply absorbing new thriller"

Publishers Weekly